GHOST OF THE BAMBOO ROAD

ALSO BY SUSAN SPANN

GHOST OF THE BAMBOO ROAD

A HIRO HATTORI NOVEL

SUSAN SPANN

SEVENTH
STREET
BOOKS®

Published 2019 by Seventh Street Books®

Cover image Shuttersotck
Cover design by Nicole Sommer-Lecht
Cover design © Start Science Fiction

Inquiries should be addressed to
Start Science Fiction
101 Hudson Street, 37th Floor, Suite 3705 Jersey City, New Jersey 07302
Phone: 212-431-5455
www.seventhstreetbooks.com

10 9 8 7 6 5 4 3 2 1

978-1-63388-550-9 (paperback) | 978-1-63388-551-6 (Ebook)

Library of Congress Cataloging-in-Publication Data available on file.

Printed in the United States of America

For Kerry
Who inspired—and challenged—
Hiro to investigate a ghost.

CHAPTER 1

"This doesn't look like a travel road." Father Mateo squinted at the narrow, uneven trail running up the rocky slope ahead. Patches of icy snow still clung to the base of the towering cedars along the left side of the path. On the right, a stand of broad-leafed bamboo grass grew high enough to block the view. Piles of old debris along the road, and leaning trees, suggested a landslide many months before.

The priest's irascible housekeeper, Ana, made a disapproving noise. "Hiro-*san* has missed a turn."

"We are *not* lost." Master ninja Hattori Hiro anticipated the housekeeper's next comment. "They told us that the village sits at the top of the second hill, on the old travel road." He gestured to the rocky path. "*This* road. Which has neither branched nor split since we left Hakone."

He shut his mouth abruptly as he realized the extent of his frustration. Trading the enticing hot spring baths of Hakone for a night in a freezing mountain inn had clearly annoyed him more than he expected.

Father Mateo looked back down the hill. "Perhaps we should have spent the night in Hakone . . ." He sneezed and wiped his nose with a scrap of cloth.

"An overnight stay in the village gives us a reasonable excuse to stop and find the woman stationed there." Hiro kept his words deliberately vague, but knew the priest would understand the reference to their clandestine mission.

"The *woman?*" Father Mateo dropped his voice to a whisper. "We're looking for a female ninja?"

"A *kunoichi*," Hiro corrected. "Surely you did not think all the names on the list were male." *Especially after what you saw in Iga.*

A frigid wind blew down the hill, rustling through the swath of *sasa* on the right side of the road. The bamboo grasses bowed and waved like a crowd of peasants greeting a samurai lord.

Hiro crested the slope and caught sight of a two-story building a hundred yards ahead, on the east side of the path. "You see?" He gestured toward it. "The *ryokan*."

The traditional inn had a steep thatched roof, to prevent the buildup of winter snow, and long, broad eaves that extended past the edge of its raised veranda. A signpost and a small stone lantern stood beside the two low wooden steps that led to the porch and entry.

"And that"—Hiro gestured to a single-story building across the road from the ryokan—"will be the teahouse, where we'll likely find the woman we came to see."

"Will you recognize her when you see her?" Father Mateo spoke softly, despite the deserted road.

"I should. My mother trained her, and Emiri was also a friend of . . . Neko's." Mention of his dead lover's name brought a pang of loss that clenched Hiro's chest like an iron fist. But this time, the initial sharpness faded quickly, giving him hope that eventually he could learn to remember her without pain.

For the moment, diversion would have to do.

The rest of the village had now come into view. Just past the teahouse and the inn, six peasant houses lined the road, three on either side of the earthen path. Beyond the houses, a narrow, stubbly rice field separated the humble dwellings from a large, two-story house that stood alone on the east side of the road, as if unwilling to admit that it belonged to the rural village. The quality of the carpentry and architectural style suggested a samurai mansion, though significantly more provincial than the ones in Kyoto.

Just past the mansion, the travel road reentered the forest and resumed its upward slope toward the mountain's summit. Massive cedars rose around the village, looming over the houses as if plotting to reclaim the narrow strip of land carved out of the forest by short-lived creatures foolish enough to believe it was their own.

Hiro's gaze drew back along the peasant homes. Icicles hung from the edges of the thatch and along the eaves. Smoke rose from two of the houses, but the rest looked strangely vacant.

"The village seems too small to support an inn and teahouse," Father Mateo said.

"They exist to serve the travelers. The villagers most likely work as porters on—" The final words died on Hiro's lips as he noticed a hooded figure standing at the north end of the village, where the road reentered the forest. The stranger wore pale trousers and a tunic, belted at the waist, and carried a six-foot bamboo staff. An enormous conch shell hung from a dark red cord around his neck. He stood as still as the pines that lined the path.

At the moment Hiro saw him, the stranger stepped backward and vanished into the trees.

"What is it?" Father Mateo asked.

"A *yamabushi*." Hiro did not nod or gesture. "In the forest at the far end of the road."

The Jesuit craned his neck in that direction. "I don't see him."

"He returned to the forest."

Father Mateo looked up the road as if hoping the yamabushi would reappear. "I would like to meet a mountain ascetic. Do they truly eat only foraged bark and tree roots?"

"I wouldn't know." Hiro climbed the steps that led to the ryokan's front door. "They keep to themselves—a prerequisite for hermits."

"Hm," Ana muttered. "Abandoned village . . . hermits don't seem out of place."

Her words made Hiro pause for a second look. He noted again that most of the village homes looked dark and cold. No children called or played in the street. No women talked between the houses.

"It does seem strangely quiet." Father Mateo tugged his traveling cloak more tightly around his shoulders. "Maybe we should return to Hakone after all."

"Nonsense. The ryokan is open." Hiro gestured to the glowing lantern beside the steps and rapped on the inn's front door. It gave a hollow echo, like the entrance to a long-deserted tomb.

A shiver ran up Hiro's spine. For a moment, he reconsidered returning to Hakone.

The heavy wooden door swung open, revealing an older woman dressed in pale mourning robes. Her silver hair hung down her back in a single braid. The stern, unyielding lines of her face suggested a person who rarely smiled.

A younger woman stood behind her, wearing a plain but once expensive kimono of pale gray silk and a striped blue *obi*.

The gray-haired woman bowed. "Good evening, gentlemen." She turned away. "My daughter-in-law, Kane, will see to your needs, now that she deigns to answer the door."

The younger woman stepped forward, but said nothing until her mother-in-law's retreating footsteps faded into silence. As she waited, she regarded Hiro and Father Mateo with a wary suspicion that pinched her mouth into unpleasant lines. At last she asked, "May I help you?"

Noting the swords at Hiro's waist, she added a perfunctory, "sir."

"Have you rooms available?" Hiro asked.

"You want to stay . . . tonight?" Her startled tone implied that they should not.

CHAPTER 2

The woman dropped her voice to an urgent whisper. "Do not stay with us tonight."

"Kane, did I hear the door?" A man appeared behind her. He looked about her age, with a narrow face and close-cropped hair. He also wore a pale robe, though his had the wrinkled look of clothing pulled from storage unexpectedly.

His eyes widened at the sight of Hiro and Father Mateo. "Good evening, noble sirs." He bowed, and Kane moved aside, allowing him to replace her at the door.

"Welcome to our ryokan," he said. "I am Noboru, and I see you have met my wife, Kane. May we offer you rooms for the night?"

The Jesuit returned the bow. "Thank you, Noboru-*san*. I am Father Mateo Ávila de Santos, and this is my scribe, Matsui Hiro."

Hiro noted with approval that the priest remembered the change to their cover story. Father Mateo's Japanese was far too proficient to claim the need for a translator any longer. Fortunately, most Japanese people believed the complexities of Japanese script beyond the learning capacity of foreigners.

"My scribe and I can share a room," the Jesuit continued, "but if you have a second room available, I would prefer that my housekeeper have a separate accommodation."

"Noboru . . ." the woman whispered.

"Kane-*san*, prepare the largest guest room at the front of the house for our honored guests, and the small one near the kitchen for their housekeeper"—he shifted his gaze to Father Mateo—"assuming that arrangement is acceptable?"

Ana's basket mewed.

Father Mateo's cheeks flushed pink. "We have a cat. May it stay in the room?"

"We could use the luck a cat would bring," Kane said. "Especially tonight."

"This ryokan is not unlucky," Noboru snapped.

In the silence that followed, the innkeeper forced a smile. "Of course, your cat can stay." He turned to his wife. "Show the noble gentleman's servant to her room, and then prepare the guest room for our visitors. Do not, under any circumstances, interrupt Ishiko-*san*. She needs to finish her preparations soon."

Hiro recalled the older woman in mourning robes, and suspected Kane had already violated her husband's order.

"In the meantime, I will take our honored guests to eat at the teahouse." Noboru gestured across the road.

Kane gave her husband an unreadable look, gestured to Ana, and walked away.

The Jesuit's housekeeper muttered under her breath as she crossed the threshold carrying Gato's basket.

"We do not wish to cause you trouble," Father Mateo said.

"No trouble at all!" Noboru stepped into a pair of shoes that sat beside the door. "Please leave your burdens here. My wife will take them to your room."

As he followed the innkeeper across the road, Hiro wondered what Ana would do about an evening meal for herself and Gato. He dismissed the concern almost at once. The Jesuit's housekeeper had proven herself exceedingly resourceful. Neither she nor the cat would want for food.

Yet again, Hiro noticed the unusual lack of smoke and light in the village houses, even though the sun had fallen below the trees and twilight had begun to leach the colors from the day. Bamboo shutters covered the windows of every dwelling, as if the houses closed their eyes to the road. Even the house at the far end of the street sat tightly shuttered, the large stone lanterns at its steps unlit.

Hiro felt a chill that had nothing to do with winter, accompanied by a sudden, instinctive desire to flee. He saw no obvious threats, yet his instincts screamed that he and the priest should leave at once.

Go, urged the familiar voice in his thoughts. *Go now, while you still can.*

A sprinkling of stars had appeared in the darkening sky. Faint wisps of cloud streaked the heavens like ghosts escaping the mortal realm.

Hiro never dismissed his instincts—not entirely, anyway—but saw no cause for immediate alarm. He would stay alert, warn Emiri that Oda Nobunaga's spies might have discovered her identity, ensure that she agreed to return to Iga as Hattori Hanzō wished, and continue the journey to Edo in the morning.

The teahouse itself looked solidly built, although its weathered planks showed signs of wear. Its heavy, black tile roof set it apart from the humbler village buildings. An elaborate stone lantern burned beside the wooden steps that led to the entrance, and the sign beside the door read "Bamboo Road Teahouse."

A pair of wooden plaques below the sign read *"Hanako"* and *"Masako."* Beneath them hung a set of empty hooks. Neither name matched the one on Hiro's memorized list of Iga agents, but kunoichi, like their male *shinobi* counterparts, customarily used invented names.

Father Mateo gestured to the empty set of hooks. "Is the third entertainer out tonight?"

"This house has two entertainers," Noboru said, and then repeated, "Only two."

Hiro noted the tension in the innkeeper's voice and wondered why the number of girls in the house would cause anxiety.

The door swung open so quickly that Hiro suspected the woman behind it had been watching as they crossed the street. She looked about twenty, with delicate features and long-fingered hands . . . and she was not Emiri.

The woman made a deep and graceful bow. "Good evening, gentlemen, and welcome." As she straightened, her eyes lingered on Noboru. "With respect, I did not expect you tonight."

"Good evening Hanako-*san*." The innkeeper gestured to Hiro and Father Mateo. "I have unexpected, but welcome, guests. Ishiko-*san* cannot prepare the evening meal, so I hoped . . ."

Hanako stepped back from the door with a welcoming gesture. "Please come in."

A narrow wooden bench sat to the left of the door, beside a small raised shelf that held two pairs of women's winter shoes. On the opposite wall, a monochromatic hanging scroll portrayed a scene of bamboo in the snow.

As Hiro set his shoes on the shelf, he found himself still strangely unsettled, for no identifiable reason. He looked around more closely. The scroll showed notably less finesse than most high-class teahouse art, but inferior paintings were hardly a cause for panic. He inhaled slowly. His sensitive nose detected only wood smoke, pine, and tea.

He saw no reason to refuse Hanako's hospitality, but decided not to remove his swords before following the others through the entry and into the teahouse proper.

If trouble did materialize, he intended to meet it fully armed.

CHAPTER 3

On the far side of the entry, a single step led up to a *tatami*-floored reception room with a sunken hearth at the center. A brazier in the corner filled the room with cheerful light. Sliding *shoji* in the walls on either side of the reception area led to adjacent private rooms where guests could dine at leisure. Vibrant paintings on the doors showed bamboo groves in every season of the year.

Too vibrant. Hiro inspected the art with a critical eye. *The work of an overenthusiastic amateur.*

An unadorned shoji on the far side of the room most likely led to the kitchen and other private portions of the house.

A fire burned brightly in the hearth. Above the flames, a steaming kettle hung suspended on a chain attached to a rafter hook. A teapot and a pair of cups sat on a tray beside the hearth.

"Were you expecting company?" Noboru looked embarrassed. "I did not intend—"

"This?" Hanako gestured to the brazier and the fire. "I merely wished to brighten a gloomy day, and invite good fortune, by filling the house with light. And you have come, so my efforts were successful."

She crossed to the left side of the room and paused before a shoji showing a bamboo grove in winter. Gaudy green, snow-laden stalks bent toward the bank of a frozen lake. In the background, painted far too brightly to create perspective depth, a flat-topped, snow-capped mountain rose dramatically into the sky.

Father Mateo gestured to the painted peak. "Mount Fuji?"

"You know Fuji-*san*?" Hanako clapped her hands in delight. "The painting is the work of my teacher, Yuko-*sama*, who founded the teahouse. She trained in Kyoto."

"Will we have the honor of meeting Yuko-*san* this evening?" the Jesuit asked.

"No . . ." Hanako lapsed into awkward silence, but her smile returned a moment later. "We should speak of happy things."

She knelt before the shoji, laid her hands on the screen, and drew it open. "My finest room: the Winter Grove."

A low wooden table sat at the center of the room, with a pair of square green cushions on either side. A brazier burned in one of the corners opposite the door. Yet another monochromatic scroll hung in a recessed alcove near the brazier, this one containing a poem written in flowing calligraphy that, intriguingly, showed true skill.

Most teahouses left the walls of their guest rooms unadorned to avoid distracting visitors from the subtle flavors of the food and tea, as well as the artistic merit of objects showcased in the *tokonoma*. Parting with tradition, someone—presumably Yuko—had transformed the walls into a grove of painted bamboo stalks. They reached from floor to ceiling, grouped in clusters of varying sizes, each adorned with a cap of painted snow. While rendered more skillfully than the bamboo on the outer doors, the paintings overwhelmed the room, destroying its balance and ruining the intended sense of peace.

Hiro found it curious that the brazier in this room was lit, despite Hanako's claim that she expected no visitors. However, he supposed an intelligent businesswoman would always have at least one room prepared for unexpected guests.

Despite the unpleasant decor, Hiro followed Noboru and Father Mateo across the threshold. He knelt on a cushion beside the priest, across the table from the innkeeper.

"Please make yourselves comfortable," Hanako said. "I will send Masako-*san* to entertain you while I prepare your meal." She bowed and closed the door.

"Thank you for arranging this." Father Mateo nodded to Noboru. "Although I feel I must apologize for the inconvenience. It appears this evening has an important meaning, of which we are not aware."

"Do not concern yourselves." The innkeeper made a dismissive gesture. "Hanako serves excellent food. I appreciate the opportunity to enjoy a meal here."

He gestured to the painted walls. "Quite lovely, don't you think?"

Hiro raised an eyebrow. "I have never seen their equal."

He ignored the Jesuit's sidelong glance.

A silent rapping came from the other side of the painted shoji. Moments later, the door slid open, revealing a slender, kneeling girl of about eighteen. She wore her hair in a simple arrangement accented by a pair of silver *kanzashi* adorned with dangling strings of tiny scarlet beads. An embroidered scene of snowy mountains flowed down the side of her dark kimono.

Hiro's hope of delivering Hattori Hanzō's message melted away like frost on a sunny morning. The girl before him was not Emiri either.

"Good evening." The entertainer bowed her forehead to the floor. "My name is Masako. May I have the honor of playing for you this evening?" As she straightened, she gestured to a *shamisen* on the floor beside her knees.

"Thank you, Masako-san." Noboru gestured for the girl to enter.

She crossed the threshold on her knees, lifted her instrument into the room, and closed the door. As she joined them beside the table and arranged her robes, Hiro noted that Masako moved with unusual, fluid grace.

She raised her instrument, removed a plectrum from her sleeve and began to play.

Shivering notes rose from the strings and filled the room with a haunting melody that conjured mental images of barren landscapes filled with icy trees. A shudder ran down Hiro's back as the music, skillfully played, grew even darker. The shamisen took years to learn, and even then most students played it badly. In Masako's hands, it sang like an extension of her soul.

When the song came to its quavering end, Noboru's eyes were full of tears.

Father Mateo looked down at his own scarred hands as if lost in thought.

Masako began another song, even lonelier and more haunting than the first.

As the songs continued, Hiro lost himself in the music and the memories it evoked of people he had loved, and lost, and would never see again.

Eventually Masako laid the instrument in her lap, removed the plectrum from the strings, and raised her face, which held no sign of an entertainer's usual desire for praise.

If anything, the girl seemed almost frightened.

"Thank you, Masako-*san*." Noboru wiped his eyes and looked at the other men. "Forgive my emotions. Today is the one-year anniversary of my sister's death."

Masako's hands flew to her mouth.

"Thank you for the entertainment, Masako-*san*," the innkeeper said. "Under the circumstances, perhaps I should entertain my guests with conversation instead of music, for a while at least. I believe Hanako-*san* could use your assistance with the meal."

The girl bowed politely, collected her instrument, and left the room with ill-disguised relief on her frightened face.

After the shoji slid closed behind her, Noboru continued, "Forgive my rudeness in sending away our entertainment, but I believe I owe you an explanation."

CHAPTER 4

"**Y**ou have no need to apologize, or to explain," Father Mateo said. "We deeply regret imposing on your family tonight."

"Guests are never an imposition." The innkeeper gave an uneasy laugh. "Especially in winter. My mother is preparing an offering for my sister's grave, so I would have eaten here this evening anyway."

Hiro doubted that, but dismissed the harmless lie.

"We will leave early tomorrow morning," Father Mateo said, "so you can take the offering to your sister's grave in peace."

"There is no need," Noboru replied. "My mother will take the offering tonight. In fact, she has probably gone and returned already."

"In the dark?" the Jesuit asked.

Hiro found that curious, too. Most people feared the dead too much to enter a burial ground at night.

Noboru looked at the painted wall behind them. "She wanted to prepare a special evening meal, as an offering, on the anniversary of my sister's death." In a voice too forced to be truly casual, he added, "A foolish woman's notion, but a harmless one."

"Is it safe for your mother to go alone at night?" Father Mateo indicated Hiro. "My scribe believed he saw someone in the trees as we entered the village."

"A man in white?" When Hiro nodded, Noboru said, "Zentaro-*san*, the yamabushi who lives on the mountain. He comes to the village to warn us about showing proper respect for the mountain deities. He is harmless, if not completely sane."

A quiet knock at the door announced Masako's return. The young entertainer carried a wooden tray with plates of fresh sashimi, a teapot, a saké flask, and cups for both saké and tea.

"Hanako-*san* did not know what you like to drink, so she prepared both tea and saké." Masako set the tray on the table and served the sashimi plates.

"You do not need to stay and serve," Noboru said. "But please return and play the shamisen during the final course." He turned to the others. "At least, if my guests have no objection?"

"We would enjoy the music," Father Mateo said.

When Hiro nodded his assent, Masako bowed and left the room.

"I hope you do not mind me sending her away." The innkeeper poured a cup of tea for Father Mateo and filled a saké cup for Hiro. "I enjoy her music, but do not feel like idle talk with a girl her age tonight."

Hiro did not mind. He disliked idle chatter every evening—and at other times as well.

The shinobi eyed the Jesuit's tea with silent envy as Father Mateo bowed his head in silent prayer. Hiro's *ronin* disguise required him to feign a preference for astringent saké, but in truth he preferred the fragrant warmth of tea.

Some time later, Hanako returned to present a steaming bowl of soba noodles, fish, and mountain vegetables in savory broth. Masako had clearly conveyed Noboru's request for privacy because the woman served the dishes, bowed, and left the room without a word.

Unexpectedly, the Jesuit refrained from asking his usual litany of questions about the innkeeper's village, life, and family. Instead, the three men ate in a silence that, though slightly strange, did not interfere with Hiro's enjoyment of the delicious food.

Eventually Hanako returned to replace the empty plates with bowls of rice and miso soup to complete the meal. As the teahouse owner departed, Masako entered the room with her shamisen.

The young entertainer knelt beside the table, bent over the instrument, and plucked the strings. Once again, her music conveyed a sadness that transcended words.

Also as before, she paused for only an instant between her songs.

Hiro preferred light-hearted music—or none at all—but respected

Masako's skill enough to listen without interruption, as he attempted to ignore the mental ghosts her music conjured.

The girl continued playing long after the final grains of rice and sips of soup had disappeared. Hiro had just begun to consider asking her to stop, despite the rudeness of such a request, when Hanako returned to the room to clear the bowls.

Noboru stood and bowed. "Thank you for serving us tonight."

Masako ended her song and looked up, confused.

Hanako also seemed perplexed. "You intend to leave so soon?"

Hiro rose to his feet.

Father Mateo took the hint and stood up also. "Thank you for a splendid meal."

Hiro decided to risk a final question. "This house seems large for two entertainers. Have you more apprentices as well?"

"No . . ." Hanako hesitated. "Before Yuko-*sama*—that is, before I inherited the house from her, we had two other girls as well. Regrettably, they are no longer here."

Hiro noted her discomfort. Unfortunately, a samurai would have no interest in unknown teahouse girls, making additional questions out of place. Whether or not Emiri was one of the girls Hanako referenced, it appeared the kunoichi had moved on. This happened often enough with the agents who spied for the Iga *ryu* that Hiro saw no cause for great concern. If Emiri no longer lived in the village, he and Father Mateo could continue on to Edo, and the next names on the list of Iga spies.

As they left the teahouse, Hiro discovered thick mist obscuring the village, as if clouds had descended like nesting birds to settle on the houses for the night. He followed Noboru and Father Mateo across the road, keeping close to avoid losing sight of them in the fog. He thought of the innkeeper's mother, carrying offerings to the dead, and felt a wave of relief at the lack of superstition it implied. People who did not fear the dead were few and far between.

After leaving their shoes in the ryokan's entry, Noboru led Hiro and Father Mateo into the reception room beyond, and paused before a shoji on the right side of the space. "Our finest guest room."

He drew the door open.

The six-mat room had clean tatami on the floor and a brazier glowed beside the door. Two futons lay in the center of the space, covered with winter quilts that still bore the lines of recent folding. A low wooden table sat against the wall on the far side of the room, beside a solid, wooden shoji that presumably led outside. The wall to the right of the entry featured a built-in cupboard and a small tokonoma that displayed a painting of bamboo in winter snow. Remarkably, the scroll showed even less artistic merit than the paintings in the teahouse.

"I know our country ryokan cannot compare with city inns," Noboru said with obvious pride, "but I do hope the room does not offend."

He gestured to the sliding door on the far side of the room. "You will want to keep the outer door both closed and barred tonight."

Hiro's traveling bundle, and Father Mateo's, lay on the floor beside the table, but Hiro saw no sign of the basket or the cat. "Where is Gato?"

"Most likely with Ana." Father Mateo sniffled. "And I cannot say that I object. With this cold, I can barely breathe as it is."

"If the village has no trouble with bandits," Hiro asked Noboru, "why insist that we bar the door?"

"Animals," the innkeeper answered, a little too quickly. "Nothing to worry about. Merely a precaution. May I bring you tea before you sleep?"

"No, thank you," Father Mateo said. "We do not wish to disturb you any longer."

Noboru bowed and stepped across the threshold. "Then I hope you will sleep soundly." As he closed the door, he added, "and undisturbed."

CHAPTER 5

Father Mateo stared at the door. "Did that seem strange to you?"

"No more than half a dozen other things." Hiro opened the cupboard and peered inside. A futon lay on the wooden shelf, along with a carefully folded quilt. He closed the cabinet and gestured to the tokonoma. "Like the local fascination with inferior paintings of bamboo."

"It does look a lot like the ones in the teahouse." Father Mateo paused. "A gift from the founder . . . Yuko-*san*?"

"Perhaps." Hiro studied the scroll more closely. "Although this one shows less skill. More likely, the work of an apprentice." He crossed the room, raised the pin that secured the exterior shoji, and opened the door enough to look outside.

The door opened onto a narrow ledge, more a catwalk than a true veranda, that ran the length of the ryokan. The building's eaves extended past the ledge, preventing rain from leaking beneath the door. Heavy mist obscured the view, though Hiro guessed the faint glow to the west was the lantern beside the teahouse steps on the opposite side of the travel road.

He closed the door and dropped the wooden pin back into place to secure it.

Father Mateo switched to Portuguese. "Speaking of apprentices, do you think the woman we're looking for is one of the two who moved away?"

"I suspect so," Hiro replied in kind. "She should have reported the move to the clan, but . . ." Given that he was currently also in breach of protocol and orders, he felt disinclined to criticize Emiri's choices. "We'll continue to look for her on the way to Edo."

"We could ask about her again before we leave," the priest suggested.

"Not without attracting unwanted attention."

"Something might have happened to her," Father Mateo said. "Wouldn't . . . your people . . . want to know?"

"Not at the risk of exposing my own identity," Hiro answered. "Once we get to Edo, I can send a message to my cousin, telling him that we undertook this mission ourselves, in Ringa's place, and letting him know of Emiri's disappearance."

Father Mateo seemed to accept that answer. "What animals can open an unbarred shoji? Bears?"

"They can. But normally, if a bear wants in, he'll simply break the door."

"How comforting." The Jesuit knelt beside the futon farthest from the outer wall.

Hiro removed his swords from his obi and set them on the tatami beside his futon. "More likely, the problem lies with foxes coming in to hunt for mice."

"Mice?" Father Mateo looked around as if expecting hordes of furry rodents to emerge from the walls at any moment. "If this place has mice, I think I might prefer a fox."

"Trust me, you wouldn't." Hiro lay down. "They stink."

Hiro woke to the muffled sound of urgent whispers. The room was dark, but his internal clock suggested dawn.

Father Mateo's silent breathing told him the priest still slept, but the voices outside the door made Hiro curious. Silently, he pushed his quilt aside and grasped his *wakizashi*, leaving the longer *katana* on the floor.

Despite their urgency, the voices seemed too loud for people planning an ambush.

Slipping the scabbard through his obi, he crossed to the door and slid it open just a crack.

The reception room was empty.

The voices came from the far end of a hall that led from the reception room to the rear of the ryokan. Hiro slipped out the guest room door and crept across the floor to the hallway entrance.

Half a dozen shoji opened off the right-hand wall of the narrow passage, their locations and spacing suggesting guest room entrances. At the far end of the hall, an open doorway led to another room, most likely the kitchen. A shadowed male figure stood in the opening with his back to the hall.

Flickering light and the sound of voices drew Hiro down the hall. He stopped halfway to the kitchen door, not wanting to make the speakers aware of his presence.

Unlike the living areas, which sat on a raised foundation, the ryokan kitchen sat at ground level, where the earthen floor reduced the risk of fire.

Noboru stood on the lower of the two short steps that led to the kitchen, holding a lantern. "She isn't here."

The innkeeper's words held an accusation.

"It was only a guess." Kane's whispered answer came from the kitchen. "I already told you, I went to sleep right after she left last night."

"And she told you to remain awake, so you could help clean up when she returned." Noboru hissed. "When I came home, and found you sleeping, I assumed—"

"I was tired"—a whine edged Kane's voice—"and your mother didn't want my help. She just couldn't stand the thought of me getting any rest."

"It was your duty." Noboru sounded frightened. "Now she's missing!"

"She probably just went to the latrine," Kane replied.

"I'm going to find her," Noboru said. "You start preparing breakfast for our guests."

Hiro retreated to the guest room and closed the door.

"Hiro?" Father Mateo whispered. "Is something wrong?"

"It sounds as if the innkeeper's mother did not return from the burial yard last night."

Quilts rustled as the priest sat up. "If she is missing, we should help them find her."

"We have no time to involve ourselves in other people's problems," Hiro said. "We have to warn the Iga agents on the travel road about—"

"A woman might be dead!"

"If she did not return last night, she almost certainly is dead, and will remain so—making our help entirely unnecessary."

"Hiro!" Father Mateo's disapproval carried clearly through the darkness.

Loud banging echoed through the inn as someone pounded on the ryokan's front door.

Footsteps hurried past the guest room door as Noboru murmured, "Who could that be? It's barely dawn."

Hiro retrieved his katana from the floor and thrust the long-sword's scabbard through his obi next to the wakizashi. He moved to the shoji and drew it open just as Noboru opened the inn's front door.

A wild-eyed Masako stood on the veranda. Her hair had come partially loose from its braid, and her cheeks were flushed a brilliant red. The rest of her face looked deathly pale.

She tried to speak, but her trembling lips made only a terrified whimper.

She drew a deeper breath and tried again. "It has returned, and killed Ishiko-*san*!"

CHAPTER 6

Masako stumbled across the threshold into the ryokan.

"Kane!" Noboru called, "Bring tea at once!"

Hiro emerged from the guest room. The Jesuit followed, carrying a quilt. Passing by Hiro, Father Mateo laid the blanket around Masako's shoulders. As the priest guided the trembling girl into the reception room, Noboru asked, "Where is my mother?"

"I-in the g-g-graveyard." Masako's teeth chattered. "H-Hanako-*san* sent me, this morning, to fetch the saké flask we left on Ri—on *her* grave, as an offering, yesterday."

She paused for several shuddering breaths. As her shaking subsided she continued, "I saw Ishiko-*san* beside the grave. I thought she had come to pray again this morning, so I waited for her to finish. But when she didn't move, I went closer..." Masako clasped her hands to her mouth and emitted a soft but high-pitched squeal. "She is dead! The *yūrei* killed her!"

"What is a '*dim spirit*'?" Father Mateo whispered, translating the unfamiliar term into Portuguese.

Hiro leaned toward the priest and whispered back, "A wrathful ghost that cannot leave this world until it avenges itself on those who wronged it during life."

Noboru gave them a curious look.

Hiro gestured to Father Mateo. "The foreigner has never heard of yūrei."

"Do they not have ghosts in foreign lands?" Noboru asked.

Kane arrived with a tray that held a single steaming teacup. She extended the tray to Masako, who clutched for it in desperation. Terror had stripped away the entertainer's cultivated grace, leaving behind a frightened country girl.

"Stay with her," Noboru told his wife. "I need to find my mother."

"No!" Masako startled, sloshing tea from the cup. "You must not go! The ghost will kill you too!"

"Did you see the yūrei?" Noboru asked.

"No one sees her and lives." Masako's lips quivered. "She killed Ishiko-*san*!"

"My mother may not be dead." Noboru slipped on his shoes and opened the door, letting in a swirl of misty air. "I have to go."

"We will accompany you." Father Mateo ducked into the guest room, reemerging a moment later carrying both his traveling cloak and Hiro's.

Hiro took his cloak from the Jesuit without argument. Although he had no plans to involve himself in this affair, he knew the priest would never leave for Edo while an elderly woman's body lay abandoned in the woods. The sooner they brought her back to the inn, the sooner they might return to the travel road.

"You do not fear the yūrei?" Noboru asked.

No, Hiro thought, *because they don't exist.*

"I fear for your mother's safety," Father Mateo said. "Let's go."

Although he had no fear of vengeful spirits, Hiro sincerely hoped to discover that Ishiko died of natural causes. Otherwise, he didn't stand a ghost of a chance of leaving the village until the crime was solved.

Hiro and Father Mateo followed Noboru through the village and up the forested slope to the north until a narrow path branched off the travel road. While the primary route continued uphill, Noboru turned onto the smaller trail that headed west along the mountainside.

The fog had intensified overnight, and although the atmosphere grew lighter as the sunless dawn continued, shifting mist hung over the forest like a shroud.

Enormous pines and cedars rose on all sides of the trail, with barren maples and ginkgo trees between them. Roots and stones poked through the rocky soil. Patches of half-melted snow lay banked against the tree trunks where, even on clear days, sunlight failed to reach the ground. The air smelled wet and cold, with hints of pine and the musty, decaying scent of leaves and needles mixed with frozen soil.

Noboru led the way with a confidence born of familiarity, though the undulating, rocky path was often hard to distinguish from the rest of the forest floor.

"Are those fox prints?" Father Mateo gestured to a set of paw-shaped holes in an icy patch of snow.

"Perhaps." Hiro glanced at the tracks for only a moment before he returned to searching the mist for signs of movement. Between the staring yamabushi, Noboru's warning the night before—which seemed even stranger, given his willingness to let Ishiko go to the burial ground alone—and now the woman's disappearance, Hiro had no intention of letting down his guard.

Given the nature of the trail, Ishiko would have required a lantern to find her way in the night before. Her presence would have stood out like a beacon to anyone watching from the woods. A light-weight woman with both hands burdened—one by a lantern, the other with an offering for the dead—would have made an easy target in the dark.

Noboru made a strangled noise and broke into a run.

Just ahead, a tall wooden *torii* loomed across the path. Mist swirled between the uprights of the sacred gate. Beyond it, carved stone monuments appeared and disappeared through the shifting fog. They ranged in size from knee-high slabs of stone to elaborate, five-tiered Buddhist *stupas* taller than a man. Some canted sideways, as if struggling to stand beneath the weight of time. Beyond them, at the far end of the burial yard, the sloping roof of a small mausoleum was barely visible through the mist.

A few meters past the torii, a female figure stood beside a sharp-edged monument. Chunks of ice and dead leaves clung to the curtain of long gray hair that obscured the woman's downturned face. Her life-less arms hung at her sides, almost as pale as the mourning robes that fell around her shoeless feet.

Noboru clutched the woman's shoulders. "Mother!" The word came out as a strangled cry. "Mother . . . no . . ."

The figure bent forward into his arms.

For a moment, Hiro thought the woman was alive, but as he reached Noboru's side Ishiko's hair fell away from her bloodless face. Her eyes stared sightlessly ahead, dark irises surrounded by a startling, violent shade of red instead of the expected white. Bruises on her throat suggested violent strangulation.

"Mother!" Noboru looked panic-stricken. "Help her. Please!"

Father Mateo made the sign of the cross.

"Regrettably," Hiro said, "that is impossible. She is dead."

CHAPTER 7

Other than the corpse itself, Hiro saw no signs of violence near the grave.

An empty rice bowl and the waxy remains of a burned-out candle sat atop the monument beside the corpse. A silver crack ran down the side of the bowl, indicating a careful repair of a former break. The waist-high monument was barely thicker than the bowl itself. Had a struggle taken place beside the grave, the bowl—and its now-missing offering—would have fallen.

A dirty slush of icy snow and frozen mud covered the ground. Footprints were everywhere, but none of them looked new.

"Will you help me?" Noboru asked. "I do not think I have the strength to carry her alone."

"Of course." Father Mateo helped him lift Ishiko's lifeless body, which remained almost as stiff and straight as the posts of the sacred torii at the entrance to the burial ground.

Hiro could not tell if the stiffness came from the passage of time or merely from the body spending the night in the freezing cold.

As he followed Noboru and Father Mateo back along the trail toward the village, Hiro realized, with some surprise, that he had assessed the body and the scene as if he planned to find the woman's killer.

When the men returned to the ryokan, Kane opened the door and held it as they carried the body past. She did not speak, but her gaze never left the corpse.

After slipping off their shoes in the entry, Father Mateo and Noboru carried Ishiko into the reception room. Noboru opened the door to a guest room across from the one where Hiro and Father Mateo slept. Except for the tokonoma, which held an empty vase, and the fact that only a single, unused futon rested in the center of the floor, the room appeared identical to theirs.

Father Mateo stopped at the sight of the futon. "You had a room prepared?"

"My mother had trouble climbing the stairs," Noboru said. "She slept here often, especially on the nights when she visited my sister's grave. I apologize for placing . . . her body . . . so close to your guest room . . ."

"They will be leaving this morning anyway." Kane spoke from the doorway.

As Hiro heard the words, he knew instinctively they were untrue.

After Father Mateo helped Noboru lower the corpse to the futon, the innkeeper fell to his knees.

"This is my fault."

He brushed Ishiko's hair from her face, revealing her sightless eyes. A dead leaf clung to the woman's cheek.

Kane gasped. "Red eyes . . . bare feet and trailing hair . . . she looks like a yūrei."

Noboru whirled. "Do not say such things!"

His wife seemed not to hear him. "Masako-*san* was right . . . it has returned . . ."

"Enough!" Noboru hissed. "Show respect for the dead!"

"You brought her here. Now *it* will follow . . ." Kane gestured to the corpse.

"I said *enough*." Noboru stood and faced his wife.

Kane cringed and backed away. When she reached the door, she turned and fled down the passage to the kitchen. A moment later, they heard footsteps on the creaking stairs to the second floor.

"I apologize for my wife," Noboru knelt beside the corpse once more.

"What did she mean about 'it' returning?" Father Mateo asked.

Noboru tried to close Ishiko's eyelids, but her flesh refused to yield. "A foolish superstition. Nothing more."

"Superstitions do not end in murder," the priest observed.

"I once believed that also." Noboru stood up. "Now, I am not so sure."

"Yūrei do not kill people," Hiro said, "because ghosts do not exist."

"You should leave this village now, while you still can." Noboru seemed unable to tear his gaze from his mother's body. "And hope the yūrei does not follow."

"Vengeful spirits did not kill this woman." Hiro gestured to the corpse. "Do you see the marks on her neck? The blood in her eyes? She was strangled."

Noboru continued as though he did not hear. "I should have gone with her to the burial yard. Or insisted she wait for morning . . ."

"A yūrei did not do this," Hiro repeated.

"But we can help you find whoever did," Father Mateo said.

"No." Noboru shook his head at the priest. "Every hour you remain, you put your lives at risk. You must leave at once."

"If you believe that, why did you allow us to spend the night?" Hiro asked.

"I did not think . . . did not believe it would return."

Ana appeared in the doorway. "Has something happened?"

Based on her lack of reaction to the body lying on the floor, Hiro suspected the housekeeper knew the facts, but wondered what Father Mateo intended to do about the situation.

"Your master needs to leave at once," Noboru said. "You should prepare to go."

Ana waited for the Jesuit's decision.

"We should leave," Hiro murmured in Portuguese. "We have people to warn in other towns, and this woman's death is no concern of ours." He switched to Japanese. "Pack our belongings Ana, it's time to leave."

The housekeeper did not move.

"We are not leaving," Father Mateo said in Portuguese. "These people need our help."

"He does not want our help." Hiro replied in kind.

Noboru looked puzzled but said nothing.

"We can help him learn the truth—" the Jesuit began.

"Please excuse us," Hiro said to Noboru, and gestured for the priest to leave the room.

To his relief, Father Mateo crossed the threshold without argument.

"Should I get ready to leave, or not?" Ana asked.

"Yes," Hiro said.

At the same time, Father Mateo answered, "No."

"When you make your minds up, tell me." Ana walked back toward the kitchen.

Hiro followed Father Mateo into their guest room and closed the door.

"We need to stay and help these people learn the truth," the Jesuit said.

"We have a more important task to complete," Hiro objected. "The woman we looked for here is gone, but others from my clan remain in danger. Would you risk their lives to chase a village ghost?"

"You know as well as I do that a person killed Ishiko, not a ghost."

"No!" Kane shrieked, somewhere nearby, "You'll kill us all!"

CHAPTER 8

Hiro opened the door with his left hand, keeping the right on the hilt of his katana.

Kane had her back to the guest room, but turned toward it as the door slid open.

Relief relaxed the tension from her face. "You haven't left?"

"They are leaving now," Noboru said.

Kane clasped her hands toward Hiro in supplication. "Please—sir—you must not leave. Please wait for the priest to come and appease the yūrei."

"Why does it matter whether or not we stay?" Hiro asked.

"We do not know what made the spirit angry." Kane lowered her hands. "Why it returned—"

"Which is precisely why they need to leave," Noboru interrupted. "This does not concern them."

"Are you certain? Would you risk your family for strangers?" Kane's question sounded more like a demand.

"How long will it take for the priest to conduct the ceremony?" Father Mateo asked.

"Too long," the innkeeper answered.

At the same time, Kane said, "Two days." Her eyes lit up with hope. "If we send word to the shrine in Hakone, the priest will come tomorrow."

"We can wait two days." Father Mateo sounded as if he considered the matter settled.

"With respect—" Hiro began.

The priest did not let him finish. "I can spare the time."

"Thank you." Kane bowed in gratitude. "Noboru-*san*, please send a message to Hakone Shrine and fetch the priest."

Hiro barely waited for Father Mateo to shut the guest room door behind them.

"I do not appreciate you forcing me to remain in this village against my will."

"I did not—"

"You know I cannot argue with my master." Hiro emphasized the final word.

"Forgive me, Hiro," Father Mateo said, "I did not consider that before I spoke, though it would not have changed my decision. We need—I need—to help these people."

"Why? You do not know these villagers. You owe them nothing."

"Yes, and yet . . . I made a grave mistake on Kōya. If I can free these people from their superstitions, prove there is no ghost, I can atone—"

"These villagers will believe in ghosts no matter what we do."

"Not if we find the killer and prove the ghost does not exist."

"But . . . you believe in ghosts."

The Jesuit drew back. "I do not."

"You pray to one every day."

Father Mateo wrinkled his forehead, clearly confused. The wrinkles smoothed as comprehension dawned. "The Holy Ghost is not . . . a ghost."

Hiro did not reply.

"He isn't," the Jesuit insisted. "The Creator God exists as one in three: the Father, the Son, and the Holy Spirit. But the Holy Spirit is not a ghost."

"If you say so."

"There are incorporeal beings that try to harm us," Father Mateo said, "like demons—"

"You believe in *yōkai*, but not ghosts?"

"Not the way Japanese people do." Father Mateo crossed his arms. "It's complicated."

"Clearly."

The Jesuit uncrossed his arms. "I need to help these people, Hiro. Maybe the deaths on Mount Kōya were not my fault, directly, but they weigh upon my soul. If we can bring this woman justice, and find her killer, I will feel that I have served my penance.

"Help me do this, please."

Hiro did not understand how helping a different set of people would relieve the Jesuit's guilt about Mount Kōya—guilt that Hiro believed the priest should not feel in the first place. However, brothers did not abandon one another in times of need, and he considered Father Mateo a brother even though they shared no blood.

"Two days," Hiro said, "but then we leave for Edo. We must not risk the living to help the dead."

He hoped the rumor that Oda Nobunaga's spies had learned the identities of Iga's agents along the travel road would prove a falsehood, rendering the warnings he was rushing to deliver unnecessary. But if not, he planned to snatch as many lives as possible from Oda's grasp.

"I understand, and thank you." Father Mateo bowed his head.

Now that the priest had explained his reasoning, Hiro discovered that he no longer objected so strenuously to the slight delay. A part of him did enjoy bringing killers to justice, and remaining in the village would give him time to learn more about Emiri's disappearance—if he could find a subtle way to do it.

"I suppose we should start the investigation by learning more about the village ghost." Father Mateo opened the guest room door and jumped at the sight of Noboru, who stood on the other side, hand raised as if to knock.

The innkeeper's cheeks flushed red. "I-I apologize for disturbing you." He lowered the hand to his side.

"May we help you?" Hiro asked.

"You need not stay to appease my wife. I have spoken with her and she understands."

Hiro believed the first assertion, but not the second one.

"I am a priest," Father Mateo said. "I do not fear the dead. In fact, I would like to learn more about your yūrei."

"I-I can assure you, I had nothing to do with it," Noboru stammered.

"I did not intend to imply . . ." The priest began again. "I was merely curious."

"Oh." Noboru relaxed a fraction. "We do not speak of it . . . surely you understand . . ."

The inn's front door banged open.

"Noboru!" A deep voice called. "Where are you?"

The innkeeper turned to face the entry and bowed so low that his nose almost touched his knees. "How may I serve you, Otomuro-sama?"

An enormous samurai waddled into the common room. He stood almost a full head taller than Hiro, taller even than Father Mateo. His stomach protruded above his obi as if he carried a melon in his robes, and swayed from side to side as he walked. His meaty jowls wobbled in perfect time with the lopsided, greasy topknot on his head.

He scowled at the sight of Hiro and Father Mateo. "Who are you?"

Hiro bent in a graceful bow, and held it longer than he would have liked. As he straightened, he infused his voice with the humility of a ronin. "Greetings, noble sir. I am Matsui Hiro, now in the service of Father Mateo Ávila de Santos, a priest of the foreign god, from Portugal."

He deliberately omitted any mention of his family or province of origin, enhancing the impression that he had no master, and no power, and thus represented no threat.

The portly samurai's piggish gaze slid back to Noboru. "Is it true? Has the yūrei returned?"

Noboru bowed again. "Regrettably, it appears—"

Otomuro pointed a puffy finger at the innkeeper. "This is your fault! Your family brought a curse upon this village!"

CHAPTER 9

Otomuro's outstretched finger shook. "I should have sent you away and closed this ryokan when the yūrei killed your father, but I foolishly allowed you to persuade me it was over. Now, we all must suffer the consequence of your lie!"

Noboru bowed his head. "I humbly apologize, Otomuro-*sama*. I assure you, it was not a lie. We all believed—"

"You lied! And now you will pay to pacify the ghost." The samurai lowered his shaking arm. "We must send for the priest at once."

"I will do so immediately, Otomuro-*sama*." Noboru said.

Otomuro's gaze returned to Father Mateo. "What is your business in my village?"

"My scribe and I are merely passing through on the way to Edo." Father Mateo bowed.

The samurai considered this. "Your presence may have angered the yūrei."

"With respect," the Jesuit said, "I do not believe—"

"Be silent!" Otomuro thundered. "You are the reason she returned, or part of it anyway. You will remain in the village until the priest performs the cleansing ceremony, and you will pay a fine, to me, for angering the ghost. One golden *koban* should suffice."

"One gold koban? To you?" Hiro asked.

Kane slipped back into the room, as if drawn by the samurai's shouting.

Otomuro pointed at Noboru once more. "Do not allow this man to charge you anything for staying at this cursed ryokan. As of today, the inn is officially closed."

"Closed?" Noboru asked. "For how long? Without the ryokan—"

"You will leave this village, and the yūrei will go with you!" Otomuro raised his chin triumphantly.

"Yūrei are bound to places, not to families," Kane said. Noboru shot his wife a pleading look, but she ignored him. "Even if we leave, the killing will not stop until everyone responsible for her suffering is dead."

Otomuro's mouth fell open. His cheeks flushed scarlet.

Noboru fell to his knees and pressed his forehead to the floor. "I apologize for my ignorant, ill-trained wife."

Father Mateo stepped between them. "With respect, have you considered that a person might have killed Ishiko-*san*, and not a ghost?"

Otomuro's stomach swayed as he took a step backward. "What did you say?"

"I said, what if a person—not a ghost—murdered Ishiko-*san*?" The Jesuit gestured to Hiro. "My scribe and I have investigated quite a few unusual deaths, including several in Kyoto. Every time, we discovered the real killer. With your permission, we would like to investigate this one, and discover the true cause of Ishiko-*san*'s unfortunate demise."

"Please, no." Kane fell on her knees before the samurai. "Otomuro-*sama*, do not allow it. If they anger the yūrei with disrespectful questions, she will kill us all."

"A moment ago you wanted them to stay," Noboru protested.

"To stay, but not to interfere or provoke her further." Kane gave her husband a pleading look.

"You need not fear the spirit's wrath," Father Mateo said. "I am a priest of the Creator God. My faith has a ritual of exorcism that no demon can withstand. If your village truly has an evil spirit, I can help expel it."

Otomuro turned his head so quickly that his jowls wobbled like a rooster's wattle. "Does this ritual truly work?" He looked suspicious. "I will not pay you to perform it, even if it does."

"I have no intention of requesting payment," Father Mateo said. "But I will help you only if you allow an investigation."

Otomuro laid a finger on his lips as he considered the request.

A weighty silence fell.

Just as Hiro felt certain the samurai planned to refuse, Kane gave a tiny, frightened whimper.

Otomuro's scowl returned. "I will allow the investigation, but only until the priest arrives from Hakone Shrine to perform a Shintō exorcism. After that, you must pay your fine and leave this place immediately." He scowled at Noboru. "As for you, if you want to reopen this ryokan after the exorcism, it will cost you twice as much as it did the last time. In addition to paying the priest to perform the ritual."

Noboru gasped. "Otomuro-*sama*, please, show mercy. The ceremony alone will cost every penny we have saved."

"I have decided!" The samurai raised his wobbly chins. "If you do not pay, I will burn this building down." He strutted back to the entry, stepped into his shoes, and left without closing the door behind him.

Noboru struggled to his feet as Kane lowered her face to her hands and sobbed.

Hiro gestured toward the open door. "Who was that?"

"Otomuro-*sama*?" Noboru looked at the entry as if expecting the portly samurai to return. "The second son of the eldest cousin of the Lion of Sagami."

"Who?" Father Mateo asked.

"Hōjō Ujiyasu, the local *daimyō*, is often called the Lion of Sagami," Hiro explained.

"Otomuro-*sama* keeps an eye on the travel road, on his behalf," Noboru said.

"Not that it's much of a travel road, since the typhoon." Kane stood up, walked to the entry, and closed the door.

"The traffic will return." Noboru's tone suggested the argument was not new.

Kane gave him a look of doubt mixed with unhappiness and left the room without another word.

"It will return," Noboru repeated, this time to Hiro. "When the typhoon and landslides closed the road last year, the travelers started using a detour, a temporary route, to the south. But now that the road is clear they will return. Just as you chose to come this way."

We had a reason to visit this village, Hiro thought. *Most travelers do not.*

"Why does Otomuro-*san* blame your family for the ghost?" Father Mateo asked.

"Are there truly no yūrei in your country?" Noboru replied.

"I believe the foreigner asked his question first," Hiro said pointedly.

Noboru looked through the open door at Ishiko's corpse. "I will tell you, but I would prefer to have the conversation elsewhere. I do not know how much the dead can hear. Would you accompany me to the teahouse?"

He gestured toward the entry.

"Where are you going?" Kane's demanding question made Noboru turn. She had returned to the end of the passage, with Ana on her heels.

"And what do you plan to do about their meals?" Kane continued, "Since I have to take care of everything alone, now that your mother . . ." She gestured to the room where Ishiko lay.

"My housekeeper would be happy to assist you for the next few days," Father Mateo offered. "To ease your burden."

Ana's face looked anything but happy.

Kane looked down her nose at Ana. "Can you cook?"

The housekeeper stared at the younger woman.

Noboru spoke first, and decisively. "Kane will care for Ishiko-*san*, and clean the room where my mother's body lies. However, if you do not mind your housekeeper helping with the meals, and cleaning your guest room, we would be grateful for her assistance."

"Of course," the Jesuit replied.

Ana bowed in assent, but with unusual stiffness.

"You do not need to prepare a meal this morning, except for yourselves," Noboru told his wife. "Our guests and I will eat at Hanako's teahouse."

"But I've already started rice and tea," Kane objected, "and we can't afford—"

"I am now master of this ryokan," Noboru said. "I will decide what I can, or cannot, afford."

CHAPTER 10

Outside, the ground-level mist had thinned, but the thick, pale clouds that filled the sky seemed almost close enough to touch. The air smelled dry and cold, redolent with the spice of smoke and pine.

But for that scent of smoke, Hiro might have believed the village long-deserted. No one moved in the street or around the houses. Even the scattered stubble in the rice field next to Otomuro's mansion looked abandoned and forlorn.

The teahouse door swung open as they approached.

As Hanako bowed from the entry, Hiro wondered if the woman spent all her time staring into the street or if her eerie punctuality was merely coincidental.

She straightened and clasped her hands to her chest. "Noboru-*san*, I am so sorry . . ."

Noboru returned the bow. "I know you do not customarily open the teahouse until afternoon, but I hoped . . ."

Hanako looked past him, at Hiro and Father Mateo. "Your guests require a morning meal before they leave?"

"Indeed." Noboru sounded relieved. "That is, they need a meal . . ."

"Surely they do not intend to stay?" Hanako looked at Father Mateo. "Did you not hear what happened?"

"We have offered to investigate the crime," the Jesuit replied. "To prove an angry spirit did not kill Ishiko-*san*."

Hanako covered her mouth with her hand. "Do you not understand the danger? Even to speak of her—of it—is dangerous." She turned back to Noboru. "You cannot let them stay."

"They wish to help." Noboru gestured to Father Mateo. "Also, his faith has rituals to exorcise—"

"The rituals of a foreign god might make it even angrier."

"I will also send for the priest from Hakone Shrine." Noboru's voice grew soft. He raised his hands in supplication. "Besides, Kane believes their presence may have angered the spirit. If so, it is important for them to remain until after the ceremony."

"I suppose they are your lives to risk." Hanako bowed and gestured for the men to come inside.

After they removed their shoes, she led them through the entry to the room where they had eaten the night before. As they seated themselves around the table, Hanako said, "Forgive me, but your meal will take some time to prepare. I have no help today. I sent Masako-*san* to bed—she was hysterical from shock."

"Please take your time," Noboru said, "we understand."

"And we apologize for the inconvenience," Father Mateo added.

Hanako bowed and slid the shoji closed.

Noboru folded his hands in his lap.

Hiro rested his own hands on his thighs and waited silently, hoping Father Mateo would do the same. Eventually, the silence would grow too heavy for the innkeeper to bear.

Unfortunately, the Jesuit spoke first. "Please tell us more about the village ghost."

"You truly have no yūrei in your country?" Noboru asked.

Hiro began to remind the man that they had covered this ground already, but before he could do so Father Mateo said, "We do not, but I would like to learn more about them."

"No man should wish to learn this thing," Noboru said, "and I am not qualified to teach."

"A man of samurai rank has asked you a question," Hiro interrupted. "You will tell him what he wants to know."

Noboru dipped his head in silent apology and began.

"My grandmother used to say that the human soul is barbed, like a thorny plant." He raised his hand, his fingers bent like claws. "During life, these barbs secure the soul to the body. But when a person dies, they can also catch on the fabric of this world. If that

happens, the soul is trapped like a fish in a net. It cannot pass to para-
dise, or judgment, or rebirth, until the barbs are smoothed by resolu-
tion of whatever issue trapped it here. In the case of a yūrei, the issue
is . . . revenge."

"So the village ghost once lived here?" Father Mateo asked. "Who
do you believe the spirit was, in life?"

"She was my sister," Noboru whispered.

Hiro spoke to avoid the apology he saw forming on Father Mateo's
lips. "How did your sister die?"

"It is dangerous to speak of," Noboru said.

"Surely not in daylight," Hiro countered. "In every legend I have
heard, the yūrei only manifests at night."

"We cannot risk it." Noboru clasped his hands more tightly. "If we
see her, we will die, as Mother did."

"A yūrei did not kill your mother," Hiro said. "Her injuries were
made by human hands."

"A yūrei's ghostly hands can strangle just as surely as a living
man's," Noboru countered.

Hiro found the comparison interesting, but before he could ask
another question Hanako returned to the room.

The teahouse owner carried a lacquered tray that held a teapot,
cups, and several covered bowls.

"I have prepared you soup, rice, and *tsukemono*, along with tea." She
set two covered bowls and a dish of pickled vegetables in front of each
man. "I apologize for the simple fare, but I had nothing else prepared."

"This will more than suffice," Noboru said.

"I am pleased to help in your time of need." Hanako bowed her
head. As she raised it and began to pour the tea she asked, "Shall I
bring a shamisen and play?"

"Thank you for the offer," Noboru said, "but today we prefer to
eat alone."

The smile froze on Hanako's face.

"If we require anything more, we will call you." When the woman
did not leave, Noboru added, "We need nothing more, Hanako-*san*."

Her lips turned down, but she quickly forced a smile. "As you wish."

She bowed more formally and left the room.

CHAPTER 11

After the door slid shut behind Hanako, Father Mateo bent his head in silent prayer. Hiro raised his teacup, closed his eyes, and inhaled the fragrant steam. The roasted leaves imbued the scent with unusual depth. He took a sip. The natural sweetness and rich, mellow flavor of roasted tea lingered pleasantly on his tongue.

When the Jesuit raised his head Noboru gestured to the food. "Please eat."

The larger bowls held mounds of polished rice. The smaller ones held salty miso broth with tofu cubes and slivers of fresh-cut onion floating on the steaming surface. Mingled scents of rice and onions blended with the smell of tea.

Hiro found the soup a bit too salty, but approved of the choice to add the delicate slivered onions raw, allowing the heat of the soup to cook them gently while preserving both their pungency and crunch. He alternated sips of soup with bites of rice to cut the salinity.

"Masako-*san* claimed the spirit had returned," Father Mateo said. "Has it killed before?"

"Four times. Five, if you count my mother." Noboru watched his soup as if expecting a ghost to appear in the steam. "I fear she may not be the last."

"Why would your sister return as a yūrei?" Hiro asked. "And why do you believe she will kill again?"

"It is dangerous—"

"So is refusing a samurai," Hiro warned.

Noboru did not answer.

Just as Hiro felt certain the innkeeper would call his bluff, Noboru set his soup bowl on the table. "To understand, you must know the history of our ryokan."

In Hiro's experience, most people grossly overestimated the importance of personal histories and anecdotes. However, he also understood that listening to unnecessary stories was far easier than changing someone's mind, and that even largely irrelevant stories often held a grain of useful truth.

"My mother's grandfather, Nobu, worked as a porter on the travel road. Each morning he walked to Hakone in the hope of finding a burden to carry. Most nights, he did not return until many hours after dark.

"Even as a young man, Nobu-*san* knew he did not want his sons to labor like animals through the summer heat and winter storms." Noboru reached for the teapot and refilled Father Mateo's teacup, then Hiro's, and finally his own. "He saved every coin he possibly could, and by the time his eldest son became a man, Nobu had saved enough money to build a ryokan. He continued to work as a porter until he died, but his son—my grandfather—never had to work the travel road.

"On his death bed, Nobu confessed to my grandfather that he and his wife—who had died before him—also had another child, a girl. In order to give her a better life, they apprenticed her to a teahouse in Kyoto on the day she learned to walk."

"Yuko-*san*?" Father Mateo guessed.

"Yes. After Nobu-*san* died, my grandfather found a letter his sister Yuko-*san* had sent from Kyoto many years before. He sent her a letter, inviting her to return and visit the village, so they could meet. She not only returned, but stayed."

"And built the teahouse," the Jesuit concluded.

Hiro wished the priest would let Noboru tell the story.

"My grandfather helped her pay for it, using proceeds from the ryokan." Noboru's expression shifted slightly. "Originally, it was a loan, although my father forgave the debt in exchange for my sister becoming Yuko's heir."

"But Hanako-*san* inherited the teahouse..." Hiro trailed off, obligating Noboru to explain.

"My sister died one day before Yuko-*san* died," Noboru said bitterly, "so Hanako—the most senior apprentice, after my sister—became the heir."

"And you consider forgiving the debt unjust?" Hiro prompted.

"Even had she lived, my sister was not worth enough to cancel the debt Yuko-*san* owed to my grandfather, and then my parents. When both she and my great-aunt died, and then my father, the payments should have been made to me, as the surviving son. But, as I said, the debt had been forgiven—in writing—leaving me no legal claim."

"Now Hanako owns the teahouse outright," Hiro said.

"I do not begrudge Hanako-*san* an honest inheritance," Noboru clarified. "I resent my father trading part of mine away to obtain a place for my worthless sister, who did not want to work in a teahouse, or inherit one, in the first place."

Although he did not believe in yūrei, Hiro began to understand why the villagers thought the ghost of Noboru's sister might hold a grudge.

"None of this explains why you believe your sister became a ghost," Father Mateo said. "How did she die?"

Noboru's gaze flickered to the hilts of Hiro's swords. "She had an accident. She fell, and hit her head, and died. An accident, and nothing more."

Liar. Aloud, Hiro asked, "Did she die in this room?"

"Yes." Noboru's cheeks flushed red. "That is, not in this room, but in the teahouse. She was in the kitchen, preparing tea. She slipped and fell."

"Was she preparing tea for herself, or for a guest?" Hiro asked.

"I do not know." Noboru glanced at the door as if wishing Hanako would reappear. "I wasn't here."

The flush in his cheeks would have betrayed the lie even if he had managed to meet Hiro's eyes or to control the quaver in his voice.

"Perhaps Hanako-*san* knows more about it," Hiro said.

"I don't think so," Noboru said, too quickly. "And you will upset her if you ask about the dead." After a pause he added, with false brightness, "Though of course you are free to ask her if you wish."

"You intend us to believe your sister became a yūrei after suffering an accidental death?" Hiro asked.

"If so," the Jesuit put in, "what hooked her soul to the fabric of this world?"

Noboru opened his mouth, paused, and exhaled heavily. "Do you truly believe you can set her spirit free?"

"We truly believe there are no yūrei," Hiro said. "In this village or otherwise."

"And we believe we can prove your mother was killed by a person," Father Mateo added, "not an angry ghost."

Hiro would not have made the Jesuit's assertion quite so strongly in the presence of a man who just confessed—albeit unwittingly—to having a motive for his mother's murder.

"My sister held a grudge against our parents, and Yuko-*san* as well. She never wanted to become an entertainer."

"You mentioned four other victims," Father Mateo said. "In addition to Ishiko-*san*."

"The spirit also killed Yuko-*san*, my father, and—"

The shoji slid open.

"Please excuse the interruption." Hanako bowed, entered the room, and lifted the empty bowls from the table to the tray she carried. "May I offer you more tea?"

"No." Noboru stood up, clearly relieved by the interruption. "We do not wish to impose upon your kindness any longer."

Hiro and Father Mateo took the cue and rose to their feet as well.

"I will show you out." Hanako preceded them to the doorway and handed the tray of dishes to Masako, who waited just outside the shoji. The pale girl accepted the tray with a bow and departed toward the kitchen without a word.

"Will you return for dinner?" Hanako asked as she guided them to the exit. "I have fresh eels."

"I do not know," Noboru said.

"Surely you don't expect Kane to cook . . ." She gave Hiro and Father Mateo a meaningful look. "Noboru's wife means well, but . . ."

"We will eat our evening meal at the ryokan." Noboru spoke with unexpected firmness.

"As you wish." Hanako's smile did not reach her eyes.

CHAPTER 12

Hiro paused beside the steps leading up to the ryokan. "I believe I'd like to take a walk."

Noboru paused, his hand already on the door. "Outside?"

"That is where walks customarily occur."

"But the yūrei . . ."

"As I mentioned, in the tales I've heard, yūrei do not attack in daylight," Hiro said.

"And if, as you claim, the killer is not a ghost?" Noboru asked.

Hiro laid a hand on the hilt of his katana. "I will take my chances."

Father Mateo stepped back off the porch. "A walk sounds pleasant."

"In this cold?" Noboru peered around the sheltering eaves at the cloudy sky. When the two men showed no signs of changing their minds, he shook his head and went inside.

Hiro started up the road that ran through the village.

Father Mateo matched his steps. "We're going to the burial ground, aren't we?"

Hiro did not reply.

Icicles hung from the eaves of the houses. Patches of pale, half-melted snow lay on the thatch like slices of whitefish on fermented rice. The final house before the samurai mansion appeared to be occupied only by the giant spiders whose webs connected the roof to a rotting woodpile near the door.

Behind the houses, rows of cedars loomed. Bare of branches to a height of a dozen meters, their massive trunks shed strips of bark like lepers forced to keep their distance, lest the houses catch their dread disease.

"Even if the men are working," Father Mateo murmured, "where are the women and children?" He gestured to a plume of pale gray smoke rising up from the chimney hole of Otomuro's mansion. "He would know. We should stop and ask."

"You want to knock on a samurai's door and ask what happened to commoners?"

"You don't have to make it sound so strange."

"It *is* so strange." Hiro gestured to the mansion. "Until we know which questions to ask, we are better off asking none."

"Why do you want to revisit the burial yard?" the Jesuit asked.

"I want to take a second look at something."

"What did you see?"

"Before I discuss it, I want to make sure I remember it correctly."

By the time they reached the burial ground, Hiro's fingers were numb and his toes had begun to burn from cold. He regretted agreeing to investigate Ishiko's death, and not only because of the temperatures. The dead did not care who killed them, and the survivors, at least in this village, cared only not to join the dead. Investigating the woman's death seemed pointless, and likely thankless.

He should have argued harder against the Jesuit's desire to stay.

But since he had not, he would do his best to find the killer quickly.

Hiro paused beside the grave where they had discovered Ishiko's body. The mended bowl and remains of the candle sat atop the monument, precisely as he remembered.

"Now can you tell me what you saw?" Father Mateo asked.

Hiro gestured to the monument, but as he did he noticed something else.

"An empty bowl?" the Jesuit asked.

Hiro pointed to his new discovery. "And a set of footprints heading up the mountain."

"I don't understand how the two things fit together."

"They may not," Hiro said. "But the offering bowl would not have been empty when Ishiko carried it here last night, and if an animal had eaten the food, the bowl would be lying on the ground."

"Suggesting a person emptied it." Father Mateo looked at the tracks in the snow. "Do you think the yamabushi killed Ishiko-*san* and took the offering?"

"That seems unlikely," Hiro said, "but a person made those tracks, for certain."

"Should we follow them?"

"If we don't, they'll vanish, but I want to take a closer look around before we go." He looked at the sharp-edged monument. "Did you notice anything strange about Ishiko's corpse?"

"Aside from the evidence of strangulation?"

"Her hair obscured her face, and her arms hung at her sides." Hiro paused, realizing the Jesuit lacked the cultural reference to understand. "In stories, yūrei often have unbound hair and dangling limbs."

"The killer positioned her to resemble a ghost, perhaps to reinforce the suggestion that a yūrei killed her." Father Mateo furrowed his brow. "That reminds me. How did the corpse stay standing? Muscles go limp when people die."

"Only for the first few hours," Hiro corrected, "after that, they stiffen and hold their position for quite some time. Also, the temperature dropped below freezing after dark, which would have hastened the stiffening of her joints."

"You think the killer waited around until the body froze?"

"That, or returned in the night to stand it up." Seeing nothing more of use, Hiro started toward the trail of footprints.

Father Mateo joined him, and they climbed uphill through the trees.

Hiro remained alert for any unusual sound or movement, but noticed nothing. In fact, the forest seemed deserted. He heard only the silent squish of his feet, and Father Mateo's, as they broke through the thin crust of snow and crushed the decomposing leaves beneath.

The hair on the back of Hiro's neck stood up. Once again, he felt the gaze of someone watching through the trees. He looked over his shoulder, but saw only the empty forest.

"Stay alert," he whispered in Portuguese. "If the yamabushi killed Ishiko, he might try to kill us too."

The tracks led up the hill in a switchback path that wove around clusters of bamboo grass. Several large gaps in the trail puzzled Hiro until he recognized that the person must have jumped from stone to stone across the boulders that dotted the slope like islands in a steep white sea.

After several minutes, Hiro stopped and looked around.

He had lost the trail.

He saw no stones within the range of a human leap. The field of snow around the trees, though melted thin enough to show the dirt beneath and pockmarked with the tracks of foxes, deer, and squirrels, held not a single human print.

"Is something wrong?" Father Mateo whispered.

"The tracks appear to end."

"They can't just end." The Jesuit looked down the mountain. "Do you think whoever made them reversed his course, stepping into his own footprints to hide the trail?"

"Only a shinobi . . ." Hiro paused. *Or a kunoichi.*

"Or a ghost."

"Ghosts don't leave foot—" Hiro noticed the Jesuit's smile. "That isn't funny."

"Since we've lost the trail," Father Mateo said, "I suggest we return to the village and try to learn more about Noboru's sister. I think he lied to us about her death."

"I agree." Hiro pushed his frustration away. "I believe his sister was murdered."

Father Mateo stopped. "By the person who killed Ishiko-*san*?"

"We cannot rule it out."

CHAPTER 13

As Hiro and Father Mateo approached the ryokan, the door swung open.

Kane stood in the entry, her face unusually pale. "Did either of you leave your room last night after Noboru-*san* brought you back from the teahouse?"

Hiro stepped in front of Father Mateo and climbed the veranda steps. "I suggest you change your tone."

Behind him, Father Mateo said, "I assure you we had nothing to do with Ishiko-*san*'s death."

The Jesuit's reassuring tone blew fresh air into the coals of frustration smoldering in Hiro's chest.

"With respect—" Kane began, though her voice held none.

Hiro cut her off. "There is no respectful way for a commoner to accuse a samurai. Change your tone, or I will change it for you."

"She's a woman," Father Mateo whispered in Portuguese.

Hiro rounded on the priest. "Need I remind you, *women also kill.*" He turned to Kane and shifted back to Japanese. "Have you something more to say?"

She released the door and retreated a step. "I apologize for my impulsive question. I did not intend to imply . . ."

Hiro regained control. "Precisely what did you intend?"

"I have lost . . ." She seemed to reconsider the statement. "Never mind. I should have known better. Please forgive me." She bowed and stepped away to clear the entry.

Hiro and Father Mateo left their shoes inside the door and returned to the guest room.

As Hiro slid the shoji closed behind them, Father Mateo whispered, "That was strange."

Everything about this place is strange.

"What do you think she lost?" The Jesuit asked.

"Something valuable," Hiro said.

"Do you think she believes we stole it?"

"I think she fears the consequences if she does not find it." Hiro paused. "Beyond that, we cannot make assumptions."

"Do you think she might have killed Ishiko-*san*?"

Hiro had considered the possibility, though he had not expected Father Mateo—who trusted most people far more than they deserved—to suspect it also. "Perhaps, though I consider it unlikely."

"Why?" The Jesuit seemed relieved as well as curious.

"Only a fool would risk a murder on a night when guests were present, if the ryokan is normally empty at this time of year. And though accusing us was foolish, Kane does not strike me as a fool."

"But last night was the anniversary," Father Mateo pointed out, "a date that makes it easier to blame a murder on the ghost."

Hiro laid a hand on the door. "I think it's time to meet the other residents of this village."

"Do you think they will talk to us? If they fear the ghost?"

"You told Otomuro-*san* that you know a ritual to exorcise a yūrei."

"A demon," the priest corrected, "but there is no demon here."

Hiro heard the warning in the Jesuit's tone, and worded his reply with care. "I am not asking you to lie. But if, for the sake of argument, your rite was useful . . . would you not perform it?"

"You know I would."

"Then I see no harm in telling the villagers that we seek information in order to find out if your rite can help them." Before the priest could argue, Hiro added, "How would you feel if there was a demon, and you missed it because you assumed you knew the truth?"

He felt a minor pang of conscience, knowing that Father Mateo felt a need to expunge himself of guilt over the recent events on Kōya. As he opened his mouth to withdraw the comment and apologize, someone knocked on the shoji.

Hiro opened the sliding door to see the Jesuit's housekeeper standing on the other side. She clutched a squirming Gato in her arms.

"Ana?" Father Mateo sneezed and drew a scrap of cloth from his sleeve to wipe his nose.

"Hm." The housekeeper entered the room. "I cannot cook in that sad excuse for a kitchen. Even the rats want to escape, if the hole in the wall is any indication."

"How do you know rats made the hole?" The Jesuit tucked the cloth in his sleeve again. "And if the kitchen does have rats, why bring the cat in here?"

"Rats chew holes when they can't find anything else to eat." Ana set Gato on the floor and closed the door to prevent the cat's escape. "I don't want this good cat getting hurt by a giant village rat. She's safer here with you."

Gato wound around her legs and purred.

"Did you see rats in the holes?" Hiro asked.

"The hole," Ana corrected. "Just one, in the wall behind the miso barrel."

"What kind of rat eats plaster when there's miso?" Hiro asked.

Ana sniffed. "You haven't smelled the miso."

Father Mateo looked confused. "What were you doing behind the miso barrel?"

"Cleaning." Ana crossed her arms. "I wouldn't trust that lazy girl to clean her buttocks, let alone a kitchen."

Hiro stifled a laugh that emerged as a snort.

"When I showed her the hole, she walked away without a word," Ana continued. "Didn't even care."

"Does the hole go all the way through the wall?" Hiro asked.

Ana shook her head. "About halfway, but it's large enough to hold a saké flask."

"Rats don't chew holes that big," Hiro said.

"You never listen. It's a *giant* rat." The housekeeper bent and patted Gato, who flopped on her side and purred. "You stay here, Gato. Father Mateo will keep you safe."

As she straightened, she glared at Hiro as if to suggest he was no use at all.

She opened the door and left the room, closing the shoji silently behind her.

Hiro looked at the cat. "She can stay here while we talk with the villagers." As he laid a hand on the door, he added, "But I want to see that hole before we go."

CHAPTER 14

Hiro and Father Mateo walked down the passage and paused at the top of the steps that led to the kitchen.

A large brick oven stood at the center of the room. Two covered kettles sat atop the cooking surface, sending up curls of steam that smelled of overfermented miso and spoiling fish.

On the left side of the kitchen, a sliding wooden door stood slightly ajar, allowing light and air into the room. A mostly-depleted pile of firewood sat to the left of the door, while a trio of barrels lined the wall to its right. Faint scuffmarks marred the earthen floor where Ana had pulled the barrels forward. The last one remained just far enough away from the wall for Hiro to see the edge of a hole behind it.

Ana appeared in the outer doorway, holding an armful of kindling.

"What are you doing here?" she asked.

"We could ask the same of you," Hiro said. "You claimed you could not cook in these conditions."

The housekeeper stepped inside and set the kindling on the stack beside the door. "If I don't, we'll all go hungry." Ana wiped her hands on a towel that hung from her obi.

"We came to see the rat hole," Father Mateo said.

She gestured to the barrels.

Hiro descended the steps, slipped on a pair of the kitchen sandals that sat beside them, and crossed the room. The sour smell grew worse as he approached, so he breathed shallowly as he pulled the barrel farther away from the wall to expose the hole.

Something had dug away the plaster, leaving an indentation about the size of a saké flask. Although the hole had ragged edges, he saw no obvious marks from teeth or claws.

"Why would a rat make a hole that doesn't go anywhere?" Father Mateo asked.

Hiro pushed the barrel back against the wall. "Rats did not make this hole. It looks like a hiding place to me."

"A hiding place?" The Jesuit asked. "For what?"

"Hm." Ana picked up a broom and swept the earthen floor. "The only things hiding in that hole are rats."

Hiro switched to Portuguese. "Perhaps whatever the innkeeper's wife is missing."

"We should ask her about it," the priest agreed.

"Not unless you want to spend the afternoon searching for a woman's misplaced baubles." Hiro returned to the steps, slipped off the kitchen sandals, and switched back to Japanese. "Ana, keep an eye on that hole and tell us if a rat—or anything else—appears inside it."

The housekeeper raised the broom. "If a rat appears in there, it will be the last thing he ever does."

Mist descended from the cloudy sky, swirling down to obscure all but the closest houses. Even the towering trees had turned to shadows, looming behind a foggy veil. Nothing moved on the road or between the houses.

The village seemed as dead as the woman lying in the ryokan.

Hiro squinted into the mist. For a moment, he thought he saw a shadow move at the far end of the road, near the place where the yamabushi had appeared the day before.

When he looked again, he saw only swirling fog.

With Father Mateo at his side, he crossed the strip of ground between the ryokan and the house next door. The humble, single-story building featured a steeply peaked thatch roof with a wooden beam that ran along the ridge. Overhanging eaves protected the walls from snow and rain. Unlike the ryokan, the house sat at ground level with no veranda or raised foundation. A six-inch wooden beam across the entry door created a simple threshold at the end of the muddy path that connected the house to the travel road.

As they approached, Hiro noted that all of the frozen footprints around the door were adult-sized. The door swung open before he knocked, and he wondered if every woman in the village spent her days watching the road from behind the door.

The woman who stood in the opening looked no more than twenty. Her eyes, which seemed too large for her tiny face, reminded Hiro of a deer. She wore a dark kimono hand-embroidered with flying cranes, an unusual choice for a country girl, especially in winter. But her most striking feature was the streak of pure white hair that began at the top of her head and trickled through her thick, dark braid like a waterfall over obsidian cliffs.

She bowed. "I am sorry. My husband is at work. But you can come back, if you want to see him." She clasped her hands together as she spoke.

"Perhaps we could talk with you instead." Hiro's unusually gentle tone drew a look from Father Mateo.

The woman bit her lip. She gripped her hands until her knuckles whitened.

"We mean no harm," Hiro continued. "Have you heard what happened in the burial yard last night?"

The woman dropped her voice to a whisper. "*She* came back. We must not say her name. It is not safe."

"That is precisely why we came." Hiro gestured to Father Mateo. "This man is a priest of the foreign god, from across the sea. His faith has special rites to cast out evil. He wants to help—"

"Do they work?" the woman asked eagerly. "The rites?"

"When evil is present." Father Mateo gave Hiro a sidelong glance.

"Please come in." The woman stepped away from the door, though she watched the road as if expecting an attack at any moment.

The front half of the one-room house had an earthen floor packed down by years of use until it looked and felt like stone. To the right of the door, a waist-high wooden fence enclosed a rectangular area four meters long and a little more than two meters deep. A pair of buckets sat beside a wooden gate at the near end of the fence, beside the door. One bucket held water, the other a combination of grain and straw. More rice straw covered the floor of the stall, and a coiled rope with one end tied in the shape of a halter hung from a peg attached to the wooden gate. The area emitted a distinct, and pungent, bovine smell that lingered in the air along with the more familiar scents of smoke and tatami grasses.

An earthen stove squatted near the center of the living space. It radiated pleasant warmth, if not much light. Beyond the stove, the rear half of the house contained a knee-high platform covered with tatami. A brazier on the floor beside the platform filled the house with smoky light.

The woman gestured to the tatami-covered area. "Please sit down. I will make tea."

"You don't—" Father Mateo began, but Hiro spoke over him.

"Thank you. We will wait." He led the priest to the edge of the platform, removing his shoes before stepping onto its tatami-covered surface. Switching to Portuguese, he murmured, "Do not refuse the tea, and drink it slowly."

"Why?"

"It gives us a way to control the conversation," Hiro said. "As long as tea remains in the cups, it would be impolite for her to make us leave."

CHAPTER 15

Hiro knelt near the edge of the platform, facing the stove. Father Mateo followed suit, though the Jesuit seemed uncomfortable.

As the woman bustled around preparing tea, Father Mateo gestured to the enclosure at the front of the house. "Is that a stall?" he whispered in Portuguese.

Hiro nodded.

"I thought only samurai could own horses."

"Only samurai can ride them," Hiro corrected. "But these people do not have a horse. They own an ox."

"How do you know?"

Hiro raised an eyebrow. "Given the smell, how could you not?"

Father Mateo sniffled. "With this cold, I can't smell anything at all." He pulled the cloth from his sleeve and wiped his nose again.

"Consider yourself fortunate."

Father Mateo switched to Japanese as the woman approached with a tray that held a steaming kettle and a pair of cups. "May we ask your honorable name?"

The woman bowed. "I am Mume. Kane-*san*, who lives at the ryokan, is my sister."

"And your husband?" Hiro asked.

"No, she is only my sister." Mume looked confused. "My husband is called Taso-*san*. He is a porter on the travel road."

The Jesuit laid a hand on his chest. "I am Father Mateo Ávila de Santos, and I come from a land called Portugal, across the sea. This man is Matsui Hiro, my scribe."

She furrowed her brow. "He looks like a samurai to me."

"I am samurai," Hiro said. "A scribe writes messages on behalf of someone else."

"Oh!" Mume gave Father Mateo an understanding smile. "Do not feel bad. I cannot write *kanji* either."

She set the tray on the platform and poured a cup of tea. As she handed it to Father Mateo, she said, "I am sorry about the smell. My husband has an ox."

"I do not mind." The Jesuit spoke with unusual kindness, as if speaking to a child.

Mume rewarded him with another dazzling, large-eyed smile.

"We hoped you could tell us more about the spirit that haunts your village," Hiro said.

Mume fumbled the pot and upset the second teacup, spilling tea across the tray. She gave a little cry and grabbed for the cup. "I am sorry. I am so sorry!"

Hiro helped her right the cup and held it while she poured the tea with trembling hands. Once the cup was safely filled and in his grasp, Mume wiped the tray with a towel before setting the teapot down.

Hiro inhaled the steam that rose from his teacup and waited to see if the girl would remember his question. To his surprise, she did.

"Kane-*san* says we must not talk about the ghost," she told them earnestly. "Talking about it will make her angry. She will hurt us."

Hiro noted the nonspecific feminine pronouns, but decided not to ask—for the moment—whether the undefined "she" referred to Kane or the ghost.

"We understand," Father Mateo said. "Do you and Taso-*san* have any children?"

Hiro wondered at the randomness of the question.

"The *kami* have not blessed me with a child. I wish they would. But Kane-*san* says—" She closed her mouth abruptly, leaving Hiro to wonder if Kane had told her sister not to discuss that topic either.

"Why are you asking me about the yūrei?" Mume asked. "Kane-*san* and Noboru-*san* know more about her. Because she was—" Mume clapped a hand over her mouth, as if remembering she should not talk about it. When she lowered the hand, she whispered, "Please, sir, do not say the spirit's name."

No chance of that. I do not even know it.

Hiro took a sip of tea. It contained more stem than leaf, and tasted as bitter as the scent suggested. Even so, he found the flavor strangely appealing. More importantly, he recognized that Mume had offered them the best she had. Plenty of people who owned far more showed far less hospitality.

"What if I told you yūrei are not real?" Father Mateo asked.

Mume considered the Jesuit's question. "Why do you know a rite to make them go away, if they are not real?"

Hiro hid a smile behind his teacup.

When Father Mateo did not answer, Mume bit her lip. "I am sorry. Was this a test? I am not good at tests. I always get the answers wrong. Kane-*san* used to help me, but Ishiko-*san* won't let her any more."

Hiro decided not to remind the woman about Ishiko's death. "Did you or your husband see, or hear, anything unusual last night?"

"I fell asleep right after dark, before Taso-*san* came home. Kane is not allowed to visit me. I get bored all by myself, so I go to sleep early."

"Did you wake up when Taso-*san* came home?" Hiro asked.

She gestured to the entry. "*Ushi* makes a lot of noise."

"*Ushi*...the ox?" Father Mateo clarified.

"Yes," Mume said. "He smells very bad."

"Do you know what time your husband returned?" Hiro asked.

Mume furrowed her forehead. Eventually she shook her head. "The fire had died. How long does that take?"

Long enough for a man to commit a murder, Hiro thought. "Did you and your husband know Ishiko-*san* well?"

Mume's cheeks flushed pink. "Ishiko-*san* did not like me."

Hiro sipped his tea, hoping the woman would elaborate. For all that she sounded childish, he found her answers trustworthy. He suspected she could not lie persuasively, even if she tried.

"Ishiko-*san* did not like Kane-*san* either." Mume looked from Hiro to the Jesuit. "She said girls should work all day, not chatter like a bunch of lazy monkeys." Mume blinked as her eyes filled up with tears. "I am not a lazy monkey."

"Of course not." Father Mateo raised a hand as if to pat her shoulder, but laid it in his lap again as if remembering that he should not.

Mume sniffed and wiped her tears away. "I was lucky to marry Taso-*san*. I got to stay near Kane-*san*. She used to take good care of me. But now, Ishiko-*san* won't let her, so Kane-*san* has to—" This time, Mume clapped both hands over her mouth.

"What does Kane-*san* have to do?" Father Mateo asked.

Mume bit her lip and shook her head.

"We promise not to tell Ishiko-*san*," Hiro coaxed.

Mume lowered her hands. "You cannot tell Ishiko-*san*. Ishiko-*san* is dead."

"Then it no longer matters," Hiro countered.

Mume considered the comment. "That is true." She nodded, as if to herself. "Kane-*san* sneaks out to see me. But she says I must not tell. Because Ishiko-*san* would beat her if she knew."

"Did Ishiko-*san* beat your sister often?" Hiro asked.

"No," Mume said vehemently. "No."

As Hiro suspected, she was a terrible liar.

"Did Ishiko-*san* ever beat you?" Father Mateo asked.

Mume shook her head. "Taso-*san* would not let her do that. Taso-*san* does not let anyone say bad things to me. Or about me. Before we came here, sometimes people said mean things." She paused. "Because I am not smart."

She touched the place where the white streak of hair emerged from her scalp. "Kane-*san* says I hit my head when I was small. After that, I was not smart. But, Kane-*san* says, I am not stupid either."

"Kane-*san* is correct." Father Mateo smiled kindly.

"Now that Ishiko-*san* is gone, the only bad thing in this village is the yūrei." She gasped and her eyes filled up with frightened tears. "I should not have said that! She will come."

"You do not need to worry about the yūrei," Father Mateo said.

Mume clasped her hands. "Can you really make her go away?"

"We will do everything in our power to keep you safe," the Jesuit replied.

Hiro noted that, as usual, the priest refused to make an idle promise, on the chance it might become a lie. He swallowed the last of his now-cold tea and set the empty cup on the tray. "Thank you for helping us. We will not inconvenience you any longer."

CHAPTER 16

As Mume shut the door behind them, Father Mateo turned to Hiro, "We forgot to ask about the other villagers."

"I did not forget." Hiro started toward the road. "Mume will tell Kane everything we talked about. Everything she remembers, anyway."

"I find it interesting that she is married." Father Mateo looked back at the house. "Do you think she has the capacity to understand . . ."

"Marriage is hardly complicated," Hiro said. "In principle, anyway. I've heard it's rather more complex in practice."

"It isn't funny, Hiro. That poor girl—"

"Looked clean, well-fed, and cared for, and she sounded competent to me. Even if she did inadvertently name her sister as a murder suspect."

"Surely you don't think Kane-*san* killed Ishiko."

Hiro noted the omission of the honorific suffix from the dead woman's name. "It would not be the first time a bride took decisive action against a tyrannical mother-in-law."

"Mume-*san* also mentioned that her husband came home late last night," the Jesuit said. "Although, I don't know what he would have done with the ox."

"He could have tied it to a tree," Hiro suggested. "The fact that he came home late did not escape my notice either, and if he does object to mistreatment of his wife, he might have held a grudge against a woman who insulted her."

"Or worse." Father Mateo's voice betrayed his disapproval. "I suspect that woman beat her daughter-in-law, and that Mume-*san* is frightened to admit it."

"Perhaps," Hiro said. "Although, until we have more evidence, I trust no one."

"Even with evidence, that won't change." The smile on the Jesuit's face suggested humor, but both men recognized the core of truth.

A path of churned but frozen earth led from the travel road to the front of the house opposite Mume's. No smoke rose from the chimney hole, but the pile of wood beside the door looked recently replenished, and no cobwebs crossed the door.

Hiro knocked and waited.

No one answered.

When no one responded to a second knock, he said, "Either no one's home or no one's going to answer."

"Let's try there instead." Father Mateo gestured to the house next door, which looked identical to the one they stood in front of, except for the thin gray line of smoke that rose from an opening in the roof.

As they approached, the door swung open. A tiny, gray-haired woman leaned one hand on a crooked walking stick. With the other, she grasped the door.

She scowled at Father Mateo. "Go away."

The Jesuit bowed. "I am Father—"

Her scowl deepened. "Are you deaf as well as dead?" She thumped her cane on the ground. "You go away. You go away right now!"

She took a backward step into her house.

The Jesuit jumped forward and stuck his foot in the opening just as the elderly woman tried to slam the door. "I am a pr—*ow!*"

The elderly woman opened the door a fraction and slammed it against the Jesuit's foot once more. When he still refused to withdraw it, she opened the door and leaned on it while she jabbed at him with her cane. "I said be gone, ghost!"

"I am not a ghost," the priest protested. "Stop slamming the door on my foot."

She slammed the door against his foot again. When it failed to produce the desired result, she looked past him at Hiro. "Why won't you take your ghost and go?"

"He is a foreigner." Hiro struggled to hide his amusement. "Not a ghost."

The elderly woman finally stopped hammering the Jesuit's foot with the door. She squinted thoughtfully at his face. "His nose is big, his face is pale, and his Japanese sounds funny. He is a ghost who does not realize he's dead."

"I assure you, I am not a ghost. I am a priest of the Creator God, from Portugal."

"You see?" The elderly woman gave Hiro a knowing look. "He does not know he's dead." She shook her walking stick at Father Mateo once again. "You died. You are a ghost. Now go away."

Hiro had an idea. "I have come to rid your village of the yūrei—"

The old woman cut him off with a snort and pointed at Father Mateo. "You cannot even rid me of this one!" She waved her hand. "I am too old to listen to your nonsense."

Father Mateo gestured to Hiro. "You cannot talk that way to a samurai. He could kill you—"

"Him?" She snorted again. "He won't kill an old woman."

Not an unarmed one, anyway, Hiro agreed to himself, impressed— and a little chagrined—that she had measured him so quickly and so well.

"But neither will I leave you in peace until you accommodate my request," he said aloud. "I need to know if you saw or heard anything unusual last night."

"Aside from three visitors coming into town on a winter evening?" The woman opened the door enough to suggest she had finished trying to shut them out. She glared at Father Mateo, who withdrew his foot with a small, embarrassed bow.

"Saku-*san!*" A voice called from the road behind them. "Saku-*san!*"

The elderly woman backed into the house and slammed the door with startling speed.

"No! Wait! Don't close the—" A wiry man slid to a stop between Hiro and Father Mateo. He wore a white tunic and trousers beneath a bulky hooded cloak woven from narrow, supple bamboo stems with the leaves left on. The straw sandals on his feet offered scant protection from the frozen ground, and he wore no socks. His long, skinny toes reminded Hiro of a tree frog's feet.

He raised a skinny arm and pounded on the woman's door. "Saku-*san*! Open this door right now! Your descendant's life depends upon it!" The conch shell hanging on a bright red cord around his neck swung sideways with the force of his knocks, but the elderly woman did not return.

Father Mateo gave Hiro a look that questioned the strange man's sanity. Hiro shrugged.

Eventually the man ceased pounding on the door and turned to Father Mateo. "Who are you?"

"I am Father Mateo Ávila de Santos, a priest of the Creator God, from Por—"

"A fellow priest!" He bowed. "I am Zentaro, humble servant of the kami and the mountains!"

He turned to Hiro. "And who are you?"

"Matsui Hiro, Father Mateo's scribe."

The yamabushi bowed again. "I am honored to meet you, Matsui Hiro the scribe and Father Mateo of Por." He laid a hand on his chest. "I am Zentaro, humble servant of the kami and the mountains."

As Noboru suggested, Zentaro's mind appeared a few bees short of a functional hive.

"Do you live near the village?" Father Mateo asked.

The question seemed to confuse the yamabushi.

Suddenly, his eyes lit up. He raised his hand, first finger extended in triumph. "I live on the mountain!" He smiled as if pleased to have found the answer. "I came to warn these people to respect Inari-*sama* and the mountain gods, and not to violate the sacred mountain by trespassing in the forest after dark." He looked over his shoulder. "Now, I must go."

As he turned to leave, the Jesuit raised a hand. "Please wait."

Unexpectedly, Zentaro did.

CHAPTER 17

Father Mateo gestured to the house. "Do you know Saku-*san*?"

Hiro hoped the Jesuit knew the woman would be listening from inside the door.

"I know many things. Things no man knows." Zentaro dropped his voice to a conspiratorial whisper. "The kami tell me."

"They tell you about Saku-*san*?" Father Mateo asked.

"Who?" Zentaro blinked.

"Saku-*san*." The Jesuit gestured to the door. "You called her name..."

Zentaro circled to his right, and then to his left. "Have you seen my walking stick?"

"You didn't have one when you arrived," Father Mateo said.

"Have I lost it again?" The yamabushi's gaze grew fixed and distant. "You should leave this village now. The mountain belongs to the kami, and the kami want it back."

Zentaro blinked, and his focus returned. He cocked his head to the side and blinked as if just noticing Father Mateo. "I know you. You arrived here yesterday, with a woman." He lowered his voice to a whisper. "Inari-*sama* told me you were coming."

"Inari-*sama*?" Father Mateo gave Hiro a questioning look.

"Inari Ōkami," Hiro said. "The Shintō god of fertility, rice, saké, and swords ... among other things."

"Saké, fertility, *and* swords?"

"Have too much of any one, and the others follow."

"Do not disrespect Inari-*sama*." Zentaro set his hands on his hips like an angry samurai.

"I assure you," Hiro said, "I have no less respect for Inari-*sama* than I do for any other kami." *And no more use for Inari than I have for the rest of them, either.*

Zentaro nodded knowingly. "His messengers tell me many things."

"Things no man knows," Hiro added drily.

"Do they speak to you also?" Zentaro looked both eager and amazed.

Instead of answering, Hiro asked, "Did you visit the burial ground last night?"

"Of course. Every morning and every evening I offer prayers to the *kami* on behalf of the living and the dead. Lately, the mountain deities have grown angry because these people do not show respect." Zentaro made a sweeping gesture that encompassed the entire village. "So far, Inari-*sama* has intervened to avert disaster, but if the ones who remain refuse to listen . . ."

Hiro tried to steer the yamabushi back on course. "What time did you visit the burial yard?"

Zentaro whipped his head around as if a voice had called out behind him. "I must go!"

Before Hiro or Father Mateo could object, he fled up the travel road toward the forest.

Hiro considered calling after him, but suspected his words would have no impact.

As Zentaro disappeared into the forest Father Mateo said, "I do not think that man is completely sane."

"It does not take great skill to fake insanity."

"Where do we go next?" Father Mateo asked. "The rest of the houses look abandoned."

"At least one of them is not." Hiro started toward the mansion.

Father Mateo followed. "Somehow, I doubt Otomuro-*san* will invite us in for tea."

"You know how I feel about assumptions," Hiro said, "and unwilling men often have far more interesting things to say than the ones who ask you in for welcome tea."

Otomuro's mansion sat on a narrow rise, looking down on the village like a magistrate sitting in judgment over a line of peasants. Carved stone lanterns standing on either side of the veranda steps bore images of crescent moons and deer.

A narrow trail of churned-up earth indicated the path Otomuro, and presumably others, took to reach the mansion from the travel road. The frozen earth did not hold footprints well, but Hiro thought he saw the marks of at least three different pairs of shoes.

"Do you think Otomuro-*san* will speak with us?" Father Mateo asked as Hiro knocked on the door.

"Samurai crave the company of others who share their noble rank. He thinks me dishonored, but even so—"

He cut himself off as the door swung open.

An elderly man in a blue-striped servant's robe blinked nearsightedly at Hiro and Father Mateo. Eventually he remembered to bow. "May I help you?"

"We have come to see Otomuro-*san*," Hiro said.

The old man turned and tottered off into the house.

Father Mateo watched him go. "Should we follow?"

"He left the door open." Hiro stepped over the threshold and left his shoes inside the door. As the Jesuit followed him inside, Hiro continued through another door and into the reception room beyond.

Aging but expensive tatami covered the floor. Their grassy scent competed with the cloying smell of incense rising from a lacquered *butsudan* that stood against the far wall of the room. The doors to the altar cabinet stood open and, inside, a pair of memorial tablets flanked a small bronze statue of a seated Buddha. An incense burner stood before the statue, sending a trickle of smoke into the air.

Braziers burned on either side of the butsudan. A third one stood, unlighted, near the tokonoma on the left-hand wall. The decorative alcove held a scroll with calligraphy flowing down it like a waterfall of deep black ink.

Hiro walked across the room to view the scroll more closely. As he finished reading the poem, he noticed the artist's name written in tiny characters on the lower left side of the scroll.

"This calligraphy looks the same as the scroll at the teahouse," Father Mateo said as he joined the shinobi before the scroll.

"I agree," Hiro confirmed, "and both poems come from the Man'yōshū, an ancient collection of Japanese verse."

"You can read it?" Father Mateo sounded impressed.

"In the rice fields of autumn, morning haze hangs above the ears of rice; my love has no end."

"A love poem?"

"Attributed, originally, to the Empress Iwanohime." Hiro switched to Portuguese. "The choice of this particular poem suggests a close relationship between the calligrapher and the recipient."

"Close, as in lovers?" Father Mateo asked. "Did the artist sign the scroll?"

"She did. The name reads 'Emiko.'"

"Emiri?" Father Mateo gave Hiro a look of startled alarm.

"Emiko," Hiro repeated, "though—" He cut himself off as Otomuro entered the room with Noboru on his heels.

Hiro found the innkeeper's presence both unusual and suspicious.

"It appears they have more courage than you think." Otomuro crossed his arms. "Have you come to steal from me as well?"

Since the samurai did not bow in greeting, Hiro did not either.

Father Mateo did. "Forgive me, Otomuro-*san*, but I must have misheard you. I thought you said—"

"I asked if you came to steal from me, as you stole from Noboru-*san*?"

The innkeeper's cheeks flushed scarlet at the mention of his name.

"Was something stolen from the ryokan?" Father Mateo asked.

"Do not deny it!" Otomuro scowled. "We know the truth."

"You may," Hiro said, "but we do not."

"You stole his savings." Otomuro gestured to Noboru. "Everything he had."

Father Mateo grasped the wooden cross that hung around his neck and raised it as if in explanation. "I am a priest of God. I do not steal." A moment later he added, "And neither does Matsui-*san*."

"Your innocent act does not fool me," Otomuro sneered. "I've known too many priests."

CHAPTER 18

"I do not steal," Father Mateo repeated more forcefully.

"Where did the money go, then?" Otomuro asked.

Noboru took a hesitant step forward. "In truth, I do not think you directly responsible. I believe your housekeeper stole the silver after my mother left for the burial yard last night, before we returned from the teahouse, while Kane slept."

"When did you discover the silver missing?" Father Mateo asked. "And why didn't you bring this matter to me directly?"

Noboru looked at the floor. "I was afraid."

"But not too afraid to accuse my servant behind my back," the Jesuit countered.

"And unjustly," Hiro added.

Noboru fell to his knees at Father Mateo's feet. "Please, have mercy. Make your servant return the silver. If not, I will lose the ryokan, and my family will starve and die."

Hiro found the reaction a bit extreme, but the innkeeper's distress looked all too real.

"Ana cannot return what she did not steal," Father Mateo said.

"Get up, you fool. The innocent do not kneel before a thief." Otomuro raised a fist to the Jesuit. "I suggest you return the silver, before you force me to take further action."

Hiro stepped between the samurai and the priest. He laid a hand on the hilt of his katana. "And I suggest you withdraw your threat, before I force you to regret it."

Noboru stood up slowly, as if hoping not to draw attention.

Otomuro glared at Hiro, but took a step backward. "Do not confuse a threat with a promise. Your foreign master has until the priest arrives from Hakone to return the money his servant stole from Noboru. If he does not, I will hang his housekeeper as a thief."

"Ana is not a thief," Father Mateo said. "I suspect the person who killed Ishiko-*san* is the one that stole the missing silver."

"Ishiko-*san* was killed by a yūrei," Otomuro said, "and vengeful spirits have no need of silver. Your servant is under arrest."

"With respect," Father Mateo replied, still calm, "I refuse to recognize the arrest."

Otomuro's jowls reddened. "You cannot refuse."

"He just did," Noboru said.

"Be silent!" Otomuro extended a hand to Hiro. "Surrender your swords, as a promise that you will not leave the village until the foreigner returns Noboru's silver."

"If you attempt to touch my swords, your hands will never touch anything again."

Otomuro pulled his hands against his chest as if the words had burned them. "You must respect my authority! Noboru, fetch Akako-*san* to guard the foreigner until we find your silver."

The innkeeper scurried from the room as if grateful for an excuse to leave.

As the front door shut behind Noboru, Otomuro said, "Will you accept the guard? Or do I have to force you?"

In different circumstances, Hiro would have found the samurai's persistence comically pathetic. At the moment, it frustrated him almost enough to force a fight.

Unfortunately, killing the local samurai would complicate his journey to Edo in ways that Hiro would rather not accommodate.

The expression on the Jesuit's face suggested he felt something similar, though when Father Mateo spoke his tone remained as calm as ever. "Provided Akako-*san* does not interfere with our investigation, we will not object to his company, at least for the afternoon."

As Hiro and Father Mateo left Otomuro's mansion, Noboru reappeared from the mist, along with a middle-aged man whose chest looked almost as broad as a saké barrel. The massive stranger's arms seemed large enough to lift an ox, and though his close-cropped hair had begun to gray, his unlined face and bright, sharp eyes made his age unusually difficult to guess.

The stranger stopped just short of the veranda. "Good morning, gentlemen. I am Akako." He bowed to Hiro and Father Mateo.

"Do not treat these thieves as men of honor," Otomuro growled from the doorway.

Father Mateo turned to the samurai. "I have told you I am not a thief."

"Guilty men proclaim their innocence the loudest," Otomuro said.

Hiro could not argue with the sentiment, despite his loathing for its current application. Instead, he ignored it. "Good morning, Akako-*san*."

"I have arrested the foreigner's housekeeper for theft," Otomuro announced. "Akako-*san*, you will guard these men. I do not want them sneaking away from the village before the woman faces judgment."

"Wouldn't it make more sense to guard the woman?" Akako asked.

Not if Otomuro thinks he can bribe the priest to save her, Hiro thought.

"Do you question my authority?" the samurai demanded.

"I am making sure I understand your orders." Akako showed an unusual lack of fear.

"If the woman does not return Noboru's coins before the priest arrives from Hakone to exorcise the yūrei"—Otomuro gestured to the Jesuit—"and her employer does not repay it on her behalf, I will hang her as a thief as soon as the ritual concludes."

"You'll hang her after the exorcism?" Akako asked. "Why not before, in case she also returns as an angry ghost?"

Hiro searched the laborer's face but saw no indication that the man had made a joke.

Otomuro's cheeks flushed red. "I have spoken. Do as I command!"

"I would like to help you," Akako said, "but I stayed home to rest today. Although perhaps, with proper compensation . . ."

Otomuro glared at the barrel-chested man. "You expect me to pay you?"

"With respect," Akako replied, "a man who expects another man to work should also expect to pay."

"Fine." Otomuro pointed to Noboru. "He will pay you a silver coin each day, to ensure these men do not leave the village. But you get paid only if they do not escape."

"Me?" The innkeeper looked taken aback. "But—"

"You will pay him. That is all." Otomuro retreated into the house and closed the door.

Noboru sighed and led the others back to the ryokan.

"You could guard them yourself, if you don't want to pay," Akako offered as they reached the inn.

"I have no time to watch them," Noboru grumbled. "I have to arrange my mother's funerary rites."

"A wise idea," Akako said. "We do not need a second angry ghost."

The innkeeper turned pleading eyes on Father Mateo. "Won't you just return the silver? It cannot mean much to you, a wealthy priest, but it means everything to me."

"I did not take your silver, and neither did Ana," the Jesuit replied, "and, despite what you say, I am not a wealthy man. However, I will help you find the thief."

Noboru shook his head. "We would have heard an intruder, and no one but your servant—aside from Kane and me—knew where the coins were hidden."

"How did Father Mateo's housekeeper learn where the coins were hidden?" Hiro asked.

"I do not know," Noboru said, "but I heard her showing you our hiding place in the kitchen wall."

"If you heard her," Hiro countered, "then you also know she attributed that hole to a hungry rat."

Noboru crossed his arms. "A ruse to disguise her crime."

"Why would she need a ruse," the Jesuit asked, "since no one had accused her?"

Hiro could think of several reasons, but offered none.

Akako indicated the priest. "Have you considered he might be telling you the truth? That someone else did steal your silver?"

"You're not supposed to take his side," Noboru said. "Just watch them conduct their investigation, and do not let them leave the village. I have things to do."

CHAPTER 19

Akako followed Hiro and Father Mateo into their guest room. The Jesuit closed the door and gave the laborer a curious look. "If you think we're innocent, why agree to guard us?"

"For the silver." Akako pulled his kimono aside. Enormous purple, green, and yellow bruises marked his chest and shoulder. "Last week I startled Taso's ox. I don't blame the beast for kicking, but I can't carry a load until this heals a little more. A man who doesn't work can't eat, and I have my mother to think of, as well as myself. This is an easy way to earn a coin."

"Not if we kill you in order to escape," Hiro said.

Akako gave him an appraising look. "You won't."

"I am samurai. I could kill you just to test my sword."

"And some men would," the laborer agreed, "but you are not among them."

"A dangerous gamble," Hiro said.

Akako smiled. "With respect, a man does not survive long on the travel road without learning to tell the difference between a reasonable samurai and one who looks for any excuse to test his sword."

"Have you lived in the village long?" Father Mateo asked.

"I was born here, and still share my mother's house. My son Chitose lives in the house next door."

"And your wife?"

"She died in childbirth." Akako spoke with good-natured calm. "When Chitose began to look for a wife, I let him have the house I built for his mother, and moved back in with Saku."

"Saku-*san* is your mother?" Father Mateo frowned. "We met her this morning. She thinks that I'm a ghost."

"She does not see well anymo—" Akako blinked in surprise as Gato emerged from under the table, stretched, and padded across the room. He knelt and extended a hand to the cat. "*Neko-chan*, how did you get inside?"

"She belongs to us," the Jesuit replied.

Akako looked at the priest as Gato butted her head against his hand and purred. "I never thought Ishiko-*san* would let a cat inside the ryokan. She hated them."

Hiro found it strange that the porter did not question why the Jesuit traveled with a cat. However, Japanese people often considered foreigners strange, and Akako could have simply accepted this as yet another example of foreign eccentricity.

Gato arched her back and turned in a circle, offering her side and back. Akako ran a tentative hand across her fur and broke into a smile as her purr increased.

"Feel free to go about your investigation." Akako scratched behind Gato's ears and along her jaw. "In fact, I'll gladly help you if I can."

"Can you tell us about the village ghost?" Father Mateo asked.

"It is not merely a ghost. It is a yūrei—more specifically, an *onryō*." Akako spoke as casually as if discussing the previous evening's meal.

"There is a difference?" the Jesuit knelt on the tatami.

"All yūrei are ghosts, but not all ghosts are yūrei." Akako continued scratching Gato's ears. "Japan has many different kinds of ghosts."

"How do you tell them apart?"

"By what they do," the laborer replied, "or what they want. A yūrei seeks to resolve some matter left unfinished during life. Some yūrei seek vengeance—"

"But some do not?" Father Mateo leaned forward slightly.

"Some wish to continue living. Others do not realize they're dead."

"Which kind is the on—on—" Father Mateo struggled with the unfamiliar word.

"On-ry-ō." Akako pronounced the word slowly and carefully. "A yūrei that holds a grudge."

"I thought all yūrei were vengeful spirits."

"In a manner of speaking, yes, but as I mentioned, some are worse than others. Sometimes a soul gets lost or stuck on its way to the afterlife. For example, if a family cannot afford a proper funeral, the spirit of the deceased will wander the earth until someone performs the proper rites on its behalf. Such yūrei, though disturbed, do not usually cause any serious harm."

"And the other kind?" Father Mateo asked.

Akako lowered his voice. "Onryō bear a grudge against the living, and refuse to leave this world until they have revenge. A woman who dies a violent death may become an onryō."

"But Noboru's sister died in an accident—"

"Who told you that?" Akako's eyes flashed with sudden anger.

"Noboru-*san*." Hiro intervened.

Akako clenched his jaw. His hand drew into a fist, provoking a curious look from Gato. "Noboru-*san* lied. Riko-*san* was murdered. Though I suppose I should be impressed that he dared to mention her, or her death, at all."

"She was murdered?" Hiro repeated. "How?"

Akako studied the Jesuit's face, and Hiro's. "With respect, I find myself in a difficult position. While I cannot refuse to answer your question, a truthful answer requires me to make serious accusations against a samurai."

Hiro knelt beside Father Mateo. "Unless the man is in this room, no one will take offense."

"The man in question would disagree, if he learned that I spoke to you of his crimes."

"If Otomuro-*san* dislikes the way the truth makes him appear, he should change his behavior," Father Mateo said pointedly.

"How do you know that I speak of Otomuro-*san*?" Akako asked.

"This village has only one samurai." Father Mateo's expression grew grave. "What did he do to Noboru's sister?"

"Everything," Akako said, "and nothing. To understand, you must hear the entire story."

For the second time in as many days, Hiro found himself doubting the veracity of those words. But once again, he found himself required to listen.

CHAPTER 20

Akako settled back on his heels in the manner of a man about to tell a lengthy tale. "Otomuro-san came from a wealthy family, but his father squandered most of their fortune on gambling and prostitutes. When his father died, Otomuro-san's elder brother joined the daimyō's service as a warrior, but Otomuro-san . . . well, you can see he isn't much for exercise, martial or otherwise."

"How do you know so much about his history?" Father Mateo asked.

Akako shrugged. "The truth will follow a man like a hungry wolf on the trail of a fox.

"The daimyō sent Otomuro-san to this village, to watch the travel road and collect the taxes, but Otomuro-san spent most of his time inside the teahouse, watching entertainers. He demanded Yuko-san pay her taxes in food and entertainment instead of silver, and he always wanted Riko-san to provide the entertainment." Akako lowered his voice. "I think he liked the fact that he could force the girl to entertain him, in order to show her family that he controlled this village—not that they ever cared what happened to her, one way or the other."

"He forced her to . . . entertain him?" Father Mateo looked ill.

"Riko-san was not a prostitute," Akako clarified. "Yuko-san refused to sell her girls that way. She claimed it reduced their value. And then, last year, Otomuro-san's brother came to visit."

"The one who served the daimyō?" Father Mateo asked.

Akako nodded. "He came to the village at the end of every year, to collect the tax receipts. Last year, Otomuro-san took him to the teahouse. As always, he demanded Riko-san.

"At some point in the evening Otomuro-san's brother demanded more than the girl desired to give, and this time, Yuko-san did not prevent it." Akako's expression darkened. "I do not know exactly why. I was not in the village that night. If I had been . . ."

"You could not have saved her from a samurai's demands." Father Mateo's voice held disapproval, though not for the laborer.

"The brother dragged her through the street to Otomuro's house. The entire village heard her screams, but no one intervened. When he finished with her, he threw her into the street like refuse. He had beaten her so badly that she had to crawl back to the teahouse on her hands and knees.

"Even then, not a single person in this village had the courage to speak against a samurai," Akako finished with disgust.

"Not even her parents?" Father Mateo sounded horrified.

"Risk a samurai's fury over a girl? And a twin at that?" Akako gave a bitter laugh.

"A twin?" The Jesuit repeated. "Riko was Noboru's twin?"

Once again Akako nodded. "That's why her parents gave her up so cheaply."

"Because she was a twin?" Father Mateo looked confused.

"The younger twin, and a girl." Akako paused. "Bad luck. Her parents apprenticed her to Yuko-*san* as soon as she could walk and, after that, pretended not to know her. They wouldn't even speak to her in the street. As she grew older, even Yuko-*san* looked down on her, because Riko-*san* was not as lovely as Hanako-*san*, or as skilled on the shamisen as young Masako."

"And yet, she remained the teahouse owner's heir?" Hiro asked.

At the sound of her master's voice, Gato stretched, stood up, and padded over to sit in front of him. He reached out a hand and stroked her coat.

"Yes. They were blood. There was also a rumor about a forgiven debt, but I cannot say for sure if that part's true."

"Did Riko-*san* recover from her injuries?" Father Mateo hesitated, as if uncertain whether he wanted to know the answer.

Akako shook his head. "The following morning Yuko-*san* discovered her dead, still wearing the bloody kimono from the night before.

"The night after Riko-*san* died of her injuries, Otomuro-*san*'s brother died in his sleep—or so Otomuro-*san* claimed. It seemed strange, even at the time, but no one dared to question the word of a samurai. Later, when we realized Riko-*san* had returned to avenge herself upon the village, Otomuro-*san* admitted that his brother was the onryō's first victim."

"The second was Yuko-*san*?" Father Mateo asked.

"She died the day after Riko did," Akako confirmed. "And then, a little more than three months later, Noboru's father died, on the night the landslide destroyed the travel road and killed the teahouse girl who tried to run. He was having dinner at the teahouse—it had become Hanako's teahouse then—when he suddenly screamed his daughter's name, clutched at his chest, and fell down dead."

"Did you see it happen?" Hiro asked.

Akako shook his head. "The girl who saw it happen ran away in terror. She's the one who died in the landslide. Most of the people in the village believed the yūrei caused the landslide too. They moved away afterward, to flee her wrath."

"That's why so many houses now stand vacant."

"They moved away because they feared a ghost?" Hiro found that difficult to believe.

Gato mewed and climbed into his lap. He stroked her absently.

"The storm occurred on the hundredth day after Riko-*san* died," Akako said. "A typhoon struck the mountain at nightfall. During the night, a massive landslide buried the travel road. It took months to clear the damage and reopen the road, and the traffic has not returned. Most travelers still prefer to take the detour, to the south."

"You mentioned the other teahouse girl who died," Father Mateo prompted.

"Emiko-*san*," Akako confirmed. "She ran away that night. The landslide buried her. Most people think the yūrei caused the slide so the girl would not escape."

"Her name was Emiko?" Father Mateo repeated.

Akako nodded. "The mountain collapsed on her as she tried to flee."

"What killed Noboru's father?" Hiro asked.

"The yūrei came for him, and his heart gave out."

"Heart failure has many causes," Hiro said, "and both typhoons and landslides happen every year, without the aid of ghosts."

"Perhaps," Akako countered, "but when four people die in as many months—and then Ishiko-*san*, on the one year anniversary of Riko's death, coincidences start to look suspicious."

"Yet you do not seem frightened," Hiro said.

"She has no reason to seek revenge against me. I played no part in her death, and neither insulted nor abused her while she lived."

Hiro continued stroking Gato's fur. "Between a string of strange but natural occurrences and the revenge of an angry ghost, I find the former a far more reasonable explanation."

"People have seen the yūrei wandering in the trees at night," Akako said, "and some claim to have heard her wailing."

"Have you seen her?" Hiro asked.

"My mother has."

Hiro set the cat on the floor and stood up. "Then I would like to speak with her about it."

Akako rose. "I do not know if she will speak to you, but we can try."

The door to the house Akako shared with Saku opened as they approached.

The ancient, scowling woman pointed her walking stick at Hiro. "Are you stupid?"

He stopped short, too startled to reply.

Saku thumped the stick on the ground. "I told you to take your foreign ghost and go."

"I am not a ghost," Father Mateo protested.

"They are inves—" Akako paused. "They want to hear about Riko-san."

"Samurai do not care about teahouse girls." Saku shifted her gaze to Father Mateo. "And neither do the dead."

"I serve a holy . . . spirit"—the Jesuit choked on the word—"who judges the living and the dead. He commands me to care about everyone."

"You serve the god of ghosts?" Saku looked dubious.

Hiro hoped the Jesuit would let the error pass, although he worried that the recent murders on Mount Kōya might hamper Father Mateo's ability to allow misunderstandings about his faith to go uncorrected. Unwilling to take the risk, he intervened. "Is it true that you have seen the yūrei?"

"If you talk to us," the Jesuit added, "we will go away."

Saku squinted at the priest as if considering the offer.

Hiro prepared to argue, but the elderly woman took a step backward and beckoned them inside. "I will tell you what I saw." She jabbed her cane at Father Mateo as he crossed the threshold. "But I don't serve tea to ghosts."

CHAPTER 21

The interior of Saku's home looked almost identical to Mume's one-room house across the road, except that it lacked a stall and the accompanying scent of ox. A fire glowed in the base of the square brick oven that squatted at the center of the open space at the front of the house. Behind it, a brazier burned beside the raised, tatami-covered platform that served as the primary living space. A trio of wooden chests sat against the rear wall of the house. Based on their sizes and location, they probably contained both clothes and bedding.

Smoke from the oven and brazier filled the house with a faint, aromatic haze. Beneath it, Hiro noted the faded, lingering scents of older fires, aging wood, and fish.

Saku tottered over to the platform, leaning heavily on her gnarled cane. When she reached the edge, she stepped out of her sandals and knelt on the tatami.

Although she offered no invitation, Akako gestured for Hiro and Father Mateo to join his mother, and then followed them across the room.

Once everyone had taken a seat on the platform, Akako said, "They want to hear about the night you saw the yūrei in the forest."

"It happened shortly after the landslide killed Emiko-*san*." The elderly woman shook her head. "Wouldn't surprise me if that one returned as a yūrei too."

She fiddled with the cane that lay beside her on the tatami. "Late one night, on the way to the latrine, I saw the yūrei gliding through the trees. Her hair hung loose around her face. She wore a pale kimono and she glowed with greenish light. Luckily, she did not turn or notice me."

"Do you see her often?" Hiro asked.

Saku sniffed disdainfully. "I know better than to test my luck. I stay inside at night." She paused, then added, "but sometimes I hear her wailing in the woods."

"Deer and foxes also sound like women wailing," Hiro said.

The elderly woman fixed him with a stony gaze. "I grew up on this mountain. I can tell a *kitsune* from a yūrei."

"And you have seen this spirit only once," Hiro said.

"I saw her twice." Saku spoke with a slight breathlessness. "About a month ago, I thought I heard footsteps behind the house." She raised the cane with a trembling hand and pointed it at the lone, slatted window at the rear of the house, which faced the woods. "I thought it was a robber, and crept to the window, planning to beat him with my cane. Instead, I saw the yūrei floating at the edge of the woods. She was staring at the house, with her hair falling loose around her and a pale kimono that glowed a sickly green."

"If she floated, how did you hear her footsteps?" Hiro asked.

"I know what I saw." Saku's hand trembled even more violently as she lowered the cane to her lap. "Believe me or not. It changes nothing."

"We believe you," Father Mateo said quickly. "Did the spirit do anything when she saw you watching?"

"I did not stay to watch!" Saku looked at the Jesuit as if he had suggested she run naked through the snow. "I ducked down and prayed to the Buddha that the yūrei had not seen me."

A shout came from the street outside. "Akako-*san*!"

Akako turned his head. "That sounds like Noboru-*san*." He slipped on his shoes, crossed the floor, and opened the wooden door as rapid footsteps approached the house.

Noboru appeared in the doorway. "Where are the strangers? You were supposed to watch them."

"I have watched them." Akako gestured to Hiro and Father Mateo. "At the moment, I'm watching them talk with Saku-*san*."

"Otomuro-*san* ordered you not to let them leave."

"I believe he meant the village," Akako replied. "He said nothing about confining them to the ryokan."

"If they run away, you'll pay the price," Noboru threatened.

"Time to go," Father Mateo murmured in Portuguese. As he slipped his feet back into his shoes he switched to Japanese. "Thank you for your hospitality, Saku-*san*."

"Anything to make you leave." Both the insult and Saku's voice had notably less force.

Hiro stepped into his shoes and followed the Jesuit to the door.

"Do you believe she saw a ghost?" Father Mateo asked Hiro in Portuguese as they followed Akako back to the ryokan.

"I believe that she believes it." Hiro wondered who, or what, Saku had seen in the forest. Her words and bearing did not suggest a lie. The terror in her eyes, and her trembling hands, were all too real.

The mist had mostly burned away, but a grayish haze hung over the sky, giving the sunlight a sickly cast. The weakened beams did little to warm the air, which hovered just above freezing. Icy mud crackled and squelched beneath Hiro's shoes. Unlike many portions of the travel road, this section had no stone cobbles to prevent it from becoming a quagmire after a rain or a winter thaw.

Noboru stood on the porch of the ryokan, holding the door and waiting for them to enter.

Hiro stopped at the foot of the steps. "I would like to speak with the yamabushi who lives on the mountain. Where can we find him?"

"Most likely, talking to a tree." Akako snickered.

Noboru pressed his lips together in disapproval. "No one knows where he lives, or if he even has a home. We see him only when he comes here threatening doom. Stop wasting time. Just go inside and wait for the priest to arrive from Hakone."

"He may have seen the person who killed your mother."

"We know what happened to my mother," Noboru said sharply. "A man who talks to boulders cannot help you."

"Will it hurt to let them look for him?" Akako asked.

"Otomuro-*san* ordered them not to leave the village!"

"He arrested the servant," Akako said, "and neither you nor I have the legal right to restrain a samurai."

"Why are you helping them?" Noboru grumbled.

"Because doing nothing is what caused the yūrei to curse this village," Akako said.

"And angering her will only make it worse!" Noboru countered.

Akako gazed at the innkeeper, impassive as a stone.

"Fine. But it's on your head if they escape." Noboru went inside the inn.

As the door banged shut behind him, Hiro started up the street with Father Mateo at his side.

Akako followed. "Do you really want to see Zentaro, or were you just tired of sitting around inside?"

"A bit of both," Hiro said. "Do you know how to find him?"

Akako gestured toward the hazy peak. "I don't think he ever leaves the mountain. Beyond that? No one knows."

"Does anyone else live up there with him?"

Akako shook his head. "In the winter, no one climbs above the burial yard except to go over the pass on the travel road. Since the landslide, only about a dozen people have even made that trip. The pass is icy and dangerous. The newer route is safer—even without considering the ghost."

"Then the tracks we followed earlier probably do belong to Zentaro." Hiro started up the mountain path. "I'd like to take another shot at following them, before they melt away."

CHAPTER 22

The three men returned to the burial yard and followed the tracks up the mountainside. In addition to muting the sunlight, the chilly haze preserved the snow beneath the trees and left the tracks unchanged.

Father Mateo gestured to the tracks. "He moves back and forth across the slope, almost as if he's looking for something."

"More likely, trying to avoid the snow," Akako said. "He wears no *tabi*, even in winter."

Once again, Hiro placed his feet in the tracks wherever possible. Where the tracks disappeared, he attempted to trace the yamabushi's leaps from stone to stone. He hoped, this time, he would not lose the trail.

"We could make better time by heading directly up the hill," Akako suggested. "You can see the tracks without following them so closely."

Hiro continued walking in the yamabushi's tracks. "If the route has a purpose aside from the wanderings of a disordered mind, we might not see it if we deviate. You can follow a more direct path if you wish, but stay behind me so you don't confuse the trail."

The porter fell back, allowing Hiro to move ahead.

Father Mateo slowed his pace to match Akako's steps. Hiro approved of the decision. Despite his occasional blunders—or perhaps because of them—Father Mateo had a knack for obtaining useful information, especially from commoners who would not speak freely in front of a samurai. Hiro kept his eyes on the tracks, but listened carefully to the conversation in his wake.

"Does Zentaro-*san* come to the village often?" Father Mateo asked.

"Before Riko died, we rarely saw him," Akako said. "But since the landslide, he comes down from the mountain at least a couple of times a week. He claims the kami send him to warn us, but I've noticed that things go missing when he appears."

"Missing?" Father Mateo repeated. "You didn't mention he might be a thief."

"Because the things he steals—if he takes them, I don't know for sure—they have no value. A broken bowl, a leaking teapot with a crack, that kind of thing."

"Have you asked him about it?"

"I'm not even sure he takes them," Akako said. "And if he does take broken things, who cares? Nobody wants a broken bowl."

A branch snapped farther up the hill.

Hiro stopped and raised a hand for silence.

The mist had grown thicker as they climbed. It swirled among the trees, concealing the mountaintop and making the upper slopes fade in and out of view. Its movement tricked the eye, creating the illusion of shadows moving among the trees.

A deeper shadow moved behind a tree trunk. Unlike the others, this one looked human.

In the instant it took Hiro to shift his gaze, the shadow had disappeared and the movement ceased. He wondered if both his mind and the mist were playing tricks on his perception.

He regretted that he could not conceal his approach. Alone, he might have managed to sneak up on Zentaro, though the yamabushi doubtless knew the terrain well enough to disappear at will. Unfortunately, Akako and Father Mateo moved through the forest with all the stealth and caution of drunken boars. Hiro simply had to hope that Zentaro would choose to show himself instead of fleeing.

As if summoned by Hiro's thoughts, a familiar voice rang out on the slope above him. "Welcome to the mountain!"

The mist swirled and Zentaro appeared. The yamabushi bounded down the hill like an overexcited hare, pale trousers flapping as he leaped from stone to stone, only rarely setting his feet on the icy ground.

"Hello! Hello!" He descended with startling recklessness, rarely glancing at the ground.

Hiro watched the mountain priest's descent with awed respect. Despite his own upbringing and extensive training in the mountains of Iga Province, he had never seen anyone move with such breakneck speed over icy ground without suffering a painful fall.

Father Mateo and Akako drew alongside Hiro as Zentaro arrived. The yamabushi placed his palms together and bowed. "Welcome to the mountain. May I ask your honorable names?"

Akako and Father Mateo returned the bow. Hiro gave the requisite nod, without taking his eyes from the mountain priest.

"Zentaro-*san*," the Jesuit began, "we have—"

The ascetic's mouth fell open. "How do you know my name? Did Inari-*sama* send you?"

"We have already met." Father Mateo gestured down the mountain. "In the village. Earlier today."

Zentaro tipped his head to the side and squinted. "We did?" His forehead wrinkled. "Are you certain?"

Slowly, his eyes returned to their usual shape. "I remember now. You are the ones Inari-*sama* said would come."

"Inari-*sama* told you?" Father Mateo tried to mask his disbelief.

"He warned me to beware of you." Zentaro looked at Hiro. "Trouble stalks your footsteps, and death follows in your wake."

Hiro kept his face a neutral mask. Zentaro could not possibly know the shinobi's true identity, or how many men had died at Hiro's hand. However, killers often tried to throw suspicion off themselves by making others seem like greater threats.

"Does Inari-*sama* tell you everything that happens on the mountain?" Father Mateo asked.

"Of course not," Zentaro said. "Defecating owls are no concern of mine."

"What does that have to do with anything?" Father Mateo looked confused.

"Precisely," Zentaro said.

The Jesuit turned to Hiro, even more perplexed.

"He means the mountain does not tell him everything."

"Exactly," Zentaro agreed. "Inari-*sama* does not burden his messengers with unimportant things."

"Did Inari tell you anything last night?" Hiro asked.

"You refer to Ishiko-*san*." Zentaro's face turned grim. "She should not have gone out alone at night, especially not on a night when the veil between life and death was stretched so thin." He pulled his hands apart as if stretching an invisible cord between them.

"Do you know who killed her?" Father Mateo asked.

Hiro wished the Jesuit would learn that direct questions seldom inspired honest answers. He watched the yamabushi carefully, waiting for the lie.

"I did not even know she died until this morning," Zentaro said. "I saw her body standing near the grave when I went to offer prayers for the dead."

"Then you did not visit the burial yard after dark last night?" Hiro asked.

"Wise men do not walk on this mountain after dark." Zentaro's zealous tone made the shinobi's blood run cold. "Even I return to shelter when the sun goes down."

"Because of Inari-*sama*?" Father Mateo asked.

"There are other, more dangerous, spirits on this mountain," Zentaro warned. "Things against which even Inari-*sama* cannot protect you."

"Where were you last night?" Hiro asked.

"Beneath a roof and safe from the mountain's wrath."

"Can you tell us where to find that roof?" Hiro asked.

"That would not be safe."

For whom? "Can anyone confirm your whereabouts?"

"Inari-*sama*." Zentaro made an expansive gesture. "And the kami of the mountain."

Hiro waited, but the stones and trees said nothing.

CHAPTER 23

Wind rustled the cedars. The hazy sunlight filtering through the trees faded away as a thicker cloud passed overhead.

"You should respect the mountain spirits," Zentaro said. "Do not leave the village after dark, and do not fail to honor the kami as they deserve."

"Does murdering a woman in the burial yard dishonor the mountain spirits?" Hiro asked.

Zentaro's eyes took on the light of a zealot once again. "The vengeance of the kami is not murder."

"Did Inari kill Ishiko-*san*?" The Jesuit asked.

Zentaro's mouth dropped open. He looked around, hands raised as if to ward off an attack. "Great Inari," he called to the treetops, "forgive the foreigner. He does not understand."

Lowering his face to the priest, and his voice to a hissing whisper, the yamabushi added, "Do not say such things. You do not know the risk you take."

"Did Ishiko-*san* take similar risks?" Hiro asked.

"She did not heed the warning—" Zentaro raised his face toward the mountain's peak, as if listening to voices only he could hear.

He turned back to Hiro. "The mountain calls me. I must go."

"If we need to find you again—" Father Mateo began.

Zentaro raised a hand to the trees. "Tell the mountain and I will know."

He retreated up the hill as recklessly as he had descended, leaping from stone to stone with a speed and agility Hiro would not have believed if he had not seen it.

"Are all yamabushi so . . . eccentric?" Father Mateo asked.

"A diet of bark and wild mushrooms would make any man a little strange," Akako said.

"And attract only those who were odd to begin with," Hiro added.

The Jesuit continued looking at the place where Zentaro disappeared into the mist. "Could he have killed Ishiko-*san*?"

"I care less for whether or not he *could*," Hiro replied, "than for whether or not he *did*."

"Why do you find it so hard to believe that a yūrei killed her?" Akako asked.

"As we mentioned—" Hiro began.

Father Mateo finished for him. "We do not believe in ghosts."

"But you are a priest," Akako protested.

The Jesuit drew a breath, but once again appeared to change his mind before he spoke. "God is not the same as ghosts. A man can believe in one and not the other."

Akako turned to Hiro. "But you are Japanese."

"A fact that creates no philosophical obligations."

Another gust of wind blew down the hill. Overhead, the cedars creaked in ghostly chorus.

"We may as well return to the ryokan," Hiro said. "There's nothing more to learn here at this time."

As Hiro opened the guest room door, Gato jumped off the low wooden table and greeted him with a plaintive mew. She trotted to the sliding door on the opposite side of the room, looked back at him over her shoulder, and meowed again, more urgently.

As Father Mateo and Akako knelt on the tatami, Hiro crossed the room and opened the outer door. A swirl of frigid air blew in as Gato slipped through the opening and leaped to the ground.

"It won't get lost?" Akako asked as he knelt on the tatami.

"She won't go far," Hiro said. "She hates the cold."

As if to prove his point, Gato suddenly darted back into the room and leaped into Father Mateo's lap. The Jesuit made a startled noise and raised his hands.

Gato circled once, lay down, and licked the priest's kimono.

"Hiro..." Father Mateo gave the cat a pointed look, his hands still raised to avoid making contact with her fur.

The shinobi smiled and started to close the door, but stopped, smile fading, as he noticed movement on the travel road.

A muscular figure crested the hill, his features blurred by the afternoon haze.

"Does your son wear a brown kimono?" Hiro asked.

Instead of answering, Akako stood and approached the door. He leaned past Hiro and peered through the opening. "That is Chitose." He leaned to the side as if seeking a better view. "But where is the priest?"

As they watched the road, Noboru emerged from the teahouse and met Chitose. The men exchanged bows and began a conversation.

Noboru crossed his arms and dipped his chin. He leaned forward, weight on the balls of his feet.

Hiro wished he could hear the conversation.

"Noboru-*san* looks angry," Akako mused. "Something must have delayed the priest."

Chitose bowed to Noboru and started up the road again, but paused when the teahouse door swung open. His shoulders raised and straightened, and he turned his head expectantly.

"Noboru-*san*?" Hanako's voice carried clearly through the evening air.

The innkeeper started toward the teahouse.

Chitose's shoulders slumped, and he continued on his way.

"Excuse me..." Father Mateo said pointedly.

When Hiro turned to look, the Jesuit nodded to his lap. Gato had closed her eyes and tucked her tail between her paws as if settling in for an extended nap.

"My cold is bad enough without her help." Father Mateo sniffled, though Hiro doubted the priest intended an illustration.

Hiro slid the shoji closed and crossed the room to retrieve the Jesuit of his feline burden. Gato mewed in protest.

As he set her down, the inner door slid open.

Hiro leaped to the doorway, hand on the hilt of his wakizashi, as Noboru entered the room.

The innkeeper jumped backward, raising his hands in self-defense. "Don't hurt me!" When Hiro did not draw his sword, Noboru lowered his hands and smoothed his kimono, "I came to tell you that the priest from Hakone Shrine did not return with Chitose-*san*."

"Did no one teach you to knock before you enter?" Hiro did not hide his irritation.

Noboru made a perfunctory bow. "I apologize. I saw you watching"—he gestured to the door on the opposite side of the room— "and assumed you would want to hear the news."

"That's the problem with assumptions," Hiro said. "Make enough, and eventually one will kill you."

"Do you know what happened to the priest?" Father Mateo asked, with concern.

"He is away, on a pilgrimage, but the priestesses promised to send him as soon as he returns." Noboru shifted his attention to Akako. "You may leave, for today."

The porter extended an open hand.

"You expect me to pay you now?" Noboru asked.

"Have I done what I was asked to do? You are supposed to pay a silver coin each day."

Noboru dropped a coin into Akako's palm with a silent sigh.

The porter bowed to Hiro and Father Mateo, then to Noboru, and left the room. A moment later, they heard the front door close behind him.

"I do not trust a thief to cook my evening meal," Noboru said, "so I have instructed Kane to prepare the food herself. Your servant will remain in her room instead."

"I object to you calling Ana a thief," Father Mateo replied, "but take no issue with your decision about the meal."

CHAPTER 24

"Now I understand why Noboru-*san* prefers to eat at the teahouse." Father Mateo examined the gelatinous gruel on the table before him. Halfway between liquid and solid, but not quite either, it gave off a pungent odor of rotting fish.

Hiro regarded his own, regrettably identical, meal. "It looks like Gato ate it once already."

"Please! I'm eating."

"That makes one of us." Hiro pushed his bowl away.

"I would have argued against confining Ana to her room, had I known the consequences."

Hiro breathed shallowly through his mouth. "Speaking of the teahouse, why not go over and buy ourselves a meal?"

"Wouldn't that offend our host?"

"Not as much as what would happen if I ate this." Hiro gestured to the bowl.

"It's not that bad." The Jesuit took a bite of the congealing porridge.

Bile rose in Hiro's throat. "Clearly, your illness has interfered with your sense of taste."

Gato approached the table, nose raised high as she sniffed the air. She thrust her questing nose toward Hiro's bowl and exhaled sharply, retreating so quickly that she almost stumbled in her haste.

"You see?" Hiro said. "Even she knows better than to eat it."

Father Mateo sighed. "I begin to doubt that we can solve this mystery. We have no evidence, and everyone we talk to blames a ghost."

"We have no obligation to catch this killer," Hiro reminded the priest. "We can leave for Edo any time you want to."

"And abandon Ana?"

"I said nothing about leaving her behind." Hiro stood, picked up his bowl, and opened the exterior shoji. Outside, a gentle snow had begun to fall.

"But she is under arrest . . ."

Hiro leaned halfway out the door, extended the bowl, and turned it over.

The gruel splattered the ground with a sound like vomit. Righting the bowl, Hiro withdrew into the room and closed the shoji.

"I don't believe you." Father Mateo gave him a disapproving look.

"Do you truly think so little of me?" Hiro felt pressure in his chest. He knew he held his emotions close, but had truly believed the Jesuit understood. "I give you my word, I will not leave her behind."

"I didn't mean Ana." Father Mateo gestured to Hiro's empty bowl. "You just dumped your dinner on the ground."

The pressure in Hiro's chest released in laughter. "It would have ended up there either way. I simply chose the most direct—and least unpleasant—route."

Father Mateo took another bite of gruel. "I've been thinking . . . what if the killer is also the person who stole Noboru's silver? You always say that people kill for a reason. And even if ghosts are not exactly *people*, I fail to see what Riko's spirit gains by Ishiko's death. No woman of Ishiko's status could possibly have protected Riko from the demands of a samurai. Even in death, her daughter would know that. But a thief, who Ishiko-*san* discovered in the act, could take advantage of the yūrei legend to disguise his crime."

"That would mean the murder happened in the ryokan," Hiro said. "We saw no signs of struggle in the kitchen."

"Perhaps we missed them."

Hiro shook his head. "I would have noticed. More importantly, Kane was here all night. She would have heard a struggle."

"Not necessarily," Father Mateo said. "A heavy sleeper might not wake, especially if the struggle didn't last very long, or if Ishiko-*san* did not cry out."

Gato returned to Hiro's side and pawed at his knee. When he raised his hands, the cat hopped into his lap. He stroked her fur as she circled once and lay down.

"Maybe the thief followed Ishiko-*san* to the burial ground and returned for the silver after she was dead." The Jesuit lowered his voice. "Or what if Kane is the killer?"

"She has no motive to steal the silver. As Noboru's wife, she has the benefit of it already."

"But not control over how it's spent. You heard Noboru yesterday."

"Stealing it would make it almost impossible to spend. Her husband would surely question her newfound wealth, especially so soon after his own had disappeared." Hiro rubbed one of Gato's ears. The cat leaned into his hand and her purr reached a crescendo. "Not to mention, this village has nothing to spend it on."

Father Mateo looked disappointed. "I still believe the killer is the thief."

"If all goes well, we'll learn the truth tomorrow. Executed properly, the plan I have in mind should catch the thief." *And, perhaps, the killer also.*

"You have a plan?"

Hiro explained what he had in mind, but omitted a few details to avoid an argument.

"Do you think it will work?" Father Mateo spooned the last of the gruel from his bowl and swallowed it.

"I hope so." After a moment's hesitation, Hiro added, "Though it could complicate matters if the thief is also the killer."

"Then you do think it's possible."

"Of course," Hiro said. "People kill for power, love, or money. Ishiko had neither youth nor beauty, and her death gives no one any significant power. Which makes money the likely motive."

"Kane gains power from Ishiko's death," the priest objected.

"None worth killing over," Hiro said. "Kane's husband inherits the ryokan, and he will run it as he has before. She could not spend any stolen coins without raising suspicions. Most importantly, Ishiko's death increased the work that falls on Kane's shoulders, and—as Ana pointed out—the girl seems less than fond of labor."

"Who else would have known about the silver? Otomuro-*san*?"

"A man who can levy a tax, or a fine, can steal with the law's consent."

"Hanako, then?"

"Again, she had no need to steal. Raising the price of Noboru's meals and entertainment would deprive him of his silver just as quickly, and without the risk of hanging."

"That leaves only Akako's family, Mume and Taso, and Zentaro." Father Mateo counted them off on his fingers.

Hiro raised a warning hand as footsteps approached the guest room. After a rapid knock, the door slid open.

Noboru stood on the threshold. "We have come to prepare your futon."

He stepped aside and Kane scuttled into the room.

She blinked at the sight of the empty bowls. Recovering quickly, she crossed to the built-in cabinet beside the door, slid it open, and removed the bedding.

While Kane unfolded the futons and laid them out, Noboru said, "I have been thinking. You have an obligation to return the missing silver. After all, the yūrei returned, and my mother died, because of your servant's greed."

Kane straightened. "Noboru! No! Your words will summon her again!"

CHAPTER 25

"Nonsense." Noboru gave his wife a dismissive look. "Finish your task."

"Ana did not steal your silver." Father Mateo stood up.

"And your mother died before the coins were stolen," Hiro added. *Though greed may well have factored into her death.*

"Every time she comes, she takes two victims," Kane whispered breathlessly. "*She's not finished.*"

"Enough!" Noboru snapped. "I told you already, no one else will die."

"But the priest didn't come." Kane covered her face with her hands. Her shoulders shook.

"He will be here soon." Noboru's cheeks turned red. "We can discuss this later."

Kane lowered her trembling hands and unfolded a quilt atop the closest futon. When she finished, she stood up and wiped a tear from her eye. "Will Otomuro-*san* reduce the fine, if no one else . . ." She seemed unable to complete the sentence.

"The fine?" Father Mateo echoed.

"A penalty." Noboru crossed his arms. "For the curse our family brought upon this village. It increases every time the ghost returns."

"Please," Kane begged, as her eyes filled up with tears once more, "don't talk about her. She will come."

"Take the bowls to the kitchen," Noboru said, "and get the one from their servant's room as well."

Kane grabbed the bowls and hurried from the room. As she crossed the threshold, a tear ran down her cheek and dropped into Father Mateo's empty bowl.

When she disappeared from view, Noboru bowed his head. "Once again I must apologize for Kane."

"You do not fear your sister's spirit?" Hiro asked.

"Why should I? I did not cause her death."

"And yet you lied to us about it."

Hiro turned, startled by the unusual anger in Father Mateo's voice.

"We know what Otomuro's brother did," the Jesuit said.

Noboru raised a hand to his throat. His face went pale. "Who told you? Nevermind. If you know, then you also understand why I could not tell the truth. If I accused a samurai, I would share my sister's fate."

"A fact you should remember before accusing us of angering her spirit, or attempting to force Father Mateo's housekeeper to return the silver she did not steal," Hiro replied.

Noboru forced a mirthless smile. "I suppose that means you still have no intention of replacing what was taken from me. So, I will leave you to your rest." He bowed and closed the door.

Father Mateo stared at the shoji. "Do you think that's really why he lied to us about her death? Or is he hiding something?"

"Those options are not mutually exclusive." Hiro removed his swords from his obi and set them beside his futon. "But we have a lot to do tomorrow so, tonight, let's get some sleep."

"Hiro!"

The shinobi jolted awake at Father Mateo's frightened whisper and sprang to his feet, wakizashi in hand.

The Jesuit stood beside the open veranda door. Moonlight and freezing air swirled in, along with a distant, keening wail.

Hiro saw no threats. "Have you lost your senses? Close that door."

"Th-the ghost—" Father Mateo pointed toward the teahouse as the silent keening stopped and began again.

"That is a woman," Hiro said. "Perhaps a deer. But not a ghost."

"I saw her, Hiro," the Jesuit whispered. "When I opened the door for Gato, she was out there in the snow, beside the teahouse."

"You saw the yūrei." Hiro didn't even try to disguise his disbelief.

"You don't believe me." Father Mateo shivered.

"I believe we'll freeze to death if you don't close that door."

Gato leaped back over the threshold, padded across the floor, and tried to burrow under Hiro's quilt. The distant wailing ceased.

"I'm telling you, I saw her," Father Mateo insisted. "Glowing, just as Saku said."

Hiro crossed the room and looked out the shoji. The brief snow-storm had ceased and the clouds had parted, revealing a haloed moon that illuminated the world with a silver glow. A veil of undisturbed, sparkling snow lay over the ground.

In the silence that followed the ghostly cries, not even a breath of wind disturbed the air.

"You must have imagined it," Hiro said.

"I would not believe it myself, if I had not seen her."

"What, precisely, did you see?"

Once again, the Jesuit pointed toward the teahouse. "As I opened the door, I saw a light across the road, between the teahouse and the forest. It was a woman in a pale robe, with her hair unbound. She glowed."

"Did you see her face?" Hiro asked.

"She was facing the forest, and floating in that direction. When she reached the trees, she turned and looked in this direction—and then she vanished."

"You mean she went into the forest?"

"I mean she *vanished*. The glow winked out and she was gone."

Hiro closed the door. "You saw Hanako, or Masako, walking out to the latrine."

"In a glowing robe? Floating above the ground?"

"A trick of the moonlight. Or you were still asleep."

Father Mateo gestured to the purring lump beneath Hiro's quilt. "Do you think I let the cat out in my sleep?"

"There is no yūrei," Hiro returned to his futon and set the wakizashi on the floor again. "Whatever you saw, it has a reasonable explanation." Father Mateo crossed his arms.

Hiro yawned and covered himself with the quilt. "I will prove it, tomorrow morning, when we see that woman's footprints in the snow."

Just after dawn, Hiro woke to the sound of a woman's screams.

He grabbed his sword and leaped to his feet with a nasty suspicion that Father Mateo's midnight sighting might have been more than a nightmare after all.

The Jesuit pushed his quilt aside and stood up. Like Hiro, he slept fully dressed. He hadn't even removed the wooden cross from around his neck. "Did you hear that?"

Hiro thrust his swords through his obi. Before he could answer the question, someone pounded on the ryokan's front door.

"Noboru-*san*!" an urgent voice called. "Come at once!"

"That sounds like Akako." Father Mateo started toward their door, but Hiro extended a hand to prevent him from opening it. "Wait."

Footsteps thumped overhead, down the stairs, and across the common room.

Only when he heard the front door creak on its hinges did Hiro withdraw his hand and allow the Jesuit to slide the shoji open wide enough to look through.

Akako stood on the porch, jacket askew. "Noboru-*san*, you must come now. Hanako-*san*—"

"Is she injured?" Noboru sounded terrified.

"She is fine," Akako said breathlessly, "but Masako-*san* is dead. The yūrei killed her in the night."

Noboru slipped on his shoes and ran outside, leaving the door ajar.

CHAPTER 26

"We must find out what happened to Masako!" Father Mateo headed for the entry.

Hiro closed the guest room door to prevent Gato's escape and followed the Jesuit. They crossed the street and walked around the left side of the teahouse, following Akako and Noboru's tracks in the thin veneer of snow.

A storehouse and a small latrine sat behind the teahouse, near the edge of the forest. A lantern hung from a hook beside the entrance to the latrine, but the buildings were otherwise featureless. Just past the latrine, a pair of long-limbed cedars rose into the air, their branches stretching over the small wooden building like skeletal hands reaching out to grasp the teahouse.

Akako and Noboru stood just to the right of the latrine, beside Hanako, with their backs to the travel road. They appeared to be staring at something on the ground.

From a distance the object looked like a rumpled pile of dark blue cloth, but as Hiro drew closer he recognized the form as a human.

Hanako turned at the sound of Hiro and Father Mateo's footsteps in the snow. She shook her head. "Get away. I do not want you here."

Masako lay on her back with her arms at her sides. Frost silvered her indigo robe, and thin layers of snow covered the dead girl's hands and bare feet. Ice crystals fused her hair into a stringy veil that covered her face and neck, and most of her chest as well.

Hiro noted the robe's dark color. Unless the priest had seen Masako's spirit leave her body, she was not the "ghost" Father Mateo claimed to have seen the night before.

But perhaps he had seen the killer.

Hiro gestured to the footprints on the ground, and to a single set that led into the forest. "As I told you," he said in Portuguese, "a ghost does not leave tracks."

"Get away from here!" Hanako screeched.

"Hanako-*san*, please." Akako extended a reassuring hand, but the woman backed away.

"This is their fault. I do not want to die!"

Noboru continued staring at the body, as if in shock.

More footsteps approached. Hiro turned to see Otomuro heading in their direction, in the company of a younger man that Hiro recognized as Chitose.

When he arrived, Otomuro scowled at Masako's body. "Her?" He seemed strangely offended. "What did she do to provoke the spirit's wrath?"

Hanako stabbed a finger at Father Mateo, and then at Hiro. "They are to blame. They said that . . . she . . . does not exist. They made her angry and she took revenge."

"The spirit always takes a second victim," Noboru whispered. "I did not believe . . ."

"You spoke to them about her in my teahouse." Hanako wrapped her arms around her chest. "You put us all in danger, and Masako paid the price."

Chitose stood beside Masako's body. "We should move her. It is wrong to leave her lying in the snow."

"No!" Hanako released herself and raised her hands in protest. "If you take her inside, the ghost will surely follow."

"Masako is dead." Chitose's hands clenched into fists. "Nothing can harm her anymore."

"I was not speaking of Masako," Hanako's voice grew shrill. "What if it comes for me!"

"I would like to examine the girl before you move her." Hiro knelt beside the body without waiting for an answer.

Behind him, Hanako gasped. "If you disturb her, she will become a yūrei too!"

Unfortunately, Masako's body revealed little more up close than it had at a distance. Her body lay on its back as if in sleep, except for the curtain of hair that the killer had used to veil her head and upper body. Her fingernails appeared unbroken, and Hiro saw no signs of bruising or defensive injuries on her hands. He could not see her neck through the curtain of hair, but anticipated it would show signs of strangulation, like Ishiko.

Whoever overpowered the girl had apparently done it quickly.

"Noboru!" Hanako cried. "Make him stop!"

Noboru blinked as if suddenly aware of his surroundings. "Please . . . you are upsetting Hanako-*san*."

"We are trying to help her," Father Mateo countered.

"The yūrei will return and kill us all," Hanako wailed.

Hiro rose and stepped away from the body. He had seen enough, at least for the moment.

"Take her body to the ryokan," Noboru said. "You can lay her beside my mother."

Before the innkeeper finished the sentence, Chitose bent and grasped Masako's arms. His father took the dead girl's feet, and together they lifted her off the frozen ground.

As they passed, Father Mateo made the sign of the cross and bent his head in prayer.

Hiro examined the dirty, frozen ground beneath the place where the body lay. It showed no sign of a struggle, and he saw no indication of a body being dragged across it, either. Whoever killed Masako must have carried her corpse and left it in the snow.

Unfortunately, the girl's diminutive size made that a fairly simple task. Anyone in the village, except for Saku, could have carried her with ease.

"Hanako-*san* . . ." Noboru took a step toward the entertainer, but she shied away as if his touch would burn and ran off toward the entrance to the teahouse.

When Hanako disappeared around the corner, Noboru hung his head and started walking slowly toward the ryokan.

Otomuro took a step toward Father Mateo. "What are you doing here?"

"Here?" the Jesuit looked confused.

"Do not pretend at innocence with me," the samurai accused. "There is no traffic on the travel road this time of year and, since the landslide, no one takes this route. Why did you come here?" He took a threatening step toward Hiro. "Are you spies?"

"Not good ones," Hiro replied, "if your words are true."

Otomuro seemed to have trouble deciding whether or not to take offense.

"The foreigner has business in Edo," Hiro continued. "As for the route, our map indicated this was the travel road."

"Not since the landslide," Otomuro repeated. "What kind of business does a foreigner have in Edo?"

"With respect," Hiro said, "that is his business."

"You think yourself clever," Otomuro sneered. "A worthless ronin who follows a foreigner like a dog."

Hiro squared his shoulders. "If you wish to fight me, feel free to repeat those words."

Father Mateo stepped between them. "With respect, Otomuro-*sama*, we will gladly leave the village, if you let my servant go."

Hiro glanced at the Jesuit, taking care to keep his surprise well hidden. Father Mateo never willingly walked away from a murder investigation. That said, he recognized the priest's suggestion as a wise one. Despite his distaste for failure—and abandoning an investigation constituted failure in his eyes—Ana's freedom, and the lives of Iga agents on the travel road, meant far more than saving a village from a nonexistent ghost.

"Will you repay the coins she stole?" Otomuro asked.

Father Mateo appeared to undergo a silent struggle. At last, he said, "I assure you, Ana did not steal—"

Otomuro raised a hand to silence him. "Unless you pay, your servant will suffer the maximum penalty for her crime."

"Please forgive my interruption," Hiro said. "But the discovery of Masako-*san*'s unfortunate death interrupted my master's morning prayers. Perhaps we could discuss this matter privately, as samurai, while the foreigner returns to the ryokan?"

"There is nothing to discuss if he will not pay," Otomuro declared.

"With respect," Hiro said carefully, "I believe that we could reach an understanding."

Otomuro pursed his lips as if trying to parse the meaning behind the words. "Very well." He flicked his hand at Father Mateo as if brushing away an annoying fly. "The foreigner may go. And as a token of my goodwill, he no longer requires a guard—so long as you give your word that he will not run away."

"I give you my word," Hiro said. "He will not flee and leave his servant here."

"Very well," Otomuro said. "Your master may go and say his prayers, and I will inform Akako that he need not guard you any longer."

To Hiro's immense relief, the Jesuit bowed and departed without an argument.

As Father Mateo disappeared around the corner of the teahouse, Otomuro continued, "So. Do you think I cannot recognize your kind?"

Hiro waited for the samurai to continue, fairly certain the comment related to his status as a ronin rather than his true identity.

Otomuro tried to cross his arms, though his bulk prevented him from doing more than laying one atop the other. "Don't think I cannot see the disrespect in your eyes. You think yourself superior to me, a country samurai, even though I serve a daimyō while you trail after an honorless foreign master. You think, if you snap your fingers, I will free his thieving servant free of charge."

"I would never disrespect an intelligent man." *But I will happily tell half-truths to a fool.*

"Then why did you ask to speak with me alone?" Otomuro waited expectantly.

"The foreign priest believes his housekeeper is innocent, and his religion prevents him from paying bribes. However, I do not follow the foreigner's religion."

Otomuro's gaze remained devoid of understanding.

Hiro shifted his hand to the purse that hung from his obi. "As I said, I hoped that you and I could reach a private understanding. One that would free the foreigner's servant, so my master—and the rest of us—would trouble you no longer."

Otomuro blinked.

Clearly, subtlety wasn't going to work.

Hiro leaned forward conspiratorially. "How much silver do you want to let the foreigner's housekeeper go free?"

A shrewd expression passed over Otomuro's face. "How much do you have?"

"Enough to repay what Noboru lost, as well as a generous gift in recognition of your aid."

Otomuro raised a hand and rubbed his fleshy jowls. "Very well. I desire a hundred gold koban. Or the equivalent in silver, if you wish."

Hiro chose his words with care. "It seems quite difficult to believe a rural ryokan earned so much silver."

"Everyone knows the foreign priests are wealthy," Otomuro said. "Gold coins mean nothing to a wealthy man."

"But a great deal to a greedy one."

"First you attempt to bribe me, and now you insult me." Otomuro pointed a fat finger squarely at Hiro's chest. "Your eagerness to pay reveals the truth: your master's housekeeper is guilty, as I suspected. Either the foreigner pays me one hundred and fifty gold koban, or I will hang his thieving servant in two days' time."

"A moment ago, you set the price at one hundred," Hiro said.

"Your master should pray I do not increase it further." Otomuro laughed. "Do you get the joke? The foreign priest should pray."

Hiro longed to draw his sword and carve the smile off Otomuro's face. Instead, he forced a smile. "I will deliver your message to Father Mateo."

"And when you do," Otomuro added, "remind him that, in Japan, a master is responsible for his servants' crimes. He will pay for your arrogance, and the woman's theft, and I will have my gold."

"Do not worry," Hiro said, "I will personally ensure that you receive what you deserve."

CHAPTER 27

"One hundred and fifty golden coins?" Father Mateo knelt beside the guest room table, Bible open on his lap and a horrified expression on his face. "Why did you try to bribe him?"

"You tried it first," Hiro objected.

"I offered to replace the missing silver, to get us out of here." Father Mateo closed his Bible. "When I saw Masako's body, I realized that you were right. My eyes were playing tricks on me last night. It has also become clear to me that these people do not want an investigation. I fear they might even refuse to believe the truth, no matter what evidence we manage to produce. And I fear the same might happen with the theft. While I hate allowing anyone to believe that Ana is a thief, I am not willing to risk her life for principles."

"Unless you have a hundred and fifty golden coins that I don't know about, we have no choice but to keep investigating the murders and the theft."

The Jesuit set his book on the table. "Unfortunately, it does appear that way."

Hiro looked around. "Where's Gato?"

Father Mateo pulled a scrap of cloth from his sleeve and wiped his nose. "I took her down the hall to Ana's room. She tries to sit in my lap when you're not here."

"She tries it when I am here, too." Hiro gestured to the holy book. "If you've finished talking with your god, we have a trap to set."

"This plan of yours had better work." The Jesuit stood up. "And, in the meantime, I do not want Ana learning that her life is on the line."

Pale sunshine streamed over the treetops. Its feeble brilliance sparkled on the thin veneer of snow. Only scattered wisps of cloud streaked through the clear blue sky.

Father Mateo's breath made clouds in the chilly air. "Where should we start?"

Hiro gestured to Mume's house. "We need to speak with everyone, to be certain the information reaches both the killer and the thief. We might as well start here."

The door swung open in response to Hiro's knock, but instead of the woman they expected, they found themselves facing a man of unusual height, with a heavily muscled frame that looked strong enough to wrestle bears. But for the few faint lines around his eyes, Hiro might have mistaken him for a man in his early twenties.

"Good morning gentlemen." As he bowed, a swirl of warm air escaped the house, redolent with the musky scents of wood smoke, oxen, and manure. "I am Taso. Mume mentioned your visit, and that you spoke about Ishiko-*san*."

The priest returned the bow. "Good morning. I am Father Mateo Àvila de Santos, and this is my scribe, Matsui Hiro."

Etiquette neither required nor permitted a samurai to bow to a laborer, so Hiro merely nodded.

"Thank you for honoring me with a visit," Taso replied, "but, regrettably, I doubt I can add anything to what my wife has told you."

Hiro noted the unusual refinement of the large man's speech. "You do not speak like a man who carries burdens on the travel road."

Taso's cheeks flushed pink as he dipped his head in acknowledgment. "My father works as an artisan woodcrafter in Hakone. As a child, I studied with a tutor there."

"And yet, you did not continue as an artisan." Hiro's observation carried the weight of an inquiry.

"I did not wish to spend my life inhaling lacquer fumes, and these paws"—he raised his enormous hands—"were not built for delicate joinery. I ran away as soon as I was old enough to bear a load."

"How did you end up here, if you don't mind me asking?" Father Mateo asked.

"In the village?" Taso looked up the narrow street. "One of the men I worked with on the travel road became like a father to me." His gaze returned to the Jesuit. "He had no wife, and no children, so I moved into this house with him and cared for him until he died. He left the house to me, and I remained. By then, this was my home."

Hiro shifted the conversation. "You chose not to work today?"

"My wife was frightened by what happened to Masako-*san*." Taso glanced at the teahouse. "She asked me not to leave her alone, in case the ghost returns."

"I suspect the killer is a living person and a thief, and not a yūrei," Hiro said. "Although the foreign priest intends to offer prayers tonight in the hope that the spirit will not disturb your village any longer."

He chose his words carefully, opting for partial truths in place of outright lies.

Taso looked concerned. "Was something stolen from the teahouse?"

"From the ryokan," Hiro corrected. "Noboru's silver."

"We have begun an investigation," Father Mateo added, "because I do not wish my own silver to suffer a similar fate when I go to offer evening prayers at the burial ground tonight."

Not the most subtle delivery, Hiro thought, *but it will do.*

"An unfortunate occurrence, but, with respect, silver hardly equates to a woman's life." Taso closed the door a fraction, as if hoping they would take the hint and leave.

"Otomuro-*san* authorized the foreigner's investigation," Hiro said.

Taso seemed unmoved. "Regrettably, I know nothing about any missing silver."

"What time did you come home the last two nights?" Hiro watched the laborer carefully, more interested in his reaction than his response.

Taso cast his gaze toward the sky as he thought, but lowered it to Hiro as he answered. "A couple of hours after dark."

"Which direction did you come from?"

"Hakone." Taso gestured toward the travel road. "I carried a burden over the hill for a merchant, along the detour route. I presume you've heard about the landslide."

Hiro nodded. "Did you see anyone on the road, or in the forest, when you returned?"

"After dark?" Taso shifted in the doorway. "Who would I see?"

"I give you my word, as a servant of God, that we will not identify you as the source of any information," Father Mateo said. "You may speak to us in confidence."

Hiro hadn't expected the Jesuit to realize the subtle change in the laborer's posture suggested the man knew something after all.

"A man should not make accusations without evidence." Taso looked at the houses across the street.

Mume approached him from behind. "Please tell them. Please. Just tell them what you saw."

"They asked about last night." Taso told her gently. "Last night I saw nothing."

"He has seen Chitose-*san* in the woods, at night," Mume said earnestly. "We should not go in the woods at night. The priest from the mountain told me so."

"I have seen him in the forest after dark on several occasions," Taso agreed, "when I returned from work unusually late."

"Did you ask what he was doing?" Father Mateo asked the question before Hiro could.

"Wise men do not involve themselves in other people's business." Taso crossed his massive arms. "But Chitose-*san* carries loads on the travel road all day, as I do. If he wants to hunt, or gather firewood, he must do it at night—as I do also. I have known Chitose-*san* his entire life. He would not harm, or steal from, anyone."

"Is he married?" Father Mateo asked.

"Not yet." Mume spoke eagerly. "He was going to marry a girl from Hakone. But her father changed his mind when he heard about the yūrei. Kane says—"

"We have talked about gossip." Taso's voice held gentle disapproval. "I will handle the conversation from here."

Mume bowed and returned to the back of the house, head low.

"I assure you," Taso said, "Chitose-*san* would not steal or kill."

"Do you believe a yūrei killed Ishiko and Masako?" Hiro asked.

Taso pressed his lips together. His brow furrowed. "I believe there is an evil in this village. Precisely what it is, I cannot say."

CHAPTER 28

"Why didn't we ask him more about the murders?" Father Mateo asked in Portuguese as he and Hiro crossed the road.

"He told us what he knew," Hiro replied, "or, at least, what he's willing to divulge. For the moment that will have to do."

"He seemed nervous when he talked about Chitose."

"I noticed that also." Hiro knocked on the door of Akako's house. A shuffling approached, and the door swung inward.

"You again!" Saku stabbed a gnarled finger at the Jesuit. "You need to go away. You don't belong in this world anymore."

Akako appeared behind the elderly woman. "Mother, please—"

Saku clenched her fist and shook it. "Don't 'mother' me. This village does not need another ghost."

"I am not a ghost!" Father Mateo protested.

"You are." The elderly woman leaned on her cane. "You just don't realize it yet."

"May I help you with something?" Akako asked.

"Don't talk to the ghost," Saku admonished. "If you encourage it, it will never leave."

"Mother." Akako gestured back inside the house. "Go drink your tea. I will make sure they leave."

She hobbled off, grumbling under her breath.

"I apologize for my mother," Akako said. "Sometimes her mind . . ."

"She's not the first to mistake me for a ghost." Father Mateo smiled.

"We would like to talk with you about the recent theft, and Masako's murder, as well as helping us protect the foreigner's gold," Hiro said. "Perhaps, if you are not busy . . ."

"Of course." The porter glanced over his shoulder. "With apologies . . . could we talk at the ryokan?"

"Of course," Hiro said. "I had hoped your son, Chitose, could also join us?"

Akako froze for a moment before answering. "Regrettably, he cannot. He has left for work on the travel road."

"That is not leaving." Saku shouted from the back of the house. "That is the *opposite* of leaving."

Akako ignored her. "My son will be tired when he returns this evening, but I could bring him to the ryokan tomorrow morning, if you wish?"

Hiro briefly considered talking with Akako alone, but decided against it. "Certainly." Upon reflection, he doubted Chitose's explanation for the nocturnal ramblings would get them any closer to the truth—even if the porter's son chose not to lie.

Hiro and Father Mateo returned to the ryokan.

"The more I consider it," Father Mateo said in Portuguese as he closed the guest room door behind them, "the more I suspect Chitose of the thefts, if not the killings. A man needs money to find a wife, and young men often find an easy coin more tempting than the one that requires labor."

"You now believe the thief and the killer are different people?" Hiro asked.

"I hate to admit it," the Jesuit said, "but after last night . . ."

"Do not tell me you have changed your mind, and now believe in ghosts."

Father Mateo reached up and grasped the cross that hung around his neck. "The honest answer is I do not know."

"Then let's focus on the thief." *And on leaving here as soon as possible.*

"We should find out if anything was stolen from the teahouse," Father Mateo said. "Either recently or in the past."

"Indeed. Masako may have startled the thief."

"Perhaps . . ." Father Mateo sounded doubtful.

Hiro wished he had seen what the Jesuit saw. He found it hard to believe, and profoundly disturbing, that something could change a reliable man's opinion so completely and so quickly. Even worse, the change made Father Mateo unreliable, which left Hiro feeling very much alone.

Someone knocked on the door.

"Enter," Hiro called.

Noboru opened the door. Kane stood behind him, right hand fidgeting with the hem of her obi.

"I spoke with your servant again," Noboru said. "She still refuses to confess her crime."

"You want a confession?" Hiro took a step toward the door. "I confess that I grow weary of your tiresome behavior. I confess profound dislike for your refusal to believe the truth. And I confess that, unless you learn some manners quickly, you will find yourself confessing to the judges of the afterlife."

Noboru staggered backward, jostling Kane. The collision knocked them both off balance. As they tried to avoid a fall, Hiro had an idea.

He turned to Father Mateo. "Put on your cloak. We need to find Zentaro."

"That bag of wind?" Noboru asked. "What could he possibly do to help?"

"He doesn't care about anyone but himself," Kane added. "He even steals the offerings from the graves . . ." An idea lit her eyes. "Do you think he stole our silver?"

"Nonsense," Noboru sniffed.

Hiro ignored him and answered Kane. "I accuse no man without evidence, but I do have questions for the mountain priest."

Once again, Hiro and Father Mateo walked up the deserted travel road to the forest. Thin lines of smoke rose from the roof of Saku's house, and Taso's, scenting the air with burning pine. Beyond them, shuttered houses crouched like empty tombs on either side of the narrow road.

Clouds had begun to gather in the sky, though the anemic winter sun still shone, its light more white than gold. Where sunshine reached the ground, the veil of snow grew thin and dark, discolored by the dirt beneath. Yet in the shadows of the houses, and beneath the trees, the snow remained pristine.

As Hiro and Father Mateo entered the forest, the smell of wood smoke from the village blended with the deeper, earthy scents of living pines, decaying leaves, and the faint, wet odor Hiro recognized as melting snow. As always, its distinctive smell called back a memory of himself, just five years old, trying in vain to persuade his older brother that he could smell the snow.

Since then, Hiro had learned to keep esoteric knowledge to himself.

Father Mateo stopped walking.

Hiro snapped to attention. "Did you hear something?"

"No, and that's precisely the problem. It's too quiet."

In the silence that followed, Hiro heard the muffled thump of his pulse inside his ears. His breath, and Father Mateo's, emerged as silent puffs of cloud.

Higher up the mountainside, a crow cried out and then fell silent.

As he listened to the distant ringing that the mind sometimes created in the absence of all other sound, Hiro agreed with the Jesuit. The silence did seem strange. That said, he felt no need to say so. It would cause his friend concern and, for the moment, Hiro saw no danger.

He continued walking.

Father Mateo fell in step beside him. "Why do you want to find

Zentaro? We spoke with him twice already, and . . . surely you don't think that he's the thief?"

"Akako did mention him stealing objects from the village," Hiro answered, "though I want to see him for a different reason. A man who sees what happens on the mountain may have also seen Chitose in the woo—"

A mournful cry, somewhere between a wail and a moan, came through the trees. It wavered as if in mimicry of speech.

Father Mateo looked alarmed. "That came from the direction of the burial yard."

But Hiro did not hear the words. He was already running toward the sound.

CHAPTER 29

The torii that marked the entrance to the burial yard came into view, a brilliant splash of vermilion against the snowy ground. Beyond the gate, stone monuments rose like the jagged, rotting teeth of a mountain troll.

A hooded figure dressed in white crouched next to Riko's grave, almost precisely where Ishiko's corpse had stood the day before. The figure swayed from side to side, hands clasped around a bowl of rice.

The moaning came from underneath the hood.

"Z-Zentaro," Father Mateo said, out of breath from running up the path.

At the sound of his voice, the moaning stopped. Zentaro straightened, turned, and bowed. "Inari-*sama* told me you would come again."

"And did he also tell you why?" Hiro asked.

"You seek answers."

"Will you . . . help us . . . find them?" Father Mateo panted.

Zentaro set the bowl of rice on the sharp-edged monument by Riko's grave, beside the bowl that Ishiko left the night she died. He pressed his palms together and executed a deep, reverential bow. As he straightened, he withdrew a pair of wooden chopsticks from his sleeve and stuck them upright in the bowl of rice.

Only then did he answer Father Mateo's question. "While I would like to help you, a sage once taught me that answers received without effort have no value. Every man must find his answers for himself."

He faced the grave and bowed again.

Hiro ignored the comment and the teaching. "Did you know that someone from the village walks the woods at night?"

Zentaro spun around. "Who would do such a dangerous thing?"

"While I would like to tell you," Hiro said, "regrettably, an answer received without effort has no value."

"I never liked that teaching," Zentaro muttered. His face lit up. "But if we *traded* answers, each would require an effort, and thus have value."

Hiro doubted any sage would agree with that logic, but had long since learned to accept any argument—no matter how illogical—if it produced the results he wanted.

"But not here." Zentaro looked around. "It is not safe."

"Why not?" Hiro gestured to the monuments. "If Inari cannot save us from the dead—"

"Do not mock Inari-*sama*!" Zentaro hissed. "Just one ill-spoken word could mean your death!"

"I'll risk it."

Father Mateo shot Hiro a warning look. "Have you a safer place in mind?"

"Follow me." Zentaro raised a finger to his lips. "But do not say a word until we get there."

He led them across the burial yard and up the mountainside. Wherever possible, he jumped from stone to stone instead of walking on the ground. Father Mateo tried to follow the yamabushi's trail exactly, but after the first few awkward leaps the Jesuit gave up and climbed straight up the slope through the shallow snow.

Hiro didn't bother with acrobatics, even from the start. As he followed the others up the hill, he wondered yet again if life in the mountains made ascetics strange, or if only strange men chose the ascetic life.

He decided it was likely some of both.

As they ascended, a cloud slipped over the sun. The shadows faded and the light turned gray. The temperature dropped, and the clouds that emerged with Hiro's breath grew denser and more visible. The snow grew deeper, too, and covered the top of Hiro's shoes with every step. He felt the cold in the soles of his feet. His toes began to numb.

Still Zentaro bounded up the mountain, leaping from stone to stone like a hunting fox. Behind him, Father Mateo struggled not to slip on the smaller stones and rotting leaves that lay beneath the snow.

The forest grew denser here as well, untouched by human hands. Huge cedars towered overhead, forcing the smaller maples to strain their branches for a share of light. The clumps of shoulder-high sasa grew larger, and Zentaro made broad detours to avoid them.

Eventually the yamabushi emerged in a house-sized clearing. An enormous, flat-topped boulder sat just left of center in the open space, flanked by a pair of carved stone foxes. The fox on the left appeared to hold a scroll in its mouth, while the one on the right held a spherical jewel carved from stone. An unpainted wooden torii stood in front of the stone, adorned with a rope of hemp and strips of paper folded into zigzag shapes. More folded papers hung from the trees at the edges of the clearing and from cords around the statues' necks.

Zentaro gestured to the stone. "Inari-*sama* will protect us in this holy place. At least, during daylight hours."

"Why is the mountain so dangerous after dark?" Father Mateo asked. "Does the forest have wolves? Or bears?"

"Any man can kill a bear." Zentaro dropped his voice to a whisper. "It is the kami men should fear."

"I understand the need to show respect," Father Mateo said, "but why does that require avoiding the mountain after dark?"

Zentaro gave the Jesuit a sidelong look. "I thought you claimed to be a priest."

"He does not understand the Japanese kami well," Hiro explained. "His land has only a single god."

"One kami?" The yamabushi looked as if the Jesuit had grown a second head. "Which one?"

"His name is Jehovah," Father Mateo said. "The One True God."

Zentaro turned to Hiro. "You must take this foreigner off this mountain. Now. Today. And do not let him return."

"Can you tell us—" Father Mateo began.

Zentaro spoke over him. "Inari-*sama* warned me you were dangerous. A priest who denies the kami of the mountain . . . he will cause disaster. He must leave right now."

"Not until you answer our questions." Father Mateo stood his ground. "You agreed to an exchange of information."

"I agreed to one question," Zentaro countered. "Ask it now, and go."

"How often does Chitose enter the woods at night, and what does he do?" Hiro asked.

"That is two questions. However, a single answer will cover both. I do not know."

"But you do spend nights on the mountain," Hiro pressed.

"In a cave, where my presence cannot offend the kami that walk the mountain after dark."

"And yet, you knew Chitose enters the woods at night," Hiro said. "When you came down to the village and called to Saku through the door, you mentioned her descendant's life. A reference to Chitose."

The flush began to fade from Zentaro's cheeks.

"If you spend every night in a cave, how did you know he risked the kami's anger?" Hiro asked.

The yamabushi regarded him evenly. "Because Inari-*sama* told me so."

"The deity told you." Hiro didn't even try to hide his disbelief.

"Not directly." Zentaro laid a hand on his chest. "The kitsune speak to me on his behalf."

"You talk to foxes," Hiro said.

"The kitsune told me to warn the villagers that the mountain belongs to the kami after dark," Zentaro said. "The villagers must not leave their homes, or enter the forest, after the sun goes down. When Chitose-*san* began to violate this edict, Inari-*sama* warned me, through the kitsune. Chitose-*san* ignored my words, but I hoped his grandmother would make him stop before disaster struck."

"A kitsune told you all of this?" Hiro didn't believe in talking foxes any more than he believed in ghosts or gods.

Zentaro raised his chin. "Ishiko-*san* did not believe me either, and she paid a deadly price."

"You believe a mountain deity killed Ishiko?" Father Mateo asked.

"She entered the forest after dark," Zentaro said. "She did not heed the warning."

"How long have you been talking with kitsune?" Hiro asked.

"I have answered your question." Zentaro pointed down the mountain. "You must go."

CHAPTER 30

"Do you think he truly believes the mountain deities killed Ishiko?" Father Mateo looked back up the mountain, even though they had already left the sacred clearing far behind.

Hiro continued walking. "He believes in talking foxes."

"At least he confirmed that Chitose walks in the woods at night."

"Again, if you believe the talking fox."

As they continued down the mountain, Hiro silently reviewed the evidence. Unfortunately, he concluded they knew nothing that seemed likely to unlock either the murders or the theft. At this point, he no longer cared if the killer escaped, or killed again. The superstitious villagers could keep their yūrei and their talking foxes. He wanted only to prove Ana's innocence and leave.

When they reached the village, Hiro turned off the road and headed for Saku's house.

"What are you doing?" Father Mateo asked.

Instead of answering, Hiro knocked on the wooden door.

Shuffling footsteps approached, and then fell silent. A female voice called, "Take your foreign ghost and go away!"

"For the last time, I am not a ghost!" the Jesuit returned.

Hiro doubted this time would truly be the last.

"I do not talk to ghosts!" Saku called through the door.

"We have come to see Akako," Hiro said.

"I will not open my door to that ghost again!"

Before Hiro could reply, Father Mateo gestured down the street.

Akako stood on the veranda of the teahouse, deep in conversation with Noboru and Hanako.

The woman stood with her face cast down and her shoulders low, as if she lacked the strength to stand erect. She wore a pale kimono with an obi of a slightly darker shade. Although not formal mourning clothes, the lack of bright colors doubtless paid homage to Masako's death.

Hiro started toward the teahouse with Father Mateo at his side.

Hanako noticed their approach. Without taking her eyes off the foreign priest, she whispered something to Noboru.

He left the porch and intercepted Hiro and the Jesuit.

"Forgive me." Noboru bowed. "Hanako-*san* would rather not speak with you today." He flushed. "I apologize, but . . ."

"She fears the yūrei," Father Mateo said.

Relief washed over Noboru's face. "Thank you for understanding."

Hanako opened the door and disappeared into the teahouse as Akako descended the steps to join Noboru and the other men.

"Forgive my ignorance," Father Mateo said, "but why does our presence endanger her? Surely the yūrei has no reason to seek revenge against her."

Noboru shrugged. "No man can understand the mind of a woman. Or a spirit, for that matter."

"An onryō does not need a reason," Akako said. "Hate propels it. Hate defines it. But the creature does not think about philosophical questions, or right and wrong, any more than a spider ponders poetry."

"She is a yūrō," Noboru interjected. "Not an onryō."

"No matter what you call her," the porter said, "she will continue to attack, and kill, until she sates her thirst for vengeance."

"But if she has no grudge against Hanako-*san*, our presence should create no threat," the Jesuit persisted.

"Hanako thinks if she shows kindness to a stranger it could make the yūrei angry," Noboru said. "Foolish, but—"

Akako cut him off. "She is not wrong. A show of compassion could anger the spirit, because no one in this village showed her any while she lived." He fixed Noboru with an angry glare. "And I don't speak only of the night she died. Her unanswered screams for help were merely the last in a lifelong chain of insults that began the night she left her mother's womb."

"How dare you judge what you do not understand." Noboru raised his chin. "She did not share your blood. You barely knew her." Raising a hand to cut off any possible response, Noboru turned to Father Mateo and changed the subject. "Have you found my silver yet?"

"If we had, we would have told you." Hiro paused. "Have there been any other thefts in the village, recently or otherwise?"

"No one here has anything to steal," Akako said, "except for Oto-muro-*san*."

"And Hanako," Noboru added, "but if we had a village thief, what reason would I have to accuse your servant?"

"Indeed." Hiro could think of several, but decided to let the question—and Noboru's lack of manners—pass.

"You claim you have solved mysteries, and yet you make no progress." Noboru gestured to Father Mateo. "His servant faces judgment when the priest arrives from Hakone. Do you even have a plan?"

"Right now I plan to take a nap while the foreigner says his midday prayers." Hiro turned and walked off toward the ryokan.

Father Mateo's hurried footsteps followed.

"Before you chide me for unnecessary rudeness," Hiro said in Portuguese, "remember that he started this with his wrongful accusation against Ana, and that, by law, I owe no courtesy to commoners."

"The law does not excuse a lack of manners," the priest replied in his native tongue, "and he has a point. Our time is running out."

Hiro woke from his nap with a strong sensation of something out of place.

Father Mateo knelt on the floor nearby with his scarred hands folded and his head bent down in prayer. A leather-bound Bible lay open on the floor beside the Jesuit's knees. The upper corner of the right-hand page was ripped away.

The page made Hiro recognize the cause of his discomfort. Normally, he woke with the comforting, familiar warmth and weight of Gato on his knees.

He sat up silently to avoid disturbing the priest's meditation. He did not share the Jesuit's faith, but his respect for Father Mateo extended to their differences as well as to the attributes they shared.

Hiro crossed his legs, closed his eyes, and meditated on the sounds around him. But unlike most meditation, in which men attempted to shut out the world, Hiro exercised his lesser senses, trying to identify each sound that reached his ears. He heard his own breathing, and Father Mateo's. The beams creaked overhead as someone walked across the upper floor, followed by the scratch of tiny claws in the space above the ceiling. Apparently, Ana's comments about rats had some foundation after all.

"You're awake."

Hiro opened his eyes at the Jesuit's words.

Father Mateo closed his Bible. "It occurred to me that Otomuro might have stolen the silver after all."

"Why would he take the risk?"

"Why else would he befriend Noboru?" the Jesuit countered. "Samurai do not consort with men from the common classes voluntarily. Clearly, Otomuro had something to gain from the relationship, and the only benefit I see is learning where Noboru kept his money— and, perhaps, how much he had."

"You overlook a more obvious explanation. Men require companionship. As a man with no equals in the village, Otomuro had no choice but to accept a friend of lower status. More importantly, as owner of the ryokan, Noboru had access to useful information about the people who passed along the travel road."

"No man treats a friend the way that samurai treats Noboru."

"While I appreciate your opinion, you do not understand the way a man like Otomuro thinks." Hiro raised his hands, palms up, in imitation of a scale. "One side of him craves friendship, but the other feels shame when he associates with men of lower rank." He moved his hands out of balance, and then rebalanced them. "He reassures himself about his own superiority by wielding his power—no matter how small—against the man he feels forced to call a friend."

"I did not know you thought so much about men's motivations."

Hiro lowered his hands. "An effective hunter understands all aspects of his prey."

Father Mateo sighed. "I hope, someday, you stop regarding men as prey."

"Our friendship does not change the way I view the world, or my position in it." Hiro met the Jesuit's gaze. "Any more than I believe it should change yours."

Father Mateo set his Bible on the table. "I wonder if the unknown benefactor who hired you knew his gift would bless me with far more than just my life."

"Your benefactor hired the Iga ryu, not me specifically." Hiro paused. "And I assure you, my cousin Hanzō considers me anything but a blessing."

The Jesuit laughed, and then grew serious. "What will we do if the thief decides not to come and steal my gold? I think we need a backup plan."

Someone knocked on the inn's front door. A voice called, "Kane? Kane, are you home?"

Father Mateo rose. "That sounds like Mume."

"Not our business," Hiro said.

The Jesuit had barely knelt on the floor again when someone knocked on the guest room door.

Father Mateo called, "Come in," and gave Hiro a look that suggested it was about to become their business after all.

The door slid open.

"Please forgive the interruption." Kane gestured to the woman at her side. "My sister asked to see you."

"Help me." Mume clasped her hands. "The thief has struck again."

CHAPTER 31

"When?" Father Mateo rose to his feet. "Come in and tell us everything."

Mume glanced at Kane. "I . . ."

"A married woman should not meet with two strange men alone, in a ryokan," Kane said.

Understanding softened Father Mateo's features. "Would she feel more comfortable if you remain with her?"

Instead of answering, Kane stepped across the threshold. Mume followed, still clutching her hands together but looking slightly more relieved.

"Tell us what happened," Father Mateo said again, as Kane closed the shoji.

"Our silver—all we had—is gone." Mume looked on the verge of tears.

"And you just discovered it missing?" the Jesuit asked.

"Right now—I mean, a few minutes ago." Mume bit her lip. "When I went to the latrine."

"You keep silver in the latrine?" Father Mateo seemed to find that difficult to believe.

"Not anymore," Mume replied. "It's gone."

"But you kept it there, when you had some," the Jesuit clarified.

"Taso said no one would look there for it."

"Perhaps your husband took it with him," Hiro suggested, "to keep it safe."

"He would not have left the sack behind." Mume bit her lower lip again.

Father Mateo took a step toward the door. "If you show us where it was, perhaps we can find a clue to its disappearance."

Despite his intense desire to avoid a tour of Mume and Taso's latrine, Hiro followed the others through the kitchen and out the door at the back of the ryokan.

When they reached the small, squat building adjacent to Taso's home, Mume opened the door, revealing a hole in the ground surrounded by a narrow square of wooden boards. The pungent odor of human waste that emanated from the hole made Hiro glad that winter temperatures muted smells.

In summertime, the stench would kill an ox.

Father Mateo coughed and took a step backward.

Mume gestured to a pair of beams that supported the wooden roof. "Up there. You see the sack?"

A piece of limp, dark cloth hung over the side of the nearest beam.

Hiro stepped into the narrow space, reached up, and retrieved the bag. Its weight and flexibility left no doubt that it was empty.

"Last night, that bag had thirty silver coins." Mume's voice held an edge of desperation.

"Why did you keep your silver on a beam, where anyone could see it?" Father Mateo asked.

"We hid it against the beam." Mume pointed to a dark place in the corner of the roof. "You could only see it if you knew . . ." She bit her lip, which had begun to quiver.

Hiro considered the latrine a ridiculous hiding place, but held his tongue. Shaming a woman in distress would serve no purpose.

Mume clasped her hands against her chest. "Please, sir. Ask your servant to return it."

"Ana did not steal your silver," Father Mateo said. "Even had she known where you hid it, she could not reach that beam."

"Your servant did know where it was hidden," Kane countered. "Mume and I discussed her silver after ours was stolen. We were in the ryokan kitchen, and your housekeeper was in there, cleaning, at the time."

"Kane told me to move my silver." Mume's eyes filled up with tears. "But I forgot to tell Taso. Now it's gone!" She began to cry.

"Ana did not do this," Father Mateo repeated.

"Taso will be so angry," Mume sobbed.

"I will speak to him on your behalf," Father Mateo said. "This theft is not your fault."

"If you will not acknowledge your servant's guilt, and restore my sister's silver, we will take the matter to Otomuro-*sama*," Kane threatened.

"I will not call an innocent person guilty," the Jesuit said, "but I give you my word that I will do everything in my power to catch the thief and recover your stolen silver."

"I hate to suggest this," Father Mateo told Hiro after their return to the ryokan, "but perhaps we should discuss these thefts with Ana."

"How long has Ana worked for you?" Hiro asked.

"Four years next spring."

"And has she ever given you the slightest reason not to trust her?"

"No."

"So. Does it make more sense that Ana would risk her trusted position, not to mention her life, for a handful of silver, or that someone else in this village is a thief?" He laid a hand on the door. "While you think that over, I'm going to get some exercise."

Hiro left the ryokan and walked to the empty rice field at the far end of the village near Otomuro's mansion. A thin, ice-crusted layer of snow lay over the field, obscuring the stubbly remains of the stalks beneath. Hiro entered the field, drew his katana, and began the first of the samurai weapon forms he used in place of shinobi *katas* when training where other eyes could see. For over an hour, he forced himself to concentrate on movement, form, and steel.

By the time he stopped and sheathed his sword, his muscles burned and his robe was damp with sweat. The sun rested about a hand's breadth above the pines in the west, bleached to a pale white disc by the hazy sky.

Hiro's stomach snarled like an angry wolf.

As he returned to the ryokan, he hoped this evening meal would prove more edible than the last.

In the guest room, Father Mateo knelt on the floor with the Bible in his lap. Gato perched on the edge of the table, watching the book with hungry eyes.

The Jesuit pulled a cloth from his sleeve and sneezed.

"Do you want me to take Gato back to Ana?" Hiro asked.

"Hm."

Hiro turned at the sound of the housekeeper's voice. She stood behind him, holding a laden tray.

"I see you're back in time to eat, as usual," she said.

Hiro found the insult unexpectedly reassuring. "Did you cook?"

"The innkeeper asked me to prepare the evening meal early." She stepped over the threshold. "So I can return to my room before dark."

Hiro stepped aside. As Ana passed him with the tray, he caught the pungent scent of onions and the oily, slightly fishy smell of eel past its prime.

His stomach lurched and a lump rose in his throat.

"I am sorry about his accusations," Father Mateo said, "and that they have imprisoned you unfairly."

Ana set the tray on the table. "Do not apologize for someone else's failings." She straightened. "Just find the thief so we can leave for Edo."

"We will," the Jesuit said, "I promise. Thank you for preparing this meal, despite the circumstances."

Hiro joined the Jesuit at the table.

In addition to a teapot and a pair of cups, the tray held two steaming bowls of golden broth laden with chunks of winter vegetables and topped with inch-wide strips of pale, ribbed flesh. Beside the eel-topped soup sat a pair of empty rice bowls and a covered circular container that undoubtedly held rice.

"*Unagi* soup?" Father Mateo asked.

"With eels 'fresh caught today,' if you believe the innkeeper's wife." Ana's tone suggested she did not.

Hiro swallowed against the nausea that rose in his throat. He could barely eat fresh eel without gagging, and the smell suggested the one in the bowls was anything but fresh.

"I used every onion I could find." Ana scooped Gato into her arms and started toward the door. "I hope it helps. There's also rice, but not much else."

"It is winter." Father Mateo sounded apologetic.

"And too far from Kyoto to find any decent food." Ana paused on the threshold. "I appreciate you watching Gato while I cooked. She can spend the night with me, so you don't sneeze."

"Not by her doing, anyway." Father Mateo sniffed and forced a smile.

CHAPTER 32

After Ana left with Gato, Hiro turned his attention to the food.

Tiny specks of fishy oil floated on the murky soup. Curls of steam rose off the bowls, with a distinctive fragrance that made Hiro's stomach stop its angry growling instantly.

Father Mateo said a silent blessing, raised his bowl, and took a sip. "It tastes like Portuguese fish stew."

Hiro raised his bowl, but his throat and gut rebelled.

He set the bowl back down.

Raising the teapot, he poured a cup of tea for Father Mateo and another for himself. The scent of roasted tea helped calm his stomach. He drank it slowly, savoring the deep, rich flavor and the lingering natural sweetness on his tongue.

After finishing the tea, he considered the bowl of soup once more. The strip of eel lay atop the vegetables like a corpse atop a pyre, a stinking barrier between his lips and the soup that lay beneath.

"You like eel?" he asked Father Mateo.

"This one less than most," the priest acknowledged, "but I've eaten worse."

Hiro gestured to his bowl. "Then you may have mine also."

"You need to eat."

Hiro refilled the Jesuit's teacup and then his own. "Many people live on only roasted tea and rice. I can manage for a night or two."

"If you're certain." Father Mateo reached for the second bowl. "You don't like eel?"

"I like them fine . . . in the river or the ocean."

"But isn't eel a specialty of Iga?"

"An unfortunate truth that has no bearing on my sense of taste."

Some time after they finished eating, they heard a knock on the guest room door.

"Come in," Hiro said.

The door slid open, and Kane bowed from the threshold. "I have come to take your tray."

Hiro felt relieved to see the innkeeper's wife instead of Ana. Her presence saved him needing to find an excuse to see Noboru. He stood up. "The foreigner wishes to visit the burial yard, to offer prayers for the dead. I will accompany him, to ensure his safety. Please lay out the futon for us now, while we are gone."

Kane froze, bent over the dinner tray. "He wants to go now? But it will soon be dark."

"A priest of his religion does not fear the darkness, or the dead." Hiro removed his purse from his obi, set it on the table, and drew his cloak around his shoulders.

Kane picked up the tray but did not leave the room. When the men finished fastening their cloaks, she said, "Please excuse me, but you must—"

"Foolish woman!" Noboru appeared in the doorway. "Do not attempt to tell a samurai what he should do." He bowed to Hiro and Father Mateo. "I could not help but overhear. Forgive my wife."

"But Noboru . . ." Her protest barely rose above a whisper.

"Prepare the room as he requested." The innkeeper's voice grew harsh.

Kane bowed her head in obedience, but cast a worried glance at Father Mateo as she hurried from the room.

"May we trouble you for the loan of a lantern?" Hiro asked Noboru.

"Of course. I will light one for you."

Father Mateo carried the lantern as he and Hiro left the ryokan. Although the sky still glowed with the remnants of a hazy sunset, the temperature had dropped dramatically when the sun disappeared below the trees.

A bitter wind blew down from the mountain, rustling the trees and making Hiro shiver.

"H-how long do we have to stay out here before we circle back to the inn?" Father Mateo's teeth chattered in the cold.

"Just long enough to make the thief believe we went to the burial yard."

"Then why are we heading to the teahouse?"

"To make sure the thief is aware we've left the ryokan."

"You think Hanako is the thief?"

Instead of answering, Hiro stepped up onto the teahouse's veranda.

As he hoped, the door swung open before he knocked.

Hanako wore a pale kimono adorned with hand-stitched bamboo stalks that bore a coat of embroidered snow. Silver threads shot through her dark green obi. "What are you doing here?" she shrieked. "You should not be here! She will come!"

"We merely wished to ask—" Hiro began.

Hanako raised her hands before her like a shield. "Go away!" Her voice rang clearly through the silent street. "I will not listen! I do not care what you have to say!"

Father Mateo stepped backward off the porch, but Hiro held his ground. "The foreigner is going to the burial yard, to offer prayers—"

"Then go to the burial yard, and leave me alone!" Hanako slammed the door.

"That went even better than I hoped," Hiro said as he joined the priest and they started up the road.

"You wanted her to yell." Father Mateo's voice held grudging respect. "So everyone in the village would believe we'd left for the burial yard."

Hiro smiled. "A shrieking woman finally proved useful."

"Go away, you ghost!" Saku stood in the open doorway of her home. "Stop scaring innocent women and go away!" She thumped the ground with her cane for emphasis.

Father Mateo turned to face her. "I am not a ghost."

She shook her head. "The longer it takes you to accept the truth, the harder it will be for you to go."

"I am taking him to the burial ground right now," Hiro said.

"To offer prayers." Father Mateo glared at the shinobi and repeated, "I am not a ghost."

Hiro smiled.

"See that he stays there," Saku said. "This village is cursed enough already, without a foreign ghost as well."

"If you truly believe the village cursed," Hiro commented, "why don't you leave?"

"Because it does no good!" Saku thumped the ground with her cane once more. "Only a fool attempts to outrun a yūrei. If she wants you dead, you die, and we deserve it. All of us. No one raised a finger when she screamed for help. Not even me." In a sorrowful voice she added, "I wish I had."

She pointed her cane at Hiro. "Leave this village. And take that fool ghost with you."

CHAPTER 33

"Do you think we need to talk with anyone else?" Father Mateo asked as he and Hiro continued on the travel road.

"Otomuro." The shinobi gestured to the samurai mansion at the far end of the village. Its shadowed form nestled against the trees as if trying to disappear into the night. The lanterns near the veranda steps were cold and dark, and wooden shutters barred the windows against the night. But for the sliver of light that escaped beneath the large front door, Hiro might have thought the occupants were sleeping.

"Surely he wouldn't—"

Hiro held up a hand for silence.

"What—" Father Mateo began.

"Shh." Hiro gestured toward the forest.

Silence fell.

Twilight drained the colors from the village, casting every shape in shades of darkening blue. The only movement came from the pale lines of smoke that rose from the chimneys of the ryokan, the teahouse, and the occupied village houses.

Just as Hiro decided he must have imagined the sound in the forest, it came again—a gentle, distant crunch, like footsteps moving through the snow.

It grew fainter as he listened.

"Circle around behind the houses and return to the ryokan," Hiro whispered. "Go in through the veranda door, and make sure no one sees you. Hide in the cupboard and wait for the thief."

"We are supposed to go back together," The priest objected, his voice a silent hiss.

"The plan has changed."

Father Mateo looked into the forest as if considering further argument.

The footsteps faded into silence.

"Go," Hiro whispered.

"Be careful." Father Mateo shuttered the lantern and hurried off across the empty field.

Hiro wondered whether he should have loaned the priest a sword. Then again, Father Mateo did not like weapons, and had no skill with them anyway.

Leaving the thought and the village behind, Hiro started up the mountain.

He moved as silently as he could without sacrificing the necessary speed. Gathering darkness transformed the ground beneath his feet into a ragged quilt of black and gray, with patches of indigo where the snow reflected the last of the failing light.

He stopped to listen for the footsteps.

Silence fell around him with a weight that seemed to amplify the cold. His nose felt numb, and his ears began to burn. He slipped his hands into his sleeves, hoping to keep his fingers flexible enough to make a fist or draw a sword.

He heard a faint sound in the distance, no longer clearly identifiable as footsteps but too rhythmic to be anything else.

Hiro followed the sound. As the darkness grew deeper, and the ground beneath him less distinct, only years of shinobi training allowed him to continue climbing without slipping or making a sound. Slowly, carefully, he closed the distance between himself and the crunching sound ahead.

The closer he drew, the more the weight and regularity of the footsteps made Hiro suspect he was following a man. The lack of a light or lantern suggested his quarry knew the mountain well.

A stick snapped loudly beneath his sandal.

Ahead, the footsteps stopped.

Hiro froze, right foot in the air. Slowly, he lowered it to the ground. He held his breath and waited.

The forest also seemed to hold its breath.

After almost a minute, the footsteps started up again. Hiro exhaled in relief and resumed his silent progress up the hill.

As he followed the footsteps, Hiro wondered where his quarry headed. Although he could not see well in the darkness, he knew the burial ground lay far below them on the mountainside.

A frigid wind rustled through the cedars. The branches rubbed across one another like ghostly fingers.

Despite Zentaro's claims, Hiro doubted the mountain cared about the short-lived, arrogant creatures who trespassed upon its rocky slopes.

The footsteps stopped.

A long, low moaning wavered through the night, the tortured cry of a soul bereft.

Hiro froze in place.

The moan repeated, deep at first but rising to a wail of despair. At the end, it dropped in pitch again and faded into silence.

Hiro reminded himself that he did not believe in ghosts.

He continued, raising a foot each time the wail began and stepping down at the apex of the moan, using the sound to camouflage his movements.

A glow appeared ahead of him, but it seemed too diffuse for a lantern. The color—a pale, silvery blue—looked wrong for fire.

Dense clumps of bamboo grass stood between Hiro and the light. He made his way around the thicket, stepping carefully to prevent rustling the bamboo. As he did, he recognized the bluish glow as hazy moonlight filtering through the trees into a clearing just ahead.

An eight-foot torii stood in the clearing, near a familiar, flat-topped boulder flanked by vigilant stone foxes. The footsteps had led him back to the sacred clearing where he and Father Mateo spoke with Zentaro earlier in the day.

A hooded figure knelt between the posts of the torii, facing the sacred stone.

This was no ghost.

With a moaning cry, the figure bowed its forehead to the snowy ground, arms extended toward the stone. The action gave a muted, eerie quality to the wail.

When the mourner pushed himself back to a kneeling position, his hood fell back, revealing Chitose's tear-streaked face.

The young man raised his hands in supplication.

"Please take me too. I do not want to live if she is gone."

CHAPTER 34

A gust of wind swept through the grove. The cedars creaked and swayed, their branches waving as if in response to Chitose's prayer.

The young man raised his face. His eyes looked wild, their expression halfway between terror and expectation.

As suddenly as it came, the wind disappeared.

The trees grew still. Their rustling faded into silence.

Chitose waited.

Hiro waited too.

Eventually the young man lowered his hands to his knees and bowed his head. He appeared to be praying until his shoulders began to shake with silent sobs. He curled his hands across his stomach and leaned forward.

"Why?" Chitose's wail carried through the forest. "It was not her fault!"

The agonized cry woke an answering pain in Hiro's heart. For an instant, he stood not in a grove of cedar and grasses on a mountain near Hakone, but in Iga, bathed in the blood of the only woman he had ever loved. His soul had made that sound the day Neko died.

Hiro also knew, without question, that Chitose had not killed Masako, and believed the young man had not killed Ishiko either. The exquisite pain in Chitose's voice testified to his innocence in ways not even Hiro's skepticism could deny.

The shinobi stepped into the clearing.

Chitose startled and screamed in terror. He tried to rise but slipped and fell. As he landed on the icy ground, he curled into a defensive ball.

"Have mercy!" He shielded his face with his hands. "Don't kill me! Please!"

"I have no intention of harming you." Hiro stood beside the shaking youth. "But I will point out, you did just ask to die."

Chitose lowered his arms. "You're not a kami."

"Not even close."

Chitose struggled to his feet. He brushed feebly at the dirty ice and snow that clung to his trousers. "You're the foreigner's servant."

"Scribe," Hiro corrected.

"Did you follow me to taunt my grief?"

"I most assuredly did not. However, I am curious. Why did you climb up here, in the freezing dark, to mourn a woman whose body lies across the road from your home?"

"I did not come to mourn Masako." Chitose's voice broke on the name. "I wanted Inari Ōkami to let the mountain spirits kill me too."

"Until the sight of me changed your mind?"

"I-I was frightened." Chitose sniffled. "With respect, a samurai would not understand."

"You think a samurai does not know fear?" Suspecting the young man knew better than to risk an answer, Hiro changed the subject. "You loved Masako."

Chitose sniffed again, and did not deny it.

"Did Hanako know?"

"She would not have allowed Masako-*san* to have a suitor," Chitose said. "We met at night, in secret."

Not quite as secretly as you believe.

Chitose mistook Hiro's silence for disapproval. "Please do not tell Father or Hanako-*san*. It would make them angry."

"The girl is dead. Why would they care?"

"With respect," Chitose said, "because our actions angered the kami and cursed the village. We did not go far, but we entered the forest after dark, to keep from being seen."

"You believe the gods of the mountain killed her—not the yūrei?"

"There is no yūrei. There never was. Our village is cursed by the kami of the mountain, as retribution for our refusal to show compassion to Riko-*san*."

A twig snapped in the forest. Chitose jumped and looked around. He drew his hands to his chest as if to shield himself from harm.

Hiro reached for the hilt of his katana.

He watched the edges of the clearing, looking for signs of movement in the shadows.

Nothing moved, and the sound did not repeat.

Hiro relaxed a fraction, but kept his hand on his sword. "Why would the kami blame your village for the crimes of a samurai who did not live there?"

"Have you heard the story of her death?"

Hiro did not answer.

"We did not help her," Chitose said. "We heard her screams, but did nothing, and she died."

"And you find a curse from the gods a more likely explanation than a yūrei."

"At first, I believed in the yūrei," Chitose said. "Zentaro-*san* told us otherwise, but nobody believes him. I didn't either . . . at first, but Riko-*san* would never have killed Masako-*chan*, not even as a ghost. If it wasn't a yūrei, it must have been the mountain gods."

Overhead, the rustling cedars whispered as if passing judgment on the young man's tale.

"You don't believe me," Chitose said. "I can tell from your silence. But it's true. Masako-*chan* and Riko-*san* loved one another dearly. On the night Riko died, only Masako tried to tend her wounds. Hanako would not even enter the room where Riko lay. When Riko died, Masako cried for days. She took offerings to the grave at least once a week, even when it made Hanako angry. Riko's spirit had no need for vengeance against Masako. Which leaves only the angry kami of the mountain."

Or a human killer. Hiro remembered the terrified girl carrying the news of Ishiko's death. "If what you say is true, why did she fear the yūrei?"

"All women are afraid of ghosts." Chitose punched the fist of his left hand into the palm of his right. "I never should have forced her to meet me in the woods at night. I should have been more patient. I finally had enough money saved for us to run away. We planned to leave in spring..."

He punched his fist into his palm again. "I made her meet me in the forest, even though she was afraid. We never went far—we stayed within sight of the houses—I thought it would be all right. And now she's dead." His voice cracked. "And her death is all my fault."

CHAPTER 35

"Has it occurred to you that a person might have murdered Masako?" Hiro asked. "Maybe even the person who told her not to enter the woods at night?"

"Zentaro-*san* protects the village. He would never harm us." Despite the words, a seed of doubt had sprouted in Chitose's voice.

Hiro gestured to the torii. "If the kami cursed your village, and want you dead, why didn't they take your life when you asked them to?"

"You interrupted them before they could."

"You believe the kami fear a ronin?"

Chitose said nothing, but Hiro could feel the young man's indecision.

Hiro turned to leave. "Angry kami did not kill Masako."

As he began to walk away, Chitose called, "Please, wait!"

Hiro paused to allow the younger man to catch him.

"I—I don't know the way back to the village in the dark," Chitose said.

That makes two of us, Hiro thought.

"I didn't think I would need a lan—" Chitose paused. "You don't have a lantern either. We are lost!"

"I believe I can find the way." Hiro started through the trees, and Chitose followed.

Here and there, a moonbeam pierced the treetops, giving just enough light to navigate. The two men walked through the frozen forest, footsteps crunching through the film of ice that formed atop the snow. Hiro returned his hands to his sleeves. Not that it helped. His fingers burned from exposure to the cold, and refused to warm.

"Do you really think a person killed Masako-*chan*?" Chitose asked.

"I would not have said so otherwise."

"But no one goes outside at night."

"Because of Zentaro's warnings?" Hiro asked.

"Because they fear the yūrei. That's why Masako-*san* and I thought we could meet in safety. We were supposed to meet last night, as well, but when she didn't come, I thought . . ." Chitose stifled a sob. "I thought Hanako-*san* stayed up too late for her to get away."

Hiro considered the recent deaths. Both Ishiko and Masako died outside, at night, though only the older woman violated the yamabushi's orders not to leave the village. Masako died within earshot of the teahouse—a fact that Hiro found difficult to reconcile if Zentaro was the killer. Surely the girl would have screamed at the sight of anyone emerging from the woods.

Unless . . .

"Could Hanako have discovered your affair with Masako?"

"We had no *affair*." Chitose emphasized the final word. "We only met at night to talk. I held her hand, and we kissed, but nothing more. I had no right to dishonor her by expecting more before our wedding night."

"She was a teahouse girl."

"She was not a p-prostitute!" Although he stammered from the cold, Chitose sounded angry enough that Hiro believed his words. "Hanako-*san* would never have allowed Masako-*san* to sleep in a room alone if she suspected anything. And if she knew for certain, she would have demanded payment. We were careful—"

Behind them, something moved in the forest.

Chitose drew his hands to his chest as if to shield himself against attack.

Hiro froze. He peered into the darkness as his hand crept down to the hilt of his wakizashi. In the trees, and in the dark, he did not trust the longer sword.

A shadow, deeper than the surrounding darkness, shifted between the trees.

As if aware Hiro saw it, the shadow stopped, melted into the darkness, and disappeared completely.

Hiro listened, but it made no further sounds.

The creature—or whatever it was—was gone.

Chitose wrapped his trembling hands around his body. "What was it?"

"Too small for a man," Hiro lied. "Perhaps a fox."

"A kitsune." Chitose breathed the word as if in grateful prayer. "A messenger from Inari, come to protect us."

Hiro continued down the mountain. Chitose followed.

To Hiro's relief, the younger man did not attempt any further conversation.

Here and there, narrow moonbeams broke through the forest canopy and flowed to the ground in silver streams. The layer of snow beneath the trees glowed pale blue-white where the moonlight struck. Occasionally, a line of tiny tracks revealed the path of a rabbit or a fox.

Hiro kept his guard up all the way to the village, but the shadow did not return.

After leaving Chitose outside his home, Hiro continued past the front of the ryokan, bypassing the door and entering through the shoji that opened directly into the guest room.

Two futons, each topped with a quilt, lay at the center of the empty room.

To Hiro's disappointment, both his purse and Father Mateo's still sat, undisturbed, on the wooden table.

"Mateo?" he whispered. "Are you here?"

"Hiro?" The built-in cupboard rattled as the door slid open, revealing the Jesuit. Father Mateo knelt in the waist-high space, atop an extra futon and a quilt.

The priest unfolded himself from the cupboard. "The thief never came." He drew a breath and held it, as if trying to decide whether or not to continue. "But the yūrei did."

"You saw the ghost . . . again?"

"I know how it sounds." Father Mateo ran a hand through his hair. "But I saw her."

"From inside the futon cupboard?"

"I was not in the cupboard at the time. That is, I was, but I came out." The Jesuit gestured to the veranda door. "About half an hour ago, I heard that door slide open. I waited for the jingling that would tell me the thief had grabbed a purse, but the sound never came. At first I thought I had made a mistake about the outer door, but then I felt cold air seep in around the corners of the cupboard door. When I opened it to check, the room was empty but the veranda door was open. I looked outside and saw a woman with unbound hair gliding around the corner of the ryokan."

"Did you follow her?" Hiro asked.

"By the time I reached the front of the building, she had disappeared."

"Did you see her disappear?"

"I didn't see her anywhere. She was gone."

"You saw the thief," Hiro said, "because ghosts do not exist."

"A thief would have taken our money." Father Mateo pointed to the purses on the table.

"She might have lost her nerve."

"She *glowed*."

"A trick of the moonlight. Are you certain you saw a woman?"

"As certain as I am that I see you now."

"Then the woman you saw was Hanako, Mume, or Kane," Hiro said, "though Kane probably would have come through the inner door and not the outer one."

"You are not listening." Father Mateo crossed his arms. "I know what I saw. I do not want to believe it any more than you do, but that does not change the truth."

CHAPTER 36

Hiro stared at Father Mateo, torn between his disbelief and the knowledge that the Jesuit did not lie.

"Did you learn anything in the forest?" Father Mateo asked.

Hiro briefly described his encounter with Chitose.

"Now what do we do?" The Jesuit sighed. "The trap has failed and we've made no progress."

"The trap did not fail completely," Hiro said. "I believe the thief did come, and that you merely mistook her for a ghost."

"I did not—"

Hiro raised a hand. "I know you *think* you saw a spirit, but logically speaking you must admit that a thief is far more likely."

"Not when I saw a ghost."

"As I said, if you're certain you saw a woman, walking upright, it could only have been one of three: Hanako, Mume, or Kane—and we can eliminate one of them right now." Hiro walked to the inner door and slid it open. He raised his voice. "Noboru!"

When no one answered, Hiro called again. "Noboru! Come downstairs right now!"

Footsteps thumped on the upper floor, down the staircase, and along the hall from the back of the house. The innkeeper appeared, still tying the sash around his robe. "Has something happened?"

Kane appeared behind him. She wore a dark blue robe, and her hair hung braided down her back. The braid looked slightly messy, as if slept on.

"A thief attempted to enter our guest room," Hiro said.

The innkeeper and his wife exchanged a glance.

"Tonight?" Noboru asked.

"Just now." Hiro shifted his gaze to Kane. "Can you attest to your whereabouts for the last half hour?"

"I was asleep." She glanced at her husband. "He was too."

"In truth, I was not sleeping," Noboru admitted. "I have not slept well since my mother's death, and even less so since the theft. I was lying on my futon, trying to figure out how to pay for the exorcism when the priest arrives from Hakone. However, because I was awake I can tell you that no one entered the ryokan. I would have heard the front door creak."

"The thief came in through the outer door," Hiro replied.

"Surely you do not plan to accuse my wife or me of stealing your silver while you slept," Noboru said.

"This is a ruse." Kane gestured to Hiro. "He wants us to believe another thief exists, so Otomuro-*sama* will free the foreigner's servant. He is trying to escape responsibility for her crime."

"Are you accusing me of lying?" Hiro infused his voice with indignation.

Unexpectedly, the woman held his gaze.

Before Hiro could decide how to defuse the situation, Father Mateo intervened. "Fortunately, our silver was not stolen. Perhaps, since it is late, we should all go back to sleep and discuss this more tomorrow."

"Did you believe her?" Father Mateo asked when he and Hiro had returned to their room.

"That she was sleeping? Yes. But that doesn't mean I think you saw a ghost."

Father Mateo knelt on his futon. "I don't want to believe it any more than you do, but I know what I saw."

"And what you saw has a perfectly reasonable explanation." Hiro withdrew his swords from his obi and laid them on the floor beside his futon.

"If so, what is it?"

"I don't know yet." Hiro lay down and covered himself with the quilt. "But I intend to find out first thing tomorrow morning."

Hiro woke at dawn and left the inn with Father Mateo a few minutes later.

Thick mist hung over the village, obscuring their view of the silent street. The trees beyond the houses had completely vanished in the fog.

No birdsong pierced the silence. Not a single puff of wind disturbed the trees.

Hiro checked the veranda as they left the ryokan, but someone had swept it the day before, leaving no snow to hold a footprint.

He would have to find the "ghost" another way.

"What if we wake them?" Father Mateo whispered as they walked toward Mume and Taso's house. "Maybe we should wait and come back later."

"By then he will have left for work, and she will lie." Hiro knocked on the door.

Taso opened it almost at once. He looked past them. "Has the yūrei killed again?"

Father Mateo bowed. "We apologize for disturbing you so early."

Mume stood behind her husband, wearing a pale kimono. Her hair hung down her back, unbound. She bit her lip as she stared at the visitors.

"May we speak with you alone?" Hiro directed the question to Taso. "We do not wish to disturb your wife unnecessarily."

"Mume, please pack my midday meal while I speak with these men outside. I need to leave as soon as we finish talking." He reached over the bars of the stall, patted the ox, and stepped outside. As he closed the door behind himself, he asked, "*Has* someone died?"

Hiro dispensed with subtlety. "Did your wife leave the house last night?"

"Last night?" Taso thought for a moment. "No. At least, not alone. Masako's death has frightened her so badly that she would not even use the latrine without me." He frowned. "Did something happen in the night?"

Hiro ignored his question. "Did you sleep?"

"Last night?" Taso asked. "Of course. I have to work this morning."

"Then how do you know, for certain, that your wife did not leave the house alone?"

"Because she woke me twice to guard her while she went to the latrine. With respect, what do you think she did?"

"You say Masako's death upset her," Hiro said, "and yet, she did not seem overly frightened on the morning after Ishiko died."

"My wife did not care for Ishiko-san, and with good reason. That woman knew no mercy, and showed no kindness if she could help it."

"She was cruel?" Father Mateo asked.

"Strict and selfish," Taso said, "though to Mume she seemed cruel. You may not have noticed, but my wife has an unusually gentle spirit— the result of an accident she suffered as a child. Things upset her easily, and sometimes she has trouble understanding. For example, she could not comprehend why she and Kane were not allowed to spend the afternoons together, as they had always done at their parents' home."

The comment suggested something else to Hiro. "Did Kane complain about her mother-in-law to Mume?"

Taso smiled. "All girls complain about mothers-in-law at first." His smile faded. "But Kane-san did not complain for long. I think she realized her comments upset Mume. Either that or she learned to live with Ishiko-san's imperious nature. In any event, Mume stopped begging me to intervene on Kane-san's behalf a few months ago, though she never ceased asking me to persuade Ishiko-san to allow her to spend more time with her sister."

"And, despite the woman's 'imperious nature,' you believe a yūrei killed Ishiko," Hiro said.

"Because it is the truth," Taso replied. "Riko's spirit will not rest until everyone who injured her has joined her in the grave."

"What grudge did she hold against Masako?" Hiro asked.

"I would not know. Masako did not grow up in the village, and I did not know her personally." Taso laid a hand on the door. "With respect, if there is nothing more . . ."

"I trust you are not angry with Mume about the missing silver," Father Mateo said, "and that you realize the theft was not her fault."

"What missing silver?" Taso asked.

"Oh . . ." A flush crept up the Jesuit's neck, making his scar stand out.

"Please excuse me," Taso said. "It appears I need to have a conversation with my wife."

CHAPTER 37

"If the woman you saw last night was neither Kane nor Mume, it must have been Hanako," Hiro said as he returned to the ryokan with Father Mateo.

"Unless she confessed to you in the night, that sounds like an assumption to me," the Jesuit said.

"A deduction," Hiro answered, "and one I intend to verify as soon as the hour gets late enough to talk with her."

"I have different idea," Father Mateo said in Portuguese as they entered the inn and left their shoes beside the door. "I think we need to take Ana, and Gato, and leave for Edo as soon as it gets dark."

Hiro stared at the priest in shock. "Did you just say what I think you said?"

The Jesuit continued, still in Portuguese. "Something is wrong in this village. None of the evidence points to anything useful. We failed in our attempt to trap the thief. You know as well as I do that Ana did not take that silver, but unless we can prove it, the samurai will execute her. We cannot—I cannot let that happen."

"You understand that running away will make us fugitives," Hiro pointed out, in the Jesuit's language. "You and me, as well as Ana."

"If we remain she will die, for a crime she did not commit."

Hiro could not believe what he was hearing. "Back in Kyoto, when your life hung in the balance, you refused to run. You said your god would save you."

"I said that he could save me if he wished," the Jesuit corrected, "but that, whether he did or not, I would trust him anyway."

"Yet you do not trust him to save Ana."

"Do not underestimate how difficult this is for me. Running away from responsibility goes against everything I believe, and yet . . ." He looked at Hiro through tortured eyes.

Father Mateo opened the guest room door and stopped unexpectedly.

Hiro barely avoided a collision. He craned his neck to look around the priest.

The futons and quilts had disappeared, most likely returned to the cupboard for the day. The table sat in its daytime location near the center of the room, and Ana knelt beside it, stroking Gato.

She looked up. "Hm. First they tell me to cook the meals. Then they lock me in my room. And then they change their minds again twice over. I think they both have lost their minds."

Hiro followed the priest into the room and closed the door.

"Did something happen to the morning meal?" Father Mateo asked.

Ana snorted. "I wouldn't know. I didn't get to cook it. That woman ordered me out of the kitchen, and told me to get the cat and wait in here. Didn't even give me time to wash my hands."

"Why here?" Hiro asked.

"Because she is the mistress of this ryokan." Ana's tone suggested mimicry. "And she wants to make the morning meal herself."

"But why here, and not your room?" Hiro persisted, instincts jangling.

Ana folded her arms across her narrow chest. "You tell me. Then both of us will know."

An idea blossomed in Hiro's head. "Stay here." He bent over his bundle of belongings long enough to retrieve the pair of sandals tucked within its depths, crossed the room, and opened the veranda door, letting in a swirl of frigid air and mist.

"What—" Father Mateo began.

"No time. Stay here." Hiro set the sandals on the porch, stepped out into them, and closed the door.

Hoping Father Mateo and Ana would follow his instructions, Hiro hurried along the narrow veranda away from the front of the inn.

At the back of the building, he stepped to the ground and moved along the wall of the ryokan, taking care to minimize the sound his sandals made on the icy crust of snow that covered the ground.

At the corner of the building closest to the kitchen door, he stopped and slowly peeked around at the kitchen entrance.

As he expected, the door was closed.

Normally, a cook would leave the sliding door open while preparing a meal, allowing air and light to enter the room. The door might be closed because of the cold and mist, or because Kane didn't know well enough to leave it open while she cooked—but Hiro doubted it.

The innkeeper's wife hated cooking. She would never voluntarily choose to make a meal herself. She would never send Ana out of the kitchen, let alone to wait in Hiro and Father Mateo's room, unless Kane wanted to do, or say, something the Jesuit's servant should not see or overhear.

Hiro crept to the kitchen door. As he reached it, he heard the urgent murmur of female voices, but could not make out the words. Looking down, he noticed a narrow gap between the base of the door and the wooden plank that served as a threshold.

Hiro knelt and lowered his ear to the gap, grateful for the mist that made him invisible from the travel road, but well aware that if someone emerged from the mist, he would have no time to rise or hide his actions.

It was worth the risk.

As his ear drew close to the crack beneath the door, the voices inside grew clear.

"—think it's us!" Mume sounded panicked.

"Don't be foolish." Kane sounded angry. "Just do what I say and it will be all right."

"But you said—"

"You took it too far!"

Mume tried again. "But you said—"

"It's not my fault you didn't stick to the plan," Kane snapped.

Mume wailed.

"*Be silent*," Kane hissed. "Someone will hear you."

Mume's cry became a whimper.

"Come to the burial ground tonight," Kane said, "at midnight, after your husband goes to sleep. We can talk about it then. It isn't safe to do this here."

Mume gave a terrified squeak. "B-but . . ."

"You do not need to worry about the ghost. Not anymore."

Mume whimpered again, more softly.

"Yes, I'm sure. Will you meet me? Yes or no?"

"Y-yes." Mume sniffled.

"Go home and wait. And whatever you do, do *not* let Taso know you're going to the burial ground. Do you remember what to bring? And what to wear?"

"Y-yes." Mume sniffled. "A lantern, and—"

"I don't have time to go over it. I need to serve this meal before the guests complain. Remember: not a word to anyone."

Footsteps approached the kitchen door.

Hiro jumped back and raced around the corner of the ryokan. He barely made it out of sight before the kitchen door rattled open.

"Do not forget," Kane repeated, "do not tell anyone."

As soon as Hiro heard the door begin to rattle shut again, he raced along the back of the inn and across the veranda to the guest room.

"Where did you go?" the Jesuit asked when Hiro stepped back through the door, holding his sandals in his hand.

Someone knocked on the interior door.

"Please forgive the interruption," Kane called. "May I serve your morning meal?"

Father Mateo gave Hiro a curious look as he answered, "Please come in."

The door slid open and Kane entered the room. She carried a tray upon which sat two bowls of rice, two bowls of soup, a teapot, and a pair of empty cups. Chopsticks and wooden spoons rested beside the bowls.

"Good morning," she said.

Father Mateo gestured to Ana. "Thank you for preparing the meal, although my housekeeper gladly would have helped you."

Kane raised her chin. "I prefer to make the food myself. I did not like her cooking."

Ana exhaled sharply.

Father Mateo smiled. *"De gustibus non disputandum est."*

Hiro raised an eyebrow. Although he did not speak Latin, he suspected whatever the Jesuit said was not entirely polite.

Kane ignored the foreign words and set the tray on the table. "I also searched your servant's room again and found no silver there."

"Most likely because I did not steal any," Ana retorted.

Kane continued as if the housekeeper had not spoken. "I think you must have told the truth. Your servant did not steal our silver."

"Just last night you accused us of trying to cover up Ana's theft, but a search of her room this morning changed your mind?" Even had Hiro not overheard the conversation in the kitchen, he would have found the woman's change of mind far too suspicious to believe.

"I apologize for the way my husband and I have treated you." Kane bowed. "It was your words last night that made me understand. Someone else must have stolen our silver, and Mume's. I am simply grateful that the thief did not steal yours also."

After a pause she added, "You may leave the village after breakfast, if you want to."

"Regrettably, we cannot," Hiro said. "Otomuro-*san* arrested the foreigner's servant."

"Noboru will speak to him." Kane bowed again, more deeply. "I apologize for the inconvenience this has caused you."

Hiro considered confronting her about the conversation in the kitchen, but knew the woman would not tell the truth. Mume would also lie, if pressed.

If he wanted to learn the truth, he would have to attend the midnight meeting in the burial yard.

CHAPTER 38

"I will ask my husband to speak with Otomuro-*sama* this morning." Kane shifted her gaze to Ana. "There is food in the kitchen, if you wish to eat."

She bowed once more and left the room, closing the door behind her. Ana looked at the breakfast tray with disapproval. "No egg. No tsukemono—not even a single pickled plum to accompany the soup and rice. Whoever trained that girl . . ." She opened the door and left the room, still grumbling to herself.

As the door closed after Ana, Hiro knelt beside the table.

"That bad?" Father Mateo knelt on the opposite side of the table.

Hiro looked up. "Pardon me?"

"The food. Your expression . . . does it truly smell that foul?"

Hiro glanced at the door. "She prepared it. I need know nothing more to know it's foul."

Father Mateo bent his head and closed his eyes in silent prayer.

Hiro's stomach growled, but he waited for the priest to finish praying before he reached for a bowl of soup.

The miso had separated into a cloudy bottom layer covered by an inch and a half of watery broth. A bite-sized cube of tofu rested sullenly at the bottom of the bowl, its lower half concealed by miso murk. Limp slivers that had once been onions drifted atop the broth like detritus floating on a stagnant pond.

Hiro lifted the bowl and inhaled deeply. Although the miso in the kitchen had smelled terrible, extreme dilution had disguised the worst of its rotting scent. The soup smelled mostly of dirty water, reminiscent of laundry left to soak overnight in a filthy barrel. Swallowing his disgust, Hiro gently swirled the bowl to remix its contents, raised it to his mouth, and sipped.

The tepid liquid rolled over his tongue and down his throat with a lingering flavor of old bonito flakes and mold.

He held his breath and drained the bowl in two more gulps.

When he set the bowl on the table, he noticed Father Mateo staring at him. Slowly, the Jesuit lowered his gaze to the bowl of soup that rested in his hands. "I see. It is that bad."

"It isn't good." Hiro took a bite of rice. Although no warmer than the soup, at least it tasted fresh.

Father Mateo sipped his soup. "I suspect Kane reheated last night's miso."

"It seemed older than that to me." Hiro finished his rice. He still felt hungry, but the meager meal would keep his stomach silent for an hour or two.

"So," Father Mateo said, "what did you do to make Kane change her mind?"

"Me?"

"You leave the room for five minutes, with no explanation, and suddenly she no longer believes that Ana is to blame for the missing silver?"

"Unless I miss my guess, Kane never believed that Ana was to blame." Hiro described the sisters' conversation. "I don't know exactly what they're hiding, or what they've done, but it seems fairly clear that they must be involved in the thefts, if not the murders."

"It does seem that way," the Jesuit agreed. "But . . . how did you know to find them in the kitchen?"

"I didn't," Hiro said, "but if Kane wanted the kitchen to herself so badly she was willing to cook a meal, I wanted to know the reason why."

Father Mateo set his empty soup bowl on the table. "Do you truly think they're killers as well as thieves?"

"Kane claimed they didn't need to worry about the ghost," Hiro said, "which means either that she is the killer, that she never believed in the yūrei, or that she has learned something about the situation she didn't know before."

"Maybe if we talked with her, alone or with Noboru—"

Hiro shook his head. "She will claim I made the whole thing up, and her husband will believe her. After all, I didn't actually hear them confess to anything specific."

"Then what do we do?"

"Since Ana is no longer in imminent danger, we stay here long enough to attend that midnight meeting at the burial yard and catch a thief, a killer, or possibly both. But before that, we visit Hanako and try to confirm the identity of your ghostly visitor. While we're there, I also want to ask a couple of questions about Emiko." Hiro looked at his bowl. "I suspect, as I think you do as well, that she is the missing kunoichi."

"I don't know . . ." Father Mateo hesitated. "This all seems too simple. Something feels wrong."

"Everything about this village feels wrong. But the investigation is finally going right."

When they finished with their meal, Hiro went to the door of the guest room and called for Noboru.

Footsteps hurried down the stairs from the second floor and along the hallway. A moment later, Noboru came into view. He bowed. "Good morning, Matsui-*san*."

"Good morning," Hiro said.

"Will you honor us with your presence for another night?" Noboru asked.

"Have you not spoken with your wife?" Hiro asked.

Noboru's smile grew strained. "With apologies, Kane should not have discussed the matter with you before she spoke with me. Surely, you understand . . ."

Hiro saw the opportunity he needed. "I understand that you cannot hold two men of samurai rank against their will, with no evidence but the words of a woman who now acknowledges those words were false."

Noboru turned pale.

"However," Hiro softened his tone, "under the circumstances, I will consider persuading the foreigner to remain here one more night, on one condition."

Noboru waited expectantly.

"The meals your wife prepares are inedible, and the foreigner's housekeeper claims the food in your storehouse is mostly rotten."

Noboru drew back. "My mother always managed the food. I did not know—"

Hiro ignored him. "If you wish us to remain another night, you will arrange for us to eat our meals at the teahouse across the road."

"While I deeply apologize for the insufficient fare"—Noboru bowed—"Hanako-*san* believes your presence angers the yūrei. If I may suggest—"

"You may not. Either we eat at the teahouse or I take the priest and go." Hiro turned on his heel and retreated into the guest room.

A few seconds later, he heard the front door shut as Noboru left the ryokan.

Father Mateo raised his head from his Bible. "Did it work?"

"I think so. And I don't believe Noboru knows what his wife is doing. He seemed as confused by her withdrawal of the claim against Ana as I would have been if I hadn't heard her talking in the kitchen."

Gato lay on her side near the priest. She stretched full length and waggled her paws at Father Mateo, inviting him to play. When he ignored her, she thumped her tail on the tatami.

Taking the cue, Hiro approached the cat and extended his hand. When she saw him, he hooked his fingers in imitation of a claw.

Gato rolled onto her back and raised her paws, toes spread and claws extended.

Hiro jabbed his hand like a striking snake. The cat attacked. Dodging her claws, Hiro touched Gato's forehead gently with a finger and withdrew his hand so quickly that her black and orange paws grasped only air.

Gato's pupils dilated until the color almost disappeared. Her tail thumped the tatami harder. She tensed, paws open, waiting.

Once more, Hiro touched her head.

Again she lunged and missed.

Gato laid her ears against her head and opened her mouth, revealing tiny fangs. She raised a paw expectantly.

Hiro reached for her head again, but this time she moved faster.

Gato wrapped her paws around his wrist and pulled it toward her mouth. Her claws dug into Hiro's wrist. He winced.

Her teeth clamped down on the heel of his hand, and her hind legs punched the sleeve of his kimono.

Gato's purring filled the room.

"All right, you win." Hiro tried to extricate himself, but Gato gnawed on his wrist for several seconds before surrendering her grip.

She jumped to her feet, ears back and tail lashing. When Hiro ignored her, she arched her back and meowed, as if inviting another round.

"Doesn't that hurt?" Father Mateo indicated Hiro's wrist, which bore the indentations of Gato's teeth.

He shrugged. "Not really. She likes to play."

"That doesn't look like play to me." Father Mateo pulled the cloth from his sleeve and wiped his nose.

"It's all she has, now that we're traveling and the cold keeps her mostly inside." Hiro looked from the Jesuit to the cat. "One way or another, a predator needs to hunt."

CHAPTER 39

As the Jesuit returned to his prayers, Hiro knelt, closed his eyes, and reviewed the evidence for and against Kane and Mume's guilt. Like Father Mateo, he could not shake the feeling that the facts did not add up. Kane's fear of the yūrei had seemed real. Mume seemed incapable of plotting a theft, let alone a murder. And although both women had motives to kill Ishiko, neither one had any grudge against Masako.

Not that he knew about, anyway.

He let his thoughts drift to the list of names he had memorized before leaving Iga, and to the assassins they represented. For reasons Hiro failed to understand, Hattori Hanzō seemed to believe the city of Edo would grow in influence in the years to come. Several of the agents on Hiro's list were stationed within the precincts of the northern city.

It bothered him that he did not know, definitively, if the missing Emiri was also the woman lost in last year's landslide. He suspected it, but could not allow himself to make assumptions.

"Because the last one always kills you."

Hiro's eyes popped open at the sound of Neko's voice. Father Mateo remained bent over his Bible. Gato dozed on the floor nearby. Neither one had heard the voice. And neither had he, except inside his head.

The only place he would ever hear her now, because Neko was dead. And Hiro, to his momentary sorrow, did not believe in ghosts.

Several hours later Noboru knocked on the guest room door. When Hiro answered, the innkeeper bowed.

"I have made arrangements for us to eat a meal at the teahouse across the road. Would you care to join me?"

"Now?" Hiro asked. "It won't be dark for almost three hours."

"Hanako-*san* has agreed to prepare a meal but, with apologies, she insists on serving it during daylight hours. She is afraid that, after dark, you will draw the yūrei."

"We are happy to accommodate her wishes," Father Mateo rose to his feet. "I am certainly hungry enough to eat."

Hiro agreed. "We accept your invitation."

The pale winter sun shone feebly in the afternoon sky, strong enough to burn away the worst of the mist but not enough to clear the hazy sky. The temperature remained near freezing.

Hanako opened the teahouse door as the men approached. She bowed and forced a smile. "Please come inside."

She escorted Hiro and the others to the overdecorated room where they ate on their first night in the village. As before, the painted stalks made the room feel suffocating.

Hiro knelt beside Father Mateo, across the table from Noboru. Hanako disappeared and returned with a tray that held a steaming teapot and three cups.

"I have prepared a humble meal." She set the tray on the table. "Please understand that I cannot offer as many courses, or as elaborate an offering, as . . . before."

"We appreciate your courtesy," Father Mateo answered, "and apologize for intruding upon your mourning."

"Samurai do not apologize to teahouse women," Hiro murmured in Portuguese, with a smile on his face to disguise his real meaning.

"Fortunately, I am not samurai," Father Mateo murmured back, with a smile of his own.

Hanako looked from one man to the other. When neither offered an explanation, she poured the tea, withdrew, and closed the door.

"Have you made any progress in your investigation?" Noboru asked.

"With regard to the killings or the silver?" Hiro raised his cup and inhaled the steam.

"You are the only ones who think the recent deaths a mystery." Noboru held his teacup but did not drink. "Now that my wife no longer blames your servant, I find myself in a difficult position. Without my silver, I will lose my ryokan. Otomuro-*san* will confiscate it if I cannot pay the priest to exorcise the ghost. He told me so, the day I learned about the theft."

"Is that what you were doing at his house?" Father Mateo asked.

"I hoped he would show mercy, but he refused." Noboru set his teacup on the table, still untouched. "I have heard you carry a significant sum, far more than enough to repay what I have lost. Perhaps, if I persuaded Otomuro-*san* to drop the claims against your servant . . ."

An awkward silence fell.

"Are you asking for a bribe?" Father Mateo asked.

"How much did you lose?" Hiro asked simultaneously.

"My money box held the equivalent of one hundred gold koban."

The same amount Otomuro named at first. It could not be coincidence, though the manner in which the two men planned to split the sum remained a mystery.

Hiro doubted Noboru's ryokan made ten percent of that amount in an entire year.

After a quick, short knock the door slid open.

Hanako entered, carrying a tray of sashimi arranged on three small plates. She knelt beside the table and served Noboru first, a social slight that did not escape Hiro's notice. However, at the moment, he cared more about the contents of his plate than how it got there.

The four thin slices of uncooked fish fanned out across a bamboo leaf. Their uniform size and delicacy revealed a skill that Hiro found surprising. Most women did not handle a knife that well, unless they had been trained as kunoichi.

"I am sorry about Masako's death," Father Mateo said.

"The fault is mine." Hanako filled the Jesuit's empty teacup. "I should have guessed that . . . she . . . would come for vengeance against Masako-*san*. And your disbelief did not help."

"If we made her angry, why did she kill Masako and not one of us?" Hiro asked. "And why did she not come for you?"

"When . . . she . . . lay dying, Masako-*san* refused to help me care for her. The girl refused to enter the room where she lay, because of a foolish superstition."

Father Mateo glanced at Hiro, who hoped Hanako would not notice the Jesuit's reaction to her lie.

Fortunately, the woman had not stopped talking.

"Not even Yuko-*san* could change her mind. Clearly, she remembers Masako-*san*'s refusal as an insult." Hanako dipped her head politely. "Please excuse me. I must prepare the second course."

After the woman left, Father Mateo bowed his head and said a silent blessing for the food. When the Jesuit finished, Hiro sampled the sashimi. To his immense relief, it tasted fresh and clean.

Hanako had not stayed long enough for Hiro to ask his questions about Emiko, so he decided to find out what Noboru knew. "Four entertainers seems a large number for such a remote location."

"Four?" The innkeeper echoed.

Hiro swallowed another piece sashimi. "By my count, Yuko had four apprentices: Riko, Hanako, Masako, and Emiko."

"We had more visitors before the landslide," Noboru said. "Now most of the traffic takes the detour route, but this road—the original road—will recover in the spring. It's steeper than the detour, and a little longer, but even so, this is the travel road. The detour was only temporary. Our guests will return. We merely need to wait."

Hiro thought of the straining laborers and oxen carrying goods and samurai palanquins along the travel road. Somehow, he doubted people would return to a steeper course if an easier route existed. However, he had more important things to discuss than the relative merits of the travel roads. "So the teahouse made a healthy profit."

"Yuko-*san* had earned a reputation in Kyoto, before she returned," Noboru said. "She was quite famous. Many travelers came to the village because of her."

"She was not young when she returned, then." Hiro ate his last slice of sashimi.

Noboru shrugged. "Teahouse women don't reveal their ages."

Once again, there was a knock and the door slid open.

CHAPTER 40

Hanako returned with plates of winter vegetables steamed in a savory soy-based sauce.

Hiro's mouth watered at the delicate, yet earthy, scent.

"This looks delicious," Father Mateo said as Hanako replaced his empty sashimi plate with a dish of vegetables.

"The best I could manage on such short notice."

"Will you run the teahouse alone now?" the Jesuit asked. "Or will you find an apprentice to assist you?"

"Apprentices cost money to acquire and train." Hanako looked pointedly at Noboru.

"This is not the time to speak of such things." Noboru's voice held an unexpected edge.

"Indeed." Hanako pressed her lips together, finished changing out the plates, and departed, leaving an uncomfortable silence in her wake.

Noboru ate his vegetables. The others did the same.

Hiro wondered what prompted the inappropriately charged exchange between Hanako and the innkeeper.

"Does Hanako-*san* want you to invest in the teahouse?" Father Mateo asked.

Hiro slowly turned his head, equally dismayed by the intrusive question and disappointed that the priest had overlooked a more obvious explanation: Noboru owed the teahouse money.

The innkeeper's cheeks turned red, then purple. He chewed as slowly as a turtle gnawing on a lotus root. At last, when he could delay no more, he swallowed. "After the landslide closed the travel road, Hanako-*san* approached my mother and suggested they combine the ryokan with the teahouse. She believed, if they worked together, they could encourage more visitors to return when the travel road reopened.

She also thought the shared expenses would make both businesses more profitable. Mother told Hanako-*san* that I would need to approve the decision. At the time, I agreed to consider it, but now. . ."

He shook his head and selected another vegetable from his plate.

Hiro wanted to shift the conversation back to Emiko, but failed to find an adequate bridge that would not seem suspicious.

Before he could reopen the conversation Hanako returned, this time with succulent fish filets braised in a dark, rich broth. As she served his portion, Hiro inhaled the delicious scents of mushrooms and wild onions mingling with the faint aroma of the fish.

Hiro began to ask her about Emiko, but she set his bowl on the table with a cold formality that chilled the question on his tongue. She concealed her anger well enough to avoid an obvious insult, but her reaction to Noboru's words seemed curiously out of proportion.

As he looked at his bowl, Hiro wondered if Hanako was the kind of woman who would poison every bowl at the table, or only the one she set before her victim.

He opened his mouth to make a joking comment to Father Mateo in Portuguese, but decided against it. Given their past experiences, the priest might not appreciate the humor.

Noboru began eating the moment Hanako left the room, but Hiro gave the Jesuit a warning glance and shook his head a fraction. While the shinobi doubted the teahouse woman would actually poison them, a bit of caution did no harm.

Once again, Father Mateo bent his head in silent prayer, giving Hiro time to examine the dish more closely. He smelled the broth repeatedly and carefully, running through his mental catalogue of poisons. It seemed safe. He raised his spoon and took a tiny sip.

The rich broth coated his tongue with the earthiness of mushrooms and the salty tang of fish, with the faintest hints of oil, dark vinegar, and pungent onions. Each of the flavors balanced the others perfectly. Three tiny sips confirmed no trace of any recognizable poison.

Hiro surrendered to his stomach and began to eat.

"Please forgive my ignorance of Japanese customs," Father Mateo said. "Do mothers customarily consult their sons about business matters?"

Hiro admired the facility with which the priest reopened the conversation.

"It is when they will inherit soon," Noboru replied as he took a bite of fish.

Father Mateo lowered his spoon. "But Ishiko-*san* could not have . . . I apologize, was your mother ill?"

"Not that I knew of." Noboru set his chopsticks on their rest. "But she hated the ryokan, and the constant work of caring for the strangers who slept beneath our roof. She planned to give the ryokan to me on the one-year anniversary of my father's death, at the end of her official mourning period. She intended to become a nun and spend the rest of her life in prayer and meditation." He smiled wistfully. "She wanted to distance herself from the worldly problems that consumed so many of her years."

Hanako knocked on the door once more.

Hiro raised his bowl and drained the last few savory mouthfuls as the woman entered, bearing the bowls of steamed white rice that traditionally ended a Japanese meal.

"Thank you again, Hanako-*san*, for preparing such a delicious feast," Father Mateo said.

She smiled politely and left the room.

Hiro reopened the conversation with a tactical shift in direction. "Your mother must have trusted you and Kane a great deal to entrust you with the ryokan."

Noboru looked up from his bowl of rice. "She trusted me." He set the bowl and chopsticks down. "Mother never had much regard for Kane. In fact, but for my father's intervention, she would have forbidden the match entirely."

Hiro gave the innkeeper a questioning look.

"Mother wanted me to marry an innkeeper's daughter—someone who had grown up learning to run a ryokan. She did not want to train a 'useless fool' like Kane, who came from a merchant's family where she did not have to work before she married."

"But you fell in love with Kane." Father Mateo smiled in understanding.

"From the moment I saw her at her parents' shop in Hakone during last year's New Year festival." Noboru blushed and looked down. Japanese men did not admit such foolishness. "We married a few weeks later, shortly before my father's death."

"During the mourning period for your sister?" Hiro found that odd.

"Mother insisted I take a wife to help her with the ryokan. She claimed she needed help before the summer—part of the reason she agreed to Kane in the first place."

"How did Mume come to marry Taso?" Hiro asked.

Noboru looked up. "Perhaps you did not notice, but Kane's sister is not . . . bright.

"Kane's parents agreed to let us wed as long as we could find a husband for Mume in the village. That way Kane could continue to help her sister. Taso had no wife, and was agreeable."

Noboru shrugged, as if this answered everything.

"Does Mume require much help?" Hiro took another bite of rice.

"She seems capable enough to me," Noboru said. "Prone to suggestion and overly emotional, but then, many women are. I think she clings to Kane mostly out of habit."

"They spend a great deal of time together?" Hiro spoke as if the answer did not matter.

"Not as much as Mume wanted. Mother disapproved of idle chatter, almost as much as she loathed laziness and sloppy work."

"Did Kane struggle with your mother's rules?" Father Mateo asked. "Or with adjusting to such a demanding environment . . ."

"My wife has had no problems." Noboru spoke with unusual vehemence. "Her—"

"Pardon my intrusion," Hanako called through the door as she slid it open. "May I bring more tea?"

"No, thank you." Father Mateo bowed his head. "And thank you for taking such trouble, especially under the circumstances."

Hiro again looked for a way to ask about Emiko without sounding suspicious. Unfortunately, he failed. Samurai simply did not ask about unknown, unimportant teahouse girls.

"Noboru-*san*," Hanako asked, "may I have a word with you after the meal?"

He refused to meet her gaze. "Regrettably, I have business at the ryokan."

"With respect," she persisted, "the matter is important and should not wait."

Hiro stood up. "Thank you for your courtesy." He met the Jesuit's gaze and tipped his head toward the door. "We will see ourselves out, so you may speak alone."

Father Mateo looked puzzled, but did not argue. He stood up and bowed. "Again, we thank you for the delicious meal."

Despite his offer, Hiro was intrigued that Hanako did not escort them to the door. The breach of etiquette made him even more curious about her impending conversation with Noboru.

On the teahouse veranda Hiro lowered his voice and switched to Portuguese, "Return to the inn. I want to find out what's going on."

Before the priest could argue, Hiro stepped off the veranda and hurried around the side of the teahouse as if going to visit the latrine.

CHAPTER 41

Hiro slowed his steps as he approached the slatted window outside the room where Noboru remained to talk with Hanako. He crouched beneath it, grateful that the window sat where he could not be easily seen from the village. A person watching from the ryokan could still see him, but he doubted Kane spent much time gazing out in that direction.

He hoped not, anyway.

Voices drifted out between the window slats, muffled slightly by the oiled paper covering but still audible.

"—claim it's because you're in mourning." Hanako seemed to be crying.

"I am in mourning," Noboru said, "and with the silver gone, I can't afford it."

"You never said that when your parents were alive."

"Things have changed." Irritation crept into Noboru's voice. "Kane needs—"

"Since when do you care about her needs? What about my needs?"

"Things cannot be as they were before. You want your money? Here it is."

Coins clattered on the wooden table.

"Noboru!"—the location of Hanako's voice shifted, as if in movement—"Noboru, wait! Please . . ."

She said something unintelligible.

Noboru's answer was muffled, as if he had left the room and spoke back through the doorway. Hiro caught only, " . . . a week."

"You know that is not what I mean," Hanako replied. "We could still come to an arrangement. Since you insist, we can even include

Kane-*san*. Why don't you bring her here tomorrow, for a meal, and we can talk?"

"...the foreigner and his scribe..."

"Yes. Their presence would make conversation difficult. Bring Kane for dinner after they leave the village."

This time, Noboru's response was clear. "Only for dinner. No promises."

Hiro noticed movement in the trees behind the teahouse.

One of the shadows shifted and took on a human shape.

He blinked, and it vanished.

Hiro peered into the forest, trying to decide if he had truly seen a person in the trees. And if so, who? Since the conversation between Hanako and Noboru seemed to have ended, he started toward the forest.

As he reached the trees, he caught a glimpse of a dark robe disappearing into a stand of bamboo grass. The stalks shifted into place behind the departing figure, leaving no evidence of human passage.

Hiro stopped and listened. He heard only the gentle rustling of the sasa and the distant cry of a crow announcing its territorial claims.

He debated calling out to the running figure, but decided to follow silently instead. Despite the darkness of the cloak, Hiro suspected the figure was Zentaro, and wondered why the yamabushi had exchanged his pale clothes for a dark robe that allowed him to blend into the shadows. None of the explanations that came to mind boded well for the yamabushi's innocence, and although Hiro had no plans to delay his stay in the village to catch the killer, he would not pass up the chance to unravel the mystery if he could.

He parted the bamboo grass and followed the figure into the thicket. The sasa grew higher than his head and covered a house-sized space beneath the trees. By the time he emerged on the far side of the thicket, his quarry had disappeared.

Once more, Hiro stopped to listen. As the sasa stilled, he heard faint footsteps heading up the mountain, roughly in the direction of the burial ground. He followed the sound, minimizing the crunch of his own footsteps on the icy ground to the extent he could.

Before long, the figure came into view among the trees. Its size and breadth, and the foxlike way it leaped upward on the slope, looked like Zentaro, though the hooded cloak prevented confirmation.

Hiro continued following at a distance.

At the burial ground, the hooded figure wove between the monuments with purpose. About halfway across the yard, the figure stopped and bent to pick something up from the ground beside a grave.

Hiro drew closer, ducked behind a tree, and watched.

As the figure straightened, his hood fell back, revealing Zentaro's face. The yamabushi held the halves of a broken rice bowl.

"Dangerous," he muttered. After a furtive look around that caused Hiro to draw back into the shelter of the tree, Zentaro continued across the burial ground.

Hiro skirted around the graves, hesitating near the larger monuments where he could conceal himself if the need arose. However, Zentaro seemed unaware of the shinobi's presence.

The yamabushi left the burial yard and bounded up the mountain as if suddenly on an urgent errand. Hiro had to work hard to keep Zentaro in sight without making too much noise.

As he climbed the slope, Hiro suddenly had the sensation that he, too, was being followed. The hair on his arms and neck stood up on end.

He crouched and looked around.

The trees—a mixture of cedars and maples—grew fairly close together here. The cedars' trunks remained devoid of branches to a height of at least ten meters, while the maples spread their arms considerably closer to the ground. Clusters of sasa grew between and beneath the trees, obscuring Hiro's view of the middle distance.

Overhead, a pair of crows exchanged avian insults through the trees. Aside from the noisy corvids, Hiro saw and heard no evidence of anything with eyes.

Zentaro's footsteps faded, but the feeling of being watched grew more intense.

As much as he loathed ignoring potential threats, Hiro had to choose between shaking his own pursuer—if he had one—and losing Zentaro's trail.

He took one last look around and, still seeing no one, followed the yamabushi up the mountain.

Zentaro's path diverged to the left of the sacred clearing. About a hundred meters farther up the slope, the ascetic paused at the foot of a steep, rocky face that appeared to continue all the way to the towering summit far above. Exposed tree roots wove around and through the stones near the bottom of the face, creating a natural ladder, though the trees near the base of the cliff prevented Hiro from seeing how high the "ladder" reached.

Zentaro looked around expectantly.

Hiro stepped behind the thick, rough trunk of a towering cedar. The ancient tree was large enough that he didn't need to turn sideways to conceal himself from view.

One of the crows had ceased its calling, a fact that caused no small offense if the calls of the other were any indication. Somewhere nearby, a stream or waterfall chattered over rocks.

"Hello?" Zentaro called. "Who's there?"

Hiro did not move.

"I hear you among the trees," Zentaro said.

Hiro slowed his breathing. He pressed himself against the cedar's trunk.

"Come on out. I know you're there."

Footsteps rustled the undergrowth to Hiro's left.

A fox the color of autumn leaves emerged from a cluster of bamboo grass a stone's throw from the place where Hiro stood. It had a bushy auburn coat with black-tipped ears and charcoal-colored legs. The creature headed toward Zentaro, but froze, ears pricked attentively forward, when it noticed Hiro behind the tree.

The fox lifted its muzzle to scent the air as Hiro willed the creature to ignore him.

Instead, it took a step in his direction.

Hiro held his breath.

"Is something wrong, kitsune-*san*?" Zentaro called. "What do you see?"

The fox regarded Hiro warily, took another step toward his hiding place, and barked.

CHAPTER 42

"What did you find, kitsune-*san*?" Footsteps crunched as Zentaro started toward the tree.

Hiro tried to invent a reasonable explanation for his presence behind the cedar, but quickly realized that none existed. As he prepared to confront the mountain priest, the fox gave one last yip, turned away from Hiro, and trotted up the slope toward the yamabushi.

"There you are." Zentaro's tone revealed his happy smile. "Are you hungry, kitsune-*san*? I have *inarizushi* waiting at the cave. Let's go."

Footsteps crunched in the opposite direction, fading in volume as Zentaro moved away.

Hiro exhaled slowly. He remained behind the tree for several seconds before risking a glance around the trunk.

Zentaro walked away along the base of the root-strewn cliff. The fox trotted contentedly at his side, ears cocked as if listening to the human's voice.

A twig snapped in the opposite direction.

Hiro spun around.

The forest behind him was completely empty.

Nevertheless, the sensation of being watched returned.

Hiro had never known his instincts to be wrong on this particular point. Even so, he felt a burning need to see where Zentaro and the kitsune went. He did not believe the fox could speak, any more than he believed the yamabushi could converse with trees. Still, he wanted to see what happened when they reached Zentaro's home.

He set off after them, taking care to remain at the greatest possible distance, to reduce the chance of the fox noticing his scent or the sound of his footsteps.

Less than a minute later, Zentaro paused near a crack in the cliff face.

Hiro retreated to the relative shelter of a nearby cluster of neck-high bamboo grass. He bent to conceal himself behind the stalks and peered around them.

"Please wait here." Zentaro said.

The fox sat down and rested on its haunches.

Zentaro bent almost double, stepped into the fissure in the cliff, and disappeared. A minute later, he reappeared with a wooden tray in his hands. A number of oblong, finger-sized rolls of inarizushi sat upon the tray.

Despite his recent meal, Hiro's mouth watered at the thought of delicately sweet, sticky rice wrapped firmly but gently in pockets of paper-thin fried tofu.

The fox stood up and barked at Zentaro.

"I know. Your favorite." The ascetic smiled. "Your sister told me."

The fox licked its chops, gaze fixed on the tray.

Zentaro set the tray on the ground.

The fox devoured the food in moments and looked up expectantly. When no more sushi rolls appeared, it gave a quick, sharp bark and trotted off into the trees. Hiro held his breath, but the kitsune did not even look in his direction.

Zentaro watched the fox until it disappeared. His hopeful expression changed to disappointment as he turned, bent down, and went inside the cave.

Hiro remained perfectly still. The fox had not seemed unusual, let alone divine. However, Zentaro clearly thought otherwise. Numerous legends spoke of men bewitched by foxes, some of whom had even killed on a kitsune's orders.

Zentaro had mentioned instructions from Inari's messengers.

Hiro wondered just how far those instructions went, and whether the voices that delivered them came from Zentaro's head, or from someone else.

Before he decided what to do, Zentaro reemerged from the fissure carrying a wooden staff and set off down the mountain at a purposeful pace.

Instinctively, Hiro crouched low to avoid detection, but the yamabushi's gaze did not deviate from his route.

Although tempted to follow, Hiro doubted the mountain priest intended harm to anyone, at least in daylight. The fissure in the stone—no doubt the entrance to Zentaro's hidden home—was a far more interesting proposition.

He waited behind the sasa for several minutes. When the yamabushi did not return and he could detect no other presence, Hiro hurried toward the opening in the cliff.

When he reached the rocky face, he craned his neck upward. Twenty meters above his head, the cliff face disappeared into a cloud that seemed to sit directly on the mountaintop. A trickle of water, not strong enough to be called a fall, wound down the face like a liquid snake. Around it, ferns emerged from cracks in the stone, dotting the cliff with splashes of brilliant green.

The rock wall seemed strangely out of place, rising vertically from the forest floor, until Hiro remembered the landslide that had altered the lower portion of the mountain earlier in the year. A far more ancient slide, or perhaps an earthquake, must have exposed this slab of bedrock when a portion of the mountain sheared away.

Hiro lowered his face and turned his attention to the fissure. Had he not seen Zentaro enter it, he would never have guessed it led into a cave. The opening measured barely as tall as Hiro's chest, and he had to twist his shoulders sideways to fit through it. He stuck his head inside. The opening curved away into darkness, preventing him from determining how deep the fissure went.

With a last look over his shoulder to ascertain that Zentaro had not returned, Hiro bent even lower, twisted sideways, and entered the cave.

As the light disappeared behind him, he kept the fingers of his right hand touching the rough stone wall. Maintaining contact with the wall at all times ensured that he could turn around, put his left hand on the wall, and follow it back out.

After half a dozen steps, the tunnel entrance widened slightly and curved to the left. Hiro took four more steps around the curve and discovered himself in the entrance to a circular cavern three meters high and about four meters in diameter.

He blinked in the unexpected light of the small brazier that lit the space.

Flat stones nestled on the floor, so perfectly fitted that Hiro wondered at the time and effort someone had taken to pave a cavern— until it occurred to him that ascetics had a surfeit of both time and stones. Only the small, square earthen hearth at the center of the room remained unpaved. A worn tatami sat beside the hearth, with a wooden tray upon it. On the tray, a teapot and a cylindrical wooden canister rested beside a ceramic bowl and a pair of ancient-looking chopsticks.

A vermilion Shintō shrine and an unpainted Buddhist altar sat against the wall of the cavern opposite the entrance. To their right, a bronze brazier cast a flickering glow across it all.

The small paneled doors on the butsudan were closed, preventing him from seeing its interior. A broken bowl, perhaps the one Zentaro picked up at the burial ground, sat on a narrow shelf in front of the Shintō shrine, between two unlit candles and a pair of small stone foxes that stood guard over the sacred space.

To Hiro's right, a neatly folded futon and quilted blanket sat atop another old tatami. A small wooden chest, of the type most often used for clothing, rested against the wall beyond the bedding.

To his left, a number of rickety wooden racks rested against the rough stone wall between the entrance and the altars. They held a collection of worn and broken items in various states of disrepair and mending. Brooms and bowls, teapots, cups, and lanterns lined the shelves, each neatly set in place with other objects of its kind.

Hiro recalled Akako's comment about Zentaro taking objects from the village.

It appeared the yamabushi had been taking them to mend them.

A breath of air flowed over the back of Hiro's neck.

Instinctively, he ducked—and a stronger rush of air passed through his topknot as the blow intended for his head passed harmlessly above it.

CHAPTER 43

Behind him, the attacker gave a grunt of surprise.

Hiro spun around, still crouched. He struck at the assailant's shadowed form, but his fist punched air.

His attacker had already backed away.

Hiro pulled a *shuriken* from his sleeve. He wrapped his fingers around the weapon's star-like points as he pursued the assailant back down the darkened passage.

He rounded the curve. Darkness engulfed him, but he sensed his assailant just ahead. He lunged forward. His free hand grasped a robe.

A trailing sleeve brushed over his hand. The robe tugged at his fingers as the shadowed figure tried to break away.

Hiro gripped the shuriken hard but did not strike. Instead, he gripped the robe more tightly. The attacker dragged him toward the exit, moving slowly but with determination through the narrow tunnel. Hiro followed.

As they emerged once more into the forest, Hiro kicked his right foot forward, hooked his assailant's ankle, and pushed hard with the hand that clutched the robe.

His attacker tripped and fell.

Hiro did not release his grip. Instead, he fell to a kneeling position atop of his assailant, using his weight to pin the stranger down.

Beneath him, the attacker squirmed.

Hiro drew back the hand that held the shuriken, prepared to strike. "If you want to live, stop fighting."

"Hiro!"

He jolted at his name—and because a female voice had spoken it.

Beneath him, the figure stopped struggling.

Hiro knelt atop a woman wearing pale pants beneath a long gray robe. Her gray hood concealed her hair and face, with only a slit where her eyes showed through.

"Who are you?" he demanded. "How do you know my name?"

She turned her head—as best she could, given the man kneeling on her back—and tried to look him in the eyes.

Hers looked familiar.

Suddenly, Hiro placed her voice—and wondered if he should believe in ghosts. "Emiri?"

"You remember me?" She seemed surprised.

He raised the fist that held the shuriken. "If you know me, why did you attack me?"

"I thought you went into the cave to hurt Zentaro."

"He isn't here."

"I noticed."

"And you're supposed to be dead."

"If you don't mind," Emiri said, "could we possibly have this conversation elsewhere? Preferably without your knee in my back?"

"This seems plenty comfortable to me."

She glared at him. "It won't be—for either of us—if Zentaro returns."

"You attacked me to protect him, but you don't want him to see you?"

She gave an exasperated sigh. "If he sees me in the daylight, he will realize I'm not truly a kitsune."

Hiro lowered the shuriken. "*You're* the kitsune?"

"Let me up, and I'll explain—in a safer place."

Hiro rose to his feet and offered the kunoichi his empty hand. She ignored it, stood up, and brushed the dirty snow from her clothes. When she finished, she led him back along the rocky cliff until they reached the place where tree roots created a natural ladder up the face. Emiri pulled off her hood and let it hang down her back. Then, grasping a pair of roots, she began to climb.

She moved up the wall with the speed of frequent practice.

As he watched her, Hiro considered the possibility that she planned to ambush him and drop him to his death. However, given her status as a fellow member of the Iga ryu, and the presence of her name on the list of agents he had come to warn, he found it highly unlikely that she meant him harm. He returned the shuriken to the pocket in his sleeve and started up the cliff—but watched her closely as he went.

About ten meters up the rocky face, Emiri stopped climbing. When he reached the place, Hiro discovered that she stood on a narrow, mostly level ledge that snaked around the side of the cliff. Although invisible from the ground, it was wide enough for a person with decent balance to walk along. As he looked back toward the forest floor, he realized a fall would give him definitive—if undesirable—personal knowledge about whether the dead could truly become ghosts.

Emiri beckoned for him to follow and set off along the ledge. His first step dislodged a handful of tiny pebbles that rolled out from beneath his feet and cascaded down the cliff in a clattering fall.

Emiri looked back over her shoulder, apparently more annoyed than concerned.

He laid his hand on the cliff to his right, this time for balance, and continued along the ledge.

About ten meters ahead of them, an enormous, nose-shaped stone formation overhung the ledge. A handful of ferns grew out beneath it like the living mustache of a mountain troll. Just as Hiro wondered how Emiri planned to bypass the giant stone, she bent down and disappeared. When he reached the spot, he discovered her sitting in a narrow cave beneath the rocky outcrop. The space looked large enough for two people to sit in side by side, but only barely.

Emiri beckoned for him to join her.

If the stone broke away from the cliff it would destroy the cave and crush them both. Hiro considered that unlikely, at least in the next few minutes.

He ducked and crawled beneath the stone.

Despite his normal preference for letting others begin a conversation, he had to know: "How did you find this place?"

She smiled. "I like to climb."

He did not return the smile. "Why did you abandon your assignment without sending word to Hanzō?"

"I believe that does not concern you."

"Considering that I came to this village to find you, on Hanzō's authority, I beg to disagree."

Emiri searched Hiro's face as if to judge his veracity. Eventually, she said, "I left the village after an incident at the teahouse, on the night of the typhoon."

Hiro remembered Akako's story. "You saw Noboru's father die."

"No. That happened later, after I had gone. I walked in on Hanako ... playing Noboru's flute."

It took Hiro a moment to understand what she meant, but the revelation came as no real surprise. "I wondered if their relationship went beyond the quality of her food."

Emiri nodded. "A few minutes later, she cornered me in the kitchen and threatened to ruin my reputation if I told anyone what I had seen. I went upstairs, collected my things, and fled into the storm."

"You ran away because she threatened your reputation?"

"I ran because I threatened *her*," Emiri said. "She could not risk me telling Noboru's parents about the affair. Sooner or later, she would have found an excuse to fire me, whether or not she ruined my reputation. I decided to leave on my own terms, and to leave no trail."

"Why would she care if you exposed her? She could have charged Noboru's parents for the value of her services."

"Maybe it works that way in Kyoto. In a village this small? On a travel road? Exposure would have cost Hanako more than what they could afford to pay. More importantly, it would have ruined her status as a high-class entertainer. Travelers don't pay a premium for used-up prostitutes."

"You did leave a trail," Hiro pointed out. "You left your cloak on the travel road."

"To disguise my direction. I doubled back and waited out the storm on the mountain. I didn't anticipate the landslide, or that they would be foolish enough to think a yūrei killed me. But I did not abandon my post." She smiled. "I changed myself into a kitsune."

CHAPTER 44

Hiro did not return her smile this time either.

"After the landslide blocked the travel road, I found a position as a maid in another teahouse on the detour route," Emiri said. "During the day, I normally watch the road from there. But I also needed to keep an eye on this part of the road, and since not even I can be in two places at once, I persuaded Zentaro to act as my accomplice."

"By convincing him you were a fox."

"It wasn't difficult. His dedication to Inari, and his love for the foxes of the mountain, made him easy to persuade."

"Surely he knew you from the village."

"He rarely came into the village while I lived there, and I never met him face to face. The old courtesan who owned the teahouse did not let us spend any time outside, for fear it would ruin our 'delicate complexions.'" Emiri imitated an elderly woman's disapproving tone. "She barely let us out to use the latrine during daylight hours. Even then we had to wear full makeup and kimono. Zentaro would never have recognized my face."

"The inside of a teahouse seems an ineffective place to watch a road," Hiro observed.

"Quite the opposite," Emiri countered. "Everyone of consequence stopped for a meal. At least, they did until the landslide changed the route. This original road is dead—and the village with it, though not everyone has accepted that reality."

"Speaking of death," Hiro said, "did you kill Ishiko and Masako?"

"Why would I do that?"

"To avenge Riko's death?" Hiro almost wished she had. At least it would have explained the killings.

"That wasn't me." She shook her head. "But I do disguise myself as a yūrei when I pass the village at night to meet Zentaro."

"You pass through the village dressed that way?" Hiro knew there had to be a reasonable explanation for Father Mateo's ghost.

"Through the forest near the village," she corrected, "and I try to avoid being seen at all, but since they believe Riko became a yūrei, the disguise discourages anyone from attempting to follow me."

"So you are Zentaro's 'messenger from Inari'?"

"I am, although I did not plan to be. Not initially, anyway. The night I fled the teahouse, he discovered me hiding in the woods. The typhoon was blowing too hard to risk a trip down the mountain when I left the teahouse, so I waited out the worst of the rain at the burial yard—inside the mausoleum. Zentaro found me there, and mistook me for a kitsune. Don't ask me why. I am not sure he's entirely sane."

"I am entirely sure he's not."

She tipped her head in acknowledgment. "In any event, I played along. Since then, I spend a couple of nights each week in his cave. I arrive after dark and leave before dawn, and he tells me what goes on in the village. He thinks I deliver his words to the kami." She laughed. "Hanzō is not precisely a god, but men should fear him more than they do Inari."

"And Zentaro never questions where you go or who you are?" Hiro asked the question even though his own observations of the yamabushi provided an adequate answer.

"He truly seems to believe I become a fox in the daylight hours. And seems honored to be performing a valuable service for Inari Ōkami."

"Not to mention, smitten with the messenger."

She smiled. "An unexpected benefit."

"It isn't dark right now," Hiro pointed out.

"And I wouldn't have approached his cave, except that I thought I needed to protect him."

Fair enough. "Did you tell him to keep the villagers away from the forest after dark?"

"Yes, but it did no harm. They feared the yūrei anyway."

"Could Zentaro have taken your instructions a step too far?" Hiro asked.

"What do you mean?"

"You never fully answered my question about Ishiko and Masako. Did you kill them . . . or do you know who did?"

Her expression grew serious. "I did not kill them. As to the second part of your question, I do not know. Zentaro seems completely dedicated to his yamabushi practice. I don't believe he would kill, but when I returned to the cave last night he was not there."

"What time did he return?"

"I cannot say. I fell asleep, and when I woke, he was beside me. It didn't occur to me to ask where he had been."

"And the night Ishiko died?" Hiro asked.

She sighed. "I was not here."

"I need you to find out where he was," Hiro said, "and if he killed the women to enforce Inari's ban on people walking in the forest after dark."

Emiri gestured to the ledge. "You need to leave, before the evening mist comes down the mountain. The descent is treacherous when the rocks get slippery, especially if you don't know it well."

"You are not coming?" Hiro asked.

She shook her head. "Kitsune only take on human form at night. I'll stay here until then."

"The slippery descent doesn't bother you?"

"I have plenty of practice."

As Hiro crawled out of the cave Emiri added, "You mentioned that you came on Hanzō's orders?"

He turned to face her. "Hanzō believes that Oda Nobunaga has acquired a list of Iga agents and their current posts, and wants every agent on the list to return to Iga as soon as possible, for reassignment."

"Let me guess. My name is on the list."

"I would not be here otherwise."

"I will leave tomorrow. Tonight, I'll talk with Zentaro and learn

the truth. If he killed the women, I will let you know . . . on one condition. I do not want him harmed. He would only have killed them if he
believed Inari wanted it to happen."

Hiro nodded as if in assent. He saw no reason to argue until—and
unless—the truth required it.

"He will not be happy when I go." Emiri's voice suggested she
would miss Zentaro too. In a lighter tone, she continued, "Do you have
a message I should take to Hanzō?"

Hiro thought carefully before he spoke.

To send no message would raise suspicion, but sending one created
other problems. Although he told the truth about Oda, the list, and
Hanzō's recall of the affected spies, the mission to warn Emiri and the
others was not Hiro's to fulfill. Hiro had undertaken the mission on
his own authority, after the spy originally charged with the task had
died. As far as Hattori Hanzō knew, Hiro and Father Mateo were
hiding out at the Portuguese colony in Yokoseura, many miles to the
south.

Hiro decided he could hide the truth no longer.

"Tell my cousin that his agent on Kōyasan was murdered, but not
by Oda's spies, and that I will finish warning the agents on the list
before the first spring thaw."

He considered adding that he and the priest would travel to Yokoseura as soon as they completed their mission in Edo, but decided not
to make a promise he already knew he did not intend to keep.

CHAPTER 45

"I will tell him," Emiri said. "Will your travels take you as far as Edo?"

"Possibly." Hiro had no intention of revealing more details than necessary.

"If you do reach Edo, look for an ally among the watchmen near the southernmost checkpoint as you enter the city."

"Among the daimyō's guards?"

"Among the fire watch," Emiri said. "The ones who spend the nights on the towers. When you find them, ask for Daisuke."

Hiro recognized the name, and not only because it appeared on his memorized list.

Many years before, a teenaged Daisuke had locked an even younger Hiro in a storehouse with a corpse—a mean-spirited trick that terrified Hiro to his core, but ultimately dispelled his belief in ghosts.

"You remember him," Emiri said.

"Clearly, you do not," Hiro replied, "or you would know that he is not my ally."

"You still hold a grudge for a childish prank—"

"I was a child," Hiro corrected. "Daisuke was not."

"Some people do change, you know. I would consider it a favor . . ." She hesitated. "If you can, warn Daisuke as well."

"I will not overlook him, if the opportunity presents itself."

She searched his face, but he knew it revealed nothing.

At last, she nodded. "I will find out what Zentaro knows about the recent deaths. If I discover anything useful, I will also find a way to let you know."

He did not bother to ask how she would reach him. A kunoichi could always find a way.

"Where have you been?" Father Mateo looked up from his Bible as Hiro entered the guest room. "I was starting to worry."

Hiro slid the shoji closed and bent down as Gato twined around his ankles. "About my safety, or that I would solve the mystery without you?"

He stroked the cat and smiled at the priest.

Father Mateo closed his Bible. "Both. Where have you been?"

Hiro crossed the room and knelt across from the Jesuit. "I found our missing kunoichi—and your ghost."

Father Mateo's eyes grew wide as Hiro told him about Emiri, though the priest's final reaction to the story was not what Hiro anticipated.

The Jesuit frowned. "And all this time, she has been sharing Zentaro's cave? That seems inappropriate."

"Not for a kunoichi. Or a kitsune, for that matter."

"Surely Zentaro does not believe the woman is a fox. Not truly."

"He believes he can talk to trees," Hiro said.

"If he steals objects from the village he might have taken the silver too, and murdered the women because they caught him doing it."

"That occurred to me as well. Emiri has promised to speak with him this evening."

"Won't he lie if he is guilty?" Father Mateo asked.

Gato crawled into Hiro's lap, circled, and lay down. "I do not think so. The legends say kitsune steal, and kill, without remorse. Zentaro has no reason to believe that she would disapprove."

The Jesuit lowered his voice. "Did she know anything about Kane and Mume?"

"I did not mention them to her. I plan to investigate that myself, tonight."

"You mean we will investigate tonight."

"I meant what I said," Hiro clarified. "You will stay here, in case the thief returns. And this time, open the closet as soon as the shoji rattles."

Father Mateo crossed his arms. "Why do you get to sneak around in the dark, while I have to wait in a stuffy closet?"

Hiro stifled a smile. "Because I am shinobi and you are not."

"I am not afraid."

You were when you thought you saw a ghost. "I swore an oath to protect you."

"You let me risk my life on Kōya."

"That was different."

"How?" Father Mateo continued without waiting for an answer. "I am tired of you treating me like candy that melts in the rain. I understand that some mysterious benefactor paid the Iga ryu quite handsomely to ensure my safety, but I don't care—"

"I don't either."

The Jesuit blinked. "You don't?"

"Not anymore."

"Then why do you still refuse to let me share the risk?"

Hiro thought of his older brother, and of Neko, gone forever.

Father Mateo, once so strange and foreign, had become as important to Hiro as his mother and his remaining brother, Kazu. He believed that feeling was mutual, and yet the priest seemed not to understand.

Hiro struggled against a lifetime of training that required him to suppress his emotions.

Before he could find the words to express his thoughts, the priest absolved him of the need.

"Hiro, no man wants his friends to suffer. But you cannot expect me to spend the rest of my life in a box"—Father Mateo gestured to the walls of the guest room—"because it's dangerous outside. The Bible commands us to share our burdens. You bear mine honorably. But you must let me bear my share of yours as well."

Hiro bowed his head in acknowledgment. "I will try. But tonight, you must wait in the closet for the thief."

The Jesuit opened his mouth to object, but Hiro continued, "We do not know for certain that Kane and Mume are guilty of anything. Someone must stay in case the thief returns."

Father Mateo sneezed. "All right, but please take Gato to Ana's room. If you don't, the thief will hear me sniffling from the far side of the ryokan."

An hour before midnight, Hiro stood up and approached the veranda door. He considered changing into the dark *hakama* and midnight blue shinobi tunic folded deep within his travel pack, but decided against it. The slight advantage the clothing offered did not offset the risk of revealing his true identity. He did, however, take a tiny, shielded shinobi lantern, barely large enough to hold a candle stump. He hoped the moon would make the light unnecessary, but would rather have the tools he needed than have to improvise without them.

Father Mateo joined him at the door. "I want to go with you. The thief won't come tonight, and you know it. Only a fool would steal from an occupied room."

"You need to remain here anyway." Hiro stuck his katana and wakizashi through his obi, securing the scabbards so they would not rattle. "I am trained to conceal myself in the forest. You are not."

"Then I want to learn. I understand that does not help tonight. But I want you to teach me—soon."

Hiro doubted the lessons would actually occur, but nodded anyway. He raised his hood and opened the door.

Outside, a heavy mist obscured the night. There was no moon. He could barely see the front of the ryokan through the shifting fog.

Hiro opened his lantern, lit the candle, and slid the cover closed. Slipping on his extra sandals, he left the ryokan.

CHAPTER 46

Although he had originally planned to circle behind the houses, the mist reduced visibility so greatly that he decided to risk the road. He moved cautiously, taking care to muffle his steps and to keep the lantern shielded. He listened for any movement, prepared to shutter the lantern and hide the instant he heard any footsteps other than his own.

As he approached the burial ground, he stopped and listened. He believed he had arrived before the women, but took no chances.

The forest seemed completely still. As he listened, he heard a distant hooting and a rustling in the underbrush that sounded like a rat, or perhaps a fox, but he detected no signs of any human presence. The mist felt damp and cold on Hiro's face, the silence dark and heavy like the woolen blankets Father Mateo had brought from Portugal—and promptly discarded in favor of Japanese quilts.

Hiro opened his lantern a sliver to light the way and passed beneath the torii into the burial ground. His breath plumed out in front of him and blended with the mist.

Monuments appeared before him like the teeth of a giant beast. The swirling mist created an illusion of movement, and more than once, Hiro reached for his sword, only to realize he was still alone.

He hurried past the graves and stopped in front of the mausoleum. Overhead, its curling eaves spread out like the wings of a massive owl. Wooden carvings decorated the eaves and lintels, though the details were lost to the night and fog. Beneath the eaves, a pair of iron-banded wooden doors secured the entrance to the tomb. Hiro reached for them, but paused when he felt the smooth, carved wood beneath his hand.

Almost twenty years had passed since the last time he spent the night with a corpse.

He grasped the door and pulled.

It did not open.

He heard the distant crunch of muffled footsteps far behind him in the forest.

Hiro pulled the door again and heard a soft, metallic rattle. As he raised his lantern, he saw the small iron lock that secured the doors.

Behind him, the steps grew closer.

With chagrin, he realized he had left his lock picks at the ryokan. Emiri's claim that she had spent the night in the mausoleum made him assume it would be open.

Assumptions kill.

A rapid search of his pockets revealed nothing he could use to pick the lock. He grasped the iron cylinder and pulled. The bolt held fast.

Suddenly, Hiro remembered the slender pick concealed in the sheath of his wakizashi. He had never needed it before, and, until that moment, had forgotten it was there.

He looked over his shoulder and saw the glow of a lantern near the torii.

He was out of time.

Crouching low, he shuttered his lantern completely and hurried around the side of the mausoleum. When he reached the back of the building, he pressed his back to the freezing wood. While not an ideal hiding place, it would work as long as Kane and Mume remained on the other side.

He slowed his breathing and listened to the footsteps coming through the burial yard.

The footsteps stopped in front of the mausoleum, as the glow of a lantern bled around the sides of the building.

Silence fell.

A single footstep crunched on the frozen ground.

A muffled clinking came from the front of the building, followed by the click of a lock releasing. Iron hinges creaked as the doors to the mausoleum opened.

Footsteps echoed inside the tomb, followed by muffled scraping sounds, and a clink like shifting coins.

Curiosity burned in Hiro's mind like wildfire. Only samurai had the money to construct a mausoleum for the dead, so only a samurai should have the key to the mausoleum door.

He resisted the nearly overwhelming urge to sneak around the building for a look. The risk of discovery was too great, especially since he did not know who made the sounds. Mume and Kane seemed most likely, but assumptions had already burned him once tonight.

Or possibly saved him . . .

Had he thought to bring a lockpick, he would have been inside the mausoleum when it opened.

The burning in his ears and forehead faded as they numbed. He resisted the urge to stomp the ground to warm his aching toes. His shinobi sandals lacked good insulation, and the cold leached up from the ground, through his tabi, and into his feet. He did not regret the tactical decision to leave his winter shoes on the rack in the ryokan to prevent their absence being noticed. Even so, he sorely missed their warmth.

Relentless cold seeped into Hiro's clothes. It felt as if it pierced his bones. He exhaled slowly, fighting his body's longing to shiver and generate warmth.

The sounds inside the mausoleum ceased.

Footsteps crunched on the ground. The doors creaked shut.

A second, softer, set of footsteps pattered through the burial yard, increasing in volume as they approached.

"What took you so long?" Hiro recognized Kane's whispered hiss.

"I fell sleep," Mume whispered.

Kane sighed. "At least you remembered to wear warm clothes."

"Are we going now?" Mume asked. "Last week you said we had to wait for spring."

Kane paused before answering. "I'm not going anywhere. With Ishiko dead, I'm mistress of the ryokan."

"But . . . you said . . . We had a plan."

"The plan has changed. I'm staying," Kane said. "But I counted what we have, and it's enough for you to go to Edo now, and live there for at least a year."

"But you said we were going to go together. You and me. Together."

"Not anymore." Irritation infused Kane's voice. "I told you, now that Ishiko's dead, I have changed my mind." More calmly, she added, "You could stay here too, with Taso."

"But you said I had to go."

"And now I'm telling you that you can stay."

"What about the yūrei? She will kill us!"

"I don't think so," Kane said. "We didn't live here when she died, and I think she only kills the people who hurt her when she was alive. Besides, Noboru says the priest from Hakone can make her go away forever."

"What if you're wrong?" Mume sounded on the verge of tears. "What if she kills you for stealing the silver? And me, for stealing from my husband?"

The regret Hiro felt over leaving the warmth of his guest room dissipated as quickly as a cloud of frozen breath.

"Don't be stupid. That money did not belong to Noboru until Ishiko died, and Riko's ghost doesn't care what happened to Ishiko's silver. She can't spend it. She's dead. A ghost doesn't need to be rich."

The icy chill that ran down Hiro's spine had nothing to do with temperature.

He knew who killed Ishiko and Masako.

More importantly, he knew who the killer would target next.

On the far side of the mausoleum, Mume started sobbing. "Y-you said that we would go to Edo. I don't want to go alone."

CHAPTER 47

"You don't have to go," Kane repeated. "You can stay and help me with the ryokan. Noboru will allow it, if I ask him."

"But you said that Taso does not want me," Mume wailed.

"No I didn't."

"Y-yes, you did." Mume's sobs brought on an attack of hiccups. "Y-you said he hates me because I am stupid."

Kane did not answer. Mume's sobs continued, punctuated by hiccups.

Eventually, Kane sighed. "I was wrong. He does not hate you."

"But you said . . ." Mume trailed off into a wail. "H-he does."

"I lied. I'm sorry. I thought . . . stop crying and listen."

Mume's cries became loud sniffles, which slowly stilled. She hiccupped loudly.

"Before Ishiko died, she was so mean to me," Kane explained. "She called me names and hurt me every day. I wanted to run away, but I couldn't leave you here alone. I promised our parents I would care for you, so I had to convince you to run away as well. That's why I told you Taso would hate you when he realized you're . . . not as smart as other people are. But it isn't true. I made it up, so you would run away with me."

"Y-you lied?" Mume hiccupped.

"I am sorry. I didn't mean to hurt you."

"It is bad to lie." Mume sounded angry.

"I know." Kane's voice had lost its edge. "I am sorry, Mume. Please forgive me."

"So . . .Taso does not hate me?"

"No."

"W-what about the silver?"

"We'll take Taso's silver back, and say we found it on the floor of the latrine. We can tell him the bag must have fallen off the rafters, and the silver rolled into the corners. The other coins, I'll leave inside the tomb, in case I need them in the future."

"What about the stranger's servant?" Mume asked.

"The foreigner is rich. He can afford two dozen silver coins to replace what we're missing. Once he gives them to Noboru, Otomuro-*san* will let the servant go."

Clearly, Kane did not know about the extravagant sum her husband claimed.

The hinges squeaked as the mausoleum doors swung open. Hiro heard the distinctive clink of coins, more loudly than before.

"Hold this while I lock the door." A metallic click followed Kane's words.

"How did you get the key to Otomuro-*sama*'s family tomb?" Mume asked.

"I didn't," Kane said. "His lock was broken. I replaced it with my own. Now let's go home. And do not speak of this to anyone. Not even Taso. Not even to me, unless we're here, in the burial yard, where no one else can hear us."

"I remember." Mume sounded slightly indignant. "We can only talk in secret here."

Their footsteps moved away from the mausoleum, and the glow of their lanterns faded. Although he looked forward to making Kane answer for her crimes, Hiro felt pity for Mume, and hoped her husband would overlook, or at least forgive, his wife's involvement in the theft.

He opened his own small lantern, but the flame had died. When he tried to relight it using the flint he carried in his obi, he discovered that the candle stub had burned completely down, leaving only a paper-thin layer of frozen wax too small to ignite.

Disappointed, Hiro stowed the lantern in his obi and felt his way around the side of the mausoleum in the dark. Working by feel, he removed the pick from the hilt of his wakizashi and located the lock on the mausoleum doors. It yielded quickly, despite his lack of sight. After carefully replacing the pick in his scabbard, Hiro opened the tomb, knelt down to avoid bumping his head on lanterns or other objects that might hang unseen from the ceiling, and crawled inside.

He moved forward on his knees, using one hand for balance and extending the other in front of his face to prevent a collision in the dark. His fingers brushed a large stone block. It seemed about waist-high, and had squared-off edges like a pedestal. He swept his fingers gently across the top, and stopped when he touched a funerary urn.

Kneeling upright, Hiro placed a hand on either side of the urn. He lifted it carefully. The weight seemed right for ashes, and it did not clink with hidden coins. He lowered the urn back into place, bent down, and felt around on the floor behind the pedestal.

His fingers met cloth. A bag. He grasped the fabric . . . and it jingled.

He pulled the bag into his lap. Kane mentioned twenty-four silver coins but, based on the weight, Hiro felt sure this bag held more.

He tucked the purse into his obi, crawled backward out of the mausoleum, and closed the doors, securing the lock once more.

It took him several minutes to find his way through the burial yard, and almost half an hour to retrace his steps to the village.

He had almost made it back when a woman's screams shattered the misty night.

A male voice called out in alarm, and another answered.

Hiro increased his pace. He emerged from the trees as the pale glow of a lantern bobbed through the mist. It came from the direction of Otomuro's home, and headed toward the ryokan.

Hiro followed.

He could barely see the houses on either side of the travel road as he passed by. Directly ahead, the mist glowed golden with the light of several lanterns. The deeper shadows resolved into human forms as Hiro approached.

A small crowd stood in the street near the ryokan, with Father Mateo and Mume at its center. As Hiro reached them, he realized that only Noboru was missing from the scene.

"Do not touch my wife!" Taso took a menacing step toward the priest.

Father Mateo raised his hands defensively. "I did not—"

"You did! I saw you!" Taso clenched his fists.

Father Mateo raised his own hands defensively. Just then, he noticed Hiro. "Matsui-*san* can help me explain."

Hiro raised an eyebrow. He had no idea what was going on.

Taso turned. "Why did the foreigner assault my wife?"

It was not an appropriate way for a commoner to address a samurai, but under the circumstances Hiro chose to ignore the insult. "There must be some misunderstanding. I can assure you, the foreigner means no harm."

"What's going on?" Noboru emerged from the ryokan with a lantern in his hand. "It's the middle of the—Kane? What . . . has someone seen the yūrei?"

Hiro noted the sudden fear in the innkeeper's voice.

"What *is* going on?" Otomuro demanded, still out of breath from the short, cold walk.

"If everyone would stop talking," Taso muttered, "we might all find out."

"I am certain there's a reasonable explanation," Hiro said, "but I see no reason to stand here in the cold while we discuss it. The reception room at the ryokan will hold us all, if everyone will follow me inside."

Taso scowled. "This does not concern the entire village."

"Actually, it does," Hiro said, "as I will explain as soon as we get inside."

A curious murmur rose behind him as he started toward the ryokan.

He did not look back. He knew that every one of them—including the killer—would follow.

CHAPTER 48

"We're all here." Taso gestured to the villagers gathered around the hearth of the ryokan's common room. "Now, please explain why the foreigner grabbed my wife."

"I did not grab her," Father Mateo said. "I—"

Ana entered the room from the hallway, wearing the robe in which she slept. Her hair hung down her back in a thin, gray braid, and she blinked like a child unexpectedly awakened from a deep, sound sleep.

"Hm." She looked around the room. "Has everyone in this village lost his mind?"

"It's all right, Ana," Father Mateo said, "go back to bed. It's the middle of the night."

"I noticed." As she turned away, she muttered, "Might as well make myself some tea." She glared at them over her shoulder. "The rest of you can get your own."

"I demand to know what's going on here," Otomuro declared as Ana shuffled back down the hall.

"I will gladly tell you." Hiro moved toward the samurai, as if to speak to him directly, but really to place himself between the villagers and the exit. "Father Mateo and I can now reveal who stole the missing silver, as well as who killed Ishiko and Masako. What is more, I can prove this village is not cursed, and there is no yūrei."

"How does he know?" Mume whispered to her sister.

Kane shushed her.

"No ghost?" Saku snorted. "Of all people, I would think that you'd know better."

Hiro reached into his obi, removed the bag of coins, and handed it to Noboru. "I believe you will find that holds not only what you knew was missing—twenty-four silver coins—but quite a bit more, most likely taken a little at a time in the months since your marriage."

"My marriage?" Noboru glanced briefly at Kane before he opened the bag and looked inside. His eyes grew wide. "Where did you find this?"

"Ask your wife." Hiro shifted his gaze to Kane. "Think carefully before you deny your guilt. I heard everything from behind the mausoleum."

Mume covered her mouth with her hands. "He knows. He knows."

Taso stared at his wife. "Are you involved in this?"

"Your wife is not the thief," Hiro said.

"Kane?" Noboru gave her a disbelieving look. "You stole from family?"

"Your family, not mine." She squared her shoulders. "And I only took what should have belonged to us already. Your mother never gave us a single coin to call our own."

"But why?" Noboru asked. "You never mentioned any need . . ."

"Would it have mattered? Your mother treated me like a slave, and you did nothing. She yelled at me. She called me names. She beat me. And you went off to the teahouse like you didn't even care." Kane pointed at her sister. "I also stole the coins for her."

Mume raised her hands to cover her entire face.

Taso laid a hand on her shoulder. "If you needed money, why didn't you talk to me?"

"She wanted the money to run away from you, and move to Edo," Kane said.

Taso looked crushed. He removed his hand from Mume's shoulder and stepped away. "Is this true? You want to leave me?"

Mume lowered her hands. "Kane said I had to."

"Stop lying, Mume," Kane stared at her sister as if urging her to cooperate. "Admit it. You wanted to go to Edo."

Mume nodded slowly. "I want to see Edo."

"Do you think I can't see what you're doing?" Taso narrowed his eyes at Kane. "My wife did not think of this herself. You manipulated her for selfish reasons."

Hiro was glad to see that Taso did not fall for the ruse.

Kane's cheeks turned pink, but her eyes were hard. "You act offended now, but your love for her will not last. You'll treat her just as badly as Ishiko treated me, as soon the novelty wears off and her simplemindedness ceases to amuse you."

"Your sister is not *simple*." Taso put a defensive arm around Mume's shoulders. "She is kind. And honest. Which is more than I can say of you."

"Fine, I admit it. I stole the money because I planned to run away—and take her with me." Kane's expression softened a fraction. "I promised our parents that I would take care of her. Alone, I could have lived by my wits. But I needed money in order to take her with me."

Kane looked around as if for support, but found only varying degrees of anger and disapproval.

"Mume is no longer your responsibility." Taso lowered his face to look at his wife. "I take care of her now."

Hiro suspected the laborer added the final sentence to make sure his wife would understand.

"You want to leave?" Noboru seemed to have trouble assimilating the information.

"Not any more. I changed my mind." Kane's voice took on a pleading urgency. "Everything changed when Ishiko died. I told Mume tonight that I wanted to stay in the village. Mume, tell him."

Mume frowned at her sister. "How do I know that wasn't another lie?"

Noboru looked expectantly at Hiro. "Did she say she had changed her mind?"

Among other things. Hiro saw no reason to cause more trouble with irrelevant details. "Yes, she did."

Noboru inhaled deeply as if preparing himself for an additional blow. "You said you solved the murders too. Did Kane kill my mother?"

"No," Hiro replied. "Your lover did."

CHAPTER 49

Noboru's cheeks turned red. "What—What lover?" The blush spread all the way to his ears, which turned as red as sliced tomatoes.

"You know perfectly well what I mean, and who." Hiro gestured to the woman at Noboru's side. "Hanako."

The teahouse owner stepped backward in dismay. "I am not a prostitute!"

Noboru looked stunned. "*Hanako* killed my mother?"

"Of course not," she retorted. "I was at the teahouse with you and your guests the night she died."

"So you wished us to believe," Hiro said. "While Masako entertained us with the shamisen, you left the teahouse, killed Ishiko, and hid her body in the woods. After we left for the night, you retrieved the body and posed it, to make it look like the yūrei was responsible."

"The yūrei *was* responsible," Hanako insisted. "And she will not stop until she takes revenge on everyone connected with her death."

"There is no yūrei," Hiro repeated.

Hanako looked around the room. "This stranger cannot understand—"

"On the contrary," Hiro said, "I understand you all too well. You were prettier and more talented than Riko, but she was Yuko's heir and you were merely an apprentice. You hated that she would inherit the teahouse, while you faced a life of servitude. But you found a way out. You began an affair with Noboru, thinking you could persuade him to marry you, at which point you would become the mistress of the ryokan."

"That would never have happened," Noboru said. "My mother would never have consented to me marrying a teahouse girl. Both of us

knew that, even before Mother learned about the affair and insisted—"
The innkeeper covered his mouth with his hand.

"—that you marry quickly, so Hanako knew she had no chance."
Hiro finished the sentence for him. "I suspected as much when you
told me about your marriage." *And when I eavesdropped on your conversation after the meal today, I knew for certain, about the affair at least.*

"I never did figure out how Mother learned about Hanako,"
Noboru said.

"Riko told her." The teahouse owner spit out the name as if it
tasted foul. "She was jealous, and told your mother because she knew
Ishiko would stop it."

"A grudge you held to the day she died," Hiro added. "To the point
that you even refused to help when Riko lay dying of her injuries."

"How did you know that?" Hanako demanded. "I told you
Masako—"

Hiro cut her off. "You lied, though you made the mistake of basing
the lie on a truth I heard from a more reliable source. Masako tended
Riko's wounds, while you refused to enter the room and help a dying
girl. A fact that would have guaranteed your death, had Riko truly
returned as a vengeful ghost."

"You think you know everything," Hanako sneered.

"On the contrary," Hiro said, "there are many things I do not know.
For example, did Yuko die of natural causes, or did you kill her also?"

Hanako's shoulders slumped, though her voice held no remorse.
"I found her lying dead on her futon the morning after Riko died. She
had trouble with her heart for years—it's why she left Kyoto. She kept
it a secret here, because no one pays for a sickly entertainer."

"How would you know why she left Kyoto?" Noboru asked. "You
were not here when she returned."

"She made me walk to Fujisawa twice a year to buy her medi-
cine. A week's hard walk each way, because she was too cheap to pay
for a palanquin. Before I came, she sent a servant so dear little Riko
wouldn't have to hurt her feet and ruin her complexion. Clearly, mine
weren't nearly so important."

"If you didn't kill her," Father Mateo said, "why did you blame her death on a ghost?"

"And settle for inheriting a tiny, impoverished teahouse?" Hanako pointed at Noboru. "He took my virtue and promised to make me mistress of the ryokan. Yuko's death gave me the chance to seize what I was promised, and to avenge myself on the people who tried to deprive me of what I deserved."

"You created the ghost?" Noboru was horrified. "You made up a yūrei to justify a murder?"

"The ghost is real," Saku objected. "I saw her."

"And Noboru was married before you killed Ishiko," Kane added.

Hiro ignored Saku's comment in favor of the one that did not require him to reveal Emiri's nocturnal visits. "Hanako intended to kill you too, as soon as Father Mateo and I had left the village."

"I merely invited her to dinner . . ." Hanako trailed off as if wondering how much Hiro actually knew.

"At which you planned to poison her, as you did Noboru's father," Hiro said.

"My father's heart gave out when he saw the ghost . . ." Noboru's words grew softer as he spoke.

"Is that what happened?" Hiro asked Hanako. "Or is it just a story you invented to disguise the truth? What did Emiko really see that night?"

"Noboru's back was to the door. He did not realize—" Hanako stopped abruptly. "How did you know what Emiko saw?"

"Perhaps I, too, can speak with ghosts." Hiro redirected the conversation. "Did you kill Noboru's father?"

"I poisoned his saké," Hanako said, "but he really did clutch his chest and call out Riko's name, as if he saw her in his final moments. Later, I used the story of the ghost to cover up the real reason Emiko fled—she saw me . . . with Noboru."

The innkeeper's cheeks flushed red.

"But I saw the ghost!" Saku repeated, louder than before.

Hiro had hoped to avoid this detail, but fabricated an explanation that avoided mentioning Emiri. "You saw Masako, sneaking out to meet Chitose in the woods. They were in love, but had to hide it from Hanako."

Saku narrowed her eyes suspiciously. "What I saw did not look like Masako-*san*."

"Grandmother," Chitose said, "last week you thought a tree stump was an ox."

The murmur of amusement that passed through the room made Hiro hope that no one else would question Saku's sighting of the ghost.

"I still don't understand," Noboru said. "If you wanted the ryokan, and me, why did you wait a year to kill my mother? And why did you still kill her, after I'd already married Kane?"

"I planned to kill her earlier, but after you got married I could never catch her alone." Hanako pointed at Kane. "She followed her daughter-in-law around like a dog chasing after a fleeing rat. But I knew she would take an offering to the grave on the anniversary of her daughter's death. She believed the ghost had killed her husband, and didn't want to follow him to the grave."

"But she might have taken Kane with her to present the offering," Noboru said, "or taken me along."

"I had a plan, and then the foreigner arrived, and I had to change the plan again." She glared at Noboru. "You almost ruined everything when you refused to let Masako entertain you while you ate."

"Speaking of which, why did you kill Masako?" Chitose asked. "She had no part in this at all."

For the first time, Hanako seemed uncomfortable. "Her death was a mistake."

"A mistake?" Chitose started forward.

Akako restrained his son. "Let her explain."

"A little while before Ishiko died, Noboru started acting strangely. He came to the teahouse less often, and when he did, he seemed so distant . . . I thought, with Ishiko gone, he would feel free to be with me openly, but he refused."

"My mother had just died!" the innkeeper interjected, "and I am married!"

Hanako ignored him. "A few months ago, Masako started acting strangely too. I suspected she was sneaking out at night to meet a man, but could never catch her. Then, when Noboru's behavior changed, I thought he had fallen in love with her, and that she was trying to steal him away from me."

"Masako-*chan* did not care about Noboru." Chitose's nose turned red. "It was me she loved!"

"I do not care who she loved." The regret disappeared from Hanako's voice. "I could not allow anyone to deprive me of the ryokan."

"Deprive you of the ryokan," Noboru repeated softly.

Hanako continued as if she had not heard him. "On the night it happened, Masako left the teahouse right after Noboru did. I saw them whispering near the latrine. He waited while she went inside. I couldn't watch what happened next . . . I found the rope I used to strangle Ishiko and got it ready. When Masako returned to the teahouse, I confronted her. She claimed innocence, but I knew better. So I killed her."

"Masako was afraid of the yūrei," Noboru said. "She asked me to stand guard outside the latrine, to keep her safe."

"That's the story she told me, too," Hanako admitted. "At the time, I thought it was a lie."

"I did not love Masako." Noboru looked at the floor as if embarrassed. "But you are right that I no longer loved you either. As my feelings for my wife grew stronger, the ones I felt for you withered and died." He looked up. "But I still liked your food."

"Would she really have killed me too?" Kane asked.

Hiro nodded. "She invited your husband to bring you to the teahouse for a meal. I do not think you would have survived her hospitality."

"You cannot prove that," Hanako said.

"I do not need to." Hiro turned to Otomuro. "I believe you have sufficient proof of this woman's guilt."

"Enough that we do not need a magistrate," the samurai agreed. "She will hang at dawn."

CHAPTER 50

After Otomuro led Hanako out the door, an unsettled silence filled the room.

"Well," Akako said, with an artificial lightness that fell flat, "I think we should all go home and get some sleep."

Chitose started for the door. Saku walked beside him, leaning heavily on her cane. Akako bowed to Hiro and Father Mateo before following his family from the room.

Taso removed his arm from Mume's shoulders and stepped in front of her. "I need to know the truth. Do you want to be my wife, or not?"

Mume turned her head to look at Kane.

Taso gently cupped Mume's cheek in his hand and turned her face to his once more. "Not what your sister wants. What you want." He lowered his hand. "I will not hurt you, or be angry, no matter what you say. But you need to tell the truth."

Mume started to lower her face, but raised it again. "I do not like having an ox in the house. He smells."

"If he lived outside in the winter he would freeze," Taso replied.

"Can we buy incense?" Mume asked. "To hide the smell?"

"Of course."

"Can I have a baby?" Her cheeks grew red.

Taso laughed. "I cannot promise, but I'll gladly try."

"Then I want to be your wife." Mume bit her lip. "Kane said you did not care for me. But I think you do."

"I care for you very much," Taso said gently. "Do you still want to go to Edo?"

"By myself?" Worried wrinkles appeared on Mume's forehead.

He smiled. "No, with me. Last week, I received a message from a cousin there. He has a growing business that needs a porter, and an ox, to help with deliveries. We would have a better house and a better future."

Far away from her sister's influence, Hiro silently agreed.

"Did you hear that, Kane?" Mume beamed. "I get to go to Edo after all!"

"That's nice for you. But where does this leave me?" Kane gave her husband a worried look.

"Did you truly steal the money only to escape my mother's cruelty?" Noboru asked.

"Yes. I swear it is the truth."

"Then prove it."

"How?" She spread her hands. "I gave the money back."

Noboru gestured to Hiro. "He gave it back. But you can prove your sincerity by helping me run the ryokan without complaining . . . and you can start by learning to cook a meal that's edible."

"You want me to learn to cook?" She looked aghast.

"I will hire a servant to teach and assist you."

"Why can't she just do the cooking?" Kane asked.

"As mistress of the ryokan, that duty falls to you."

Kane looked unable to believe what she was hearing. "If I do, can you forgive me?"

"I am willing to," Noboru said. "Whether or not I *can* depends on you."

The following morning, Hiro and Father Mateo prepared to leave. When Hiro set the traveling basket on the floor and opened the lid, Gato flattened her belly against the tatami and flattened her ears against her head.

"I think she knows we're leaving." Father Mateo nodded at the cat. "And doesn't like it."

"You wouldn't either, if you had to travel in a basket," Hiro said.

"Getting to ride instead of walk? I would gladly take her place."

Hiro smiled. "I suspect Ana wouldn't be quite as willing to carry you."

Before the Jesuit could respond, the ryokan's front door opened. A moment later, Otomuro appeared in the guest room's doorway, with Noboru at his back.

"Good morning," the samurai bowed to Hiro and the Jesuit. As they returned the gesture, he continued, "I have come to release your servant from her arrest, so you may leave."

Hiro raised an eyebrow but said nothing.

"Thank you for acknowledging her innocence," Father Mateo said.

When neither the samurai nor Noboru withdrew, Hiro asked, "Is there something more?"

The innkeeper looked uncomfortable. "I wanted to thank you for finding my missing silver. And to apologize for blaming your servant." He bowed. "Please forgive my error."

"All men err." Father Mateo made a gesture of benediction. "I pray that God will protect you and bless this ryokan."

"Thank you." Noboru bowed once more. "I will leave you to your preparations."

The innkeeper disappeared in the direction of the kitchen, but Otomuro lingered in the doorway.

Hiro gave the samurai a curious look.

Otomuro entered the room and closed the door. "I found your explanation for the crimes quite interesting . . . but incomplete."

"How so?" Hiro suspected he knew the answer.

"It did not account for my brother's death."

Father Mateo's curious expression suggested the priest had realized this also.

"An intentional omission," Hiro said, "as a courtesy. Because, as you know already, Hanako did not kill your brother. You did."

Otomuro's jowls wobbled. "How did you know? We were alone . . ."

"I will answer that if you explain why you demanded a hundred and fifty gold koban when you knew Noboru lost much less."

Otomuro's cheeks flushed red, like giant apples. "It is the sum I need to take my brother's place in the daimyō's service. To pay for my armor, and for the necessary gifts. Now, how did you know about my brother?"

"He abused and killed the woman you cared for." Hiro avoided the more complicated "*loved*." "Moreover, Yuko could not make a claim against your family—financial or otherwise—if he was dead."

Otomuro nodded. "It is the truth."

"Then you never believed in the yūrei?" Father Mateo asked.

"I did believe." Otomuro looked embarrassed. "I feared she would come for me, despite the fact that I tried to avenge her, because I could not—did not—prevent my brother from killing her."

He jumped as someone knocked on the door behind him.

The door slid open, revealing Ana. The Jesuit's housekeeper wore an unadorned blue kimono with an orange obi and carried a bundle across her back.

Otomuro bowed to Hiro. "As our business is concluded, I will leave you to your preparations."

Father Mateo and the shinobi returned the bow as the portly man withdrew.

Ana took his place inside the door and rested her hands on her hips. "Hm. The two of you are slower than a pair of children heading out to lessons."

"We're ready." Father Mateo hefted the bundle that held his Bible, a spare kimono, and the few additional possessions he had acquired since they left Kyoto.

Hiro's own traveling bundle, smaller and lighter than the priest's, lay at his feet. He kept his own important possessions—most of them lethal—concealed on his person.

He reached down and picked up Gato, who splayed her legs in order to avoid being placed in the basket. As he lowered her toward it, she snagged her claws on the rim and stiffened her legs against the sides. Hiro tried, but could not stuff her through the opening.

Ana laughed.

"It isn't funny," Hiro said, as Gato let out an angry yowl and bit his hand.

Ana laughed even harder.

Even Father Mateo smiled.

Hiro finally managed to loosen Gato's claws and slip her into the basket. He secured the lid and Ana picked it up.

"Onward to Edo," Father Mateo said. "Though one thing still does trouble me. You told the villagers the apparition they saw in the woods was Masako, but I saw her after Masako died."

"We discussed this," Hiro reminded him. "You saw Emiri, returning to see Zentaro."

"Emiri claimed she was not here that night—or on the night we tried to catch the thief."

"Kunoichi do not always tell the truth," Hiro pointed out, "but I can try to find her before we leave, and ask—"

"No." The word came out with unusual force. "I think I would rather believe I saw Emiri."

After an uncertain pause, the priest concluded, "after all, we have a mission to complete."

Throwing a caltrop under Oda Nobunaga's plans to seize Kyoto and the shogunate—and hopefully putting Neko's spirit to rest . . . and mine as well.

Hiro hefted his pack. "Let's get back on the road."

GLOSSARY OF JAPANESE TERMS

B

butsudan: a Buddhist shrine commonly found in Buddhist homes and temples

C

-chan: an affectionate diminutive suffix, commonly used for children, pets, and lovers. "Neko-chan" is roughly the equivalent of "kitty."

D

daimyō: a samurai lord, usually the ruler of a province and/or the head of a samurai clan

F

futon: a thin padded mattress, small and pliable enough to be folded and stored out of sight during the day

H

hakama: loose, pleated pants worn over kimono or beneath a tunic or surcoat

I

Inari: (also: Inari Ōkami) a Shintō *kami* (deity) worshipped in Japan since at least the eighth century as the patron of agriculture, fertility, rice, saké, foxes, swordsmiths, and merchants. In Shintō belief, *kitsune* (foxes) often serve as Inari's messengers.

inarizushi: (also: *inari sushi*) a type of sushi named for the Shintō deity Inari, made by stuffing sushi rice seasoned with black sesame into pockets of fried tofu (*aburaage*). According to Japanese legend, this type of sushi is a favorite meal of the *kitsune*, or foxes, who act as Inari's messengers.

K

kami: the Japanese word for "god" or "divine spirit"; used to describe the gods of Japan's indigenous Shintō faith, the spirits inhabiting natural objects, and certain natural forces of divine origin

kanji: Chinese characters used, together with the phonetic *hiragana* and *katakana* syllabaries, for writing the Japanese language

kanzashi: traditional Japanese hair ornaments or hair pins.

kata: literally, "form"; a series or pattern of movements, often used for training in martial arts

katana: the longer of the two swords worn by a samurai (the shorter one is the wakizashi)

kimono: literally, "a thing to wear"; a full-length wraparound robe traditionally worn by Japanese people of all ages and genders

kitsune: literally, "fox"; in Japanese, used to refer to both normal foxes and to the supernatural fox spirits of Japanese folklore, some of which are closely associated with the Shintō deity Inari

koban: an oval Japanese coin, generally made of gold

kunoichi: a female *shinobi*, trained in the arts of espionage and assassination

M

miso: a traditional Japanese food paste made from fermented soybeans (or, sometimes, rice or barley)

N

neko: cat

O

obi: a wide sash wrapped around the waist to hold a kimono closed, worn by people of all ages and genders

onryō: (literally: "vengeful spirit") a wrathful yūrei (ghost) that causes natural disasters and seeks revenge against the living

R

ronin: a masterless samurai

ryokan: a traditional Japanese inn

ryu: literally, "school"; shinobi clans used this term as a combination identifier and association name (Hiro is a member of the Iga ryu)

S

saké: an alcoholic beverage made from fermented rice

-sama: a suffix used to show even higher respect than *-san*

samurai: a member of the medieval Japanese nobility, the warrior caste that formed the highest-ranking social class

-san: a suffix used to show respect

sasa: broad-leafed bamboo, a variety of running bamboo

shamisen: a three-stringed Japanese instrument with a long neck and wooden body, similar to a banjo but with a smaller, drum-shaped body and without any frets on the neck

shinobi: literally, "shadowed person"; shinobi is the Japanese pronunciation of the characters that many Westerners pronounce "ninja," which is based on a Chinese pronunciation

shogun: the military dictator and commander who acted as de facto ruler of medieval Japan

shogunate: a name for the shogun's government and/or the compound where the shogun lived

shoji: a sliding door, usually consisting of a wooden frame with oiled paper panels

shuriken: an easily concealed palm-sized weapon made of metal and often shaped like a cross or star, which shinobi used for throwing or as a handheld weapon in close combat

stupa: a Buddhist monument, often made of wood or stone and used for storing sacred relics, marking graves, and other religious purposes

T

tabi: traditional Japanese socks, which have a separation between the big toe and the other toes, allowing them to be worn with sandals *tatami*: a traditional Japanese mat-style floor covering made in standard sizes, with the length measuring exactly twice its width; tatami usually contained a straw core covered with grass or rushes

tokonoma: a decorative alcove or recessed space set into the wall of a Japanese room; the tokonoma typically held a piece of art, a flower arrangement, or a hanging scroll

torii: a sacred Shintō gate that marks the entrance to a Shintō shrine or the boundary between a worldly space and a sacred one

tsukemono: (literally, "pickled things") a general term for the pickled vegetables that typically accompany a traditional Japanese meal

U

unagi: eel

W

wakizashi: the shorter of the two swords worn by a samurai (the longer one is the katana)

Y

yamabushi: a Japanese mountain ascetic, once believed to possess supernatural powers and an unusual ability to communicate with various gods and spirits.

yūrei: (literally: "dim spirit") a type of Japanese ghost, commonly believed to be the spirit of a person who died in a sudden or violent manner, which is stuck in the world of the living until the conflict that bound the spirit to this world is resolved

For additional cultural information, expanded definitions, and author's notes, visit http://www.susanspann.com

AUTHOR'S NOTE

G*host of the Bamboo Road* was inspired by my friend and fellow author, Kerry Schafer (who also writes as Kerry Anne King), whose paranormal mysteries (starting with *Dead Before Dying*) are among my favorite reads. She asked me what Hiro would do if he saw a ghost, and refused to accept "He doesn't believe in them" for an answer. This story is the result of that friendly challenge.

Japan is rich in ghostly lore, and each of the phantoms mentioned in this book features prominently in Japanese legend, as do the *kitsune*, who really are considered messengers of the deity Inari Ōkami. Inari remains a popular and revered Shintō deity throughout Japan to this day, and his primary shrine, Fushimi Inari Taisha, is famous around the world for the thousands of vermillion *torii* (sacred Shintō gates) that line its slopes.

For centuries, the mountains of Hakone represented a major barrier for people and traders traveling between the medieval capital of Kyoto and the northern city of Edo. In the early sixteenth century, Tokugawa Ieyasu would unify Japan and move the capital from Kyoto to Edo. At that time, he also unified the major travel roads between those cities, creating five official travel routes, including the famous Tōkaidō, which passed through Hakone.

Ghost of the Bamboo Road is set on Hakone's *Yusaka-michi*, a route through the mountains that predated the official Tōkaidō. Although portions of the route remain (I hiked them several times while researching the novel) the route itself has essentially become a ghost, remembered only by historians, hikers, and the occasional novelist. Landslides like the one in the story really did cause the travel routes to change, because in Hiro's time it was easier to find a new path through the steep, unforgiving mountains than to dig the trails out enough to allow the passage of heavily loaded carts and animals. This book was partially inspired, also, by my curiosity about what happened to the villages along those older roads when a landslide caused the route to shift and they became phantoms of their former selves.

In Japan, it is said that every author has a *yōkai* (ghost) story to tell.

This one is mine.

ACKNOWLEDGMENTS

Many people don't bother to read the acknowledgments section, so if you're reading this, the first thanks belongs to you.

Thank you for choosing this book from among the millions of stories and other media clamoring for your attention. I deeply appreciate you spending your valuable time with Hiro and Father Mateo, and with me.

Thanks to my agent, Sandra Bond, for so many things that it would take me pages to list them all. You were the first to believe in Hiro and Father Mateo, and you continue to be their constant champion (and mine), as well as an eagle-eyed editor who ensures that Hiro (and I) always appear at our very best on the page. Thank you for being the best business partner, and friend, an author could hope to have.

Thanks to Dan Mayer, my editor, for giving Hiro and Father Mateo a home at Seventh Street Books and for the thoughtful, attentive editing that makes the stories better than I could ever hope to make them on my own.

Thank you to Heather Webb, Kerry Schafer, Rae (R.F. James), Corinne O'Flynn, and all of the other friends who have been such an enormous help and support. As iron sharpens iron, one person sharpens another, and I am grateful for the way you keep my heart full and my skills at a katana's edge. To each of you, and to all of my other friends: I love you, and I could not do this—or anything else— without you.

Last, but certainly not least: thank you to my family. Michael and Christopher, Paula, Spencer, Robert, Lola, Anna, Matteo, Gene, Marcie, Bob, and Spencer (III): words alone are not enough. I love you deeply and appreciate your support, not only now, but in the many years before this crazy dream became reality.

If you've made it this far, thank you again for reading this page— and this book—to the end. If you like this novel, or any other, I hope you'll consider telling a friend about it. Your praise and your recommendation are the greatest rewards an author can receive.